Awards and Praise For Swimming Through Clouds

2014 B.R.A.G. Medallion Recipient
2012 Semi-Finalist Genesis Contest (YA Fiction)
2012 Finalist (2nd Place) NORWA (YA Fiction)
2012 Finalist Women of Faith Full Manuscript
2012 Finalist Wisconsin RWA Honorable Mention (YA Fiction)

"With beautifully crafted poetic prose, author Rajdeep Paulus weaves fear and tragedy, hope and romance through a story that dictates you endure emotional anguish right along with her characters. A work of art."
~USA TODAY's HEA Review, Serena Chase, author of THE RYN

"Tough and touching, resilient and raw -- Rajdeep Paulus has crafted a story of love and abuse with the deft touch of a master. SWIMMING THROUGH CLOUDS is profound, but never preachy. Paulus never allows her characters to be anything less than real and she never averts her pen from the realities that face far too many women and children."
~Tosca Lee, NY Times bestselling author of HAVAH and The Books of Mortals series with Ted Dekker

"Paulus is an exceptional writer! The essence of the human spirit is illuminated through the characters who come to life in each page. Paulus captures the heart of the reader in SWIMMING THROUGH CLOUDS."
~Diana Mao, President of Nomi Network

"Will leave you gasping for air, reaching for something steady to lean on…"
~ Jennifer Murgia, author of the ANGEL STAR series & BETWEEN THESE LINES

"Difficult to read but even more difficult to put down."
~Brown Girl Magazine Book Review

"Should be read by everyone … men and women, the young and the old."
~Masala Mommas Book Review by Angie Seth

"This patient, subtle romance is intimate and enticing."
~Talking Cranes, Book Review

"This is not a bubble-gum, high school sweetheart kind of story."
~Laura Anderson Kurk, author of GLASS GIRL and PERFECT GLASS

"SWIMMING THROUGH CLOUDS is a heart-wrenching story of both suffering and courage. This book will haunt you long after you finish it."
~Darby Karchut, author of Griffin Rising and Finn Finnegan

"I'm trapped in the middle of someone's life... And it's only just begun! I need more!!!"
~Teenage Reader

"There is much to admire about Rajdeep Paulus's writing. Poetic, raw and thought-provoking, her words will indeed send you swimming through clouds."
~Selene Castrovilla, author of THE GIRL NEXT DOOR, a GalleyCat Best YA Book (2010)

SWIMMING THROUGH CLOUDS

Rajdeep Paulus

Birch House Press
Est. 2015

SWIMMING THROUGH CLOUDS

by Rajdeep Paulus

First Edition Copyright 2013
Second Edition Copyright 2015

Cover design by Angela Llamas

Published in Association with

Birch House Press
Est. 2015

For my Sunshine. Because you know me. And love me anyway. And you promise not to give up on me. Love you more than words can say, Santhosh. When we first met, I thought this. Fifteen years later, I know for sure:

You're proof I'm God's favorite.

~ONE~

I live in the in between. Between what if and what is. It's how I manage. It's the only way I know. Everyone has their way. This is mine.

I flip my imaginary pen shut, close my invisible journal, and tuck my thoughts away in the only safe place I know exists. My heart.

A new school changes nothing in my mind—the other place I file the chapters of my story. A story no one can ever know. Instinctively, I tug at my sleeve, pulling the left one over my hand. Because my arm is where Dad prefers to write. Reminders to never step out of line.

Someone clears her throat. The brunette bus driver with smoker's breath taps the top of the seat in front of me. "Bell rings in seven minutes." Empty rows surround me—we're the last two on board. "Might want to get a move on, hon."

Move? Second week of September, and I wish I could move back. Back in time, that is. To a time when Mom made apple pie and my younger brother flew kites from the roof. A time that never existed—until I wrote it down in between my lines of reality. That's my favorite place. Leave me there. And leave me alone.

"Five, now." Coughing, Madam Bus Driver's friendly, good-morning voice dissipates like the sand in an hourglass. "And don't forget, no cell phone use in the classroom. The ban is in full effect, and they will confiscate on the first offense."

"Oh, that won't be a problem." Because, well, I don't have one.

Rising, I drag myself into school, plop my backpack next to my desk, slide into my chair, and bury my face in my arms. If I can't see the other kids, maybe they can't see me. Careful to keep my quads from brushing against the museum of chewed gum on the bottom of my table, I hug my left arm close to me when I notice a scrap of paper on the floor below. It's a little, yellow, square Post-it note. Small enough to vanish under my shoe if I had stepped on it. Juicy, circulated gossip from last week, perhaps. I squint to read the writing without moving the paper.

Talia.

My name printed neatly across the top is all I need to see before I do step on it. Who wrote this? Did Dad plant this here as a warning? That's nuts. Dad hasn't followed me to school. Or has he? Is someone else passing notes around about me? I excuse myself to the lady's room, scoop up the paper as I go, and crumple the Sticky Note in my hand to make it disappear. Then I walk-run until I stand locked behind the walls of a toilet stall. Trembling, I prop my back against the side with the least graffiti, leaning on my right arm, and open up my hand and smooth out the creases.

The Post-it reads:

Talia, Dew drop by and have lunch with me in the cafe?
L

Huh? Who is L? And how does this person know what my name means? Or maybe he or she is just a terrible speller?

Lagan. Has to be. The same tall math geek who wears his Bulls Jersey at least twice a week and would offer to tie my shoes if the teacher asked for a volunteer. I ignore the offer. And him. I avoid his eyes during the rest of first period and tell Ms. Miller, "I don't need any help with AP Chem. I understand the material. I'm good."

Good until I arrive at my locker after second period, and there's another Post-it note openly stuck to the door for anyone to see.

This one reads:

I can balance a mean cafeteria tray on one hand while spinning a b-ball with the index finger of the other. Eat lunch with me?

L

I scrunch it up in my hand. How many people have read it in passing? Do all his friends know he's leaving me notes? Did the basketball team put him up to this? Like some kind of stupid dare to test the transfer student? What would make this stranger want to have lunch with me, the strange girl?

If that isn't bad enough, when I open up my locker over the week, a new Sticky Note falls out each day.

Tuesday's boasts:

I can open up a milk carton no handed. Have lunch with me?

L

Wednesday's says:

I'll buy you lunch. Throw in two desserts. Have lunch with me?

L

A stalker is all I need to add another layer to my already complicated life. And this guy clearly has an overabundance of free time on his hands. All week, I decide to hide in the girls' bathroom and leave five minutes to eat lunch at my locker, standing and scarfing down my sandwich and guzzling down my water bottle before the bell sounds. Time is my enemy. I fear her more than the dark.

When Thursday rolls around, I spin the combination on my lock, confused that I'm half-expecting to find another sticky. My heart sinks the second the lock clicks open. What if? And before panic sets in, a little, yellow, square sheet sails down like an autumn leaf, landing on my shoe. Can this tiny Post-it be trying to direct my steps? Toward Lagan?

I don't know whether to hide or to laugh when I read Thursday's Sticky Note:

I'm in good with the cafeteria ladies. Chocolate or vanilla ice cream? Have lunch with me?

L

Leaning against my locker, I imagine the cool sensation of ice cream on my lips, and before I finish unwrapping my sandwich, a hall monitor busts me. "No eating allowed outside the cafeteria. Proceed there now, or I'll have to write you up." She stares at me, holding a pen and clipboard with the intensity of a cop dangling handcuffs.

Put the cuffs, I mean pen, away. I toss my lunch in the nearest trash bin to avoid the lunchroom. And Lagan. The short, pudgy hall monitor lady with tight red curls a little past her ears just shrugs her shoulders and returns to her post and her pile of People magazines. I'm not mad at her. She's just doing her job. I get that.

I mumble, "I'm sorry," as I walk past her down the hall and up a flight of stairs to English class.

Sinking into my chair, the bell sounds, and Ms. Benson announces the first formal writing assignment of the semester. "Well, seniors, I simply loved reading the journal entries on your summer adventures! Only two weeks in and I sense this is going to be a superb fall kick-off to the culmination of your secondary education, don't you think?"

Superb. Sure. I guess she bought the made-up story of my trip to Disney. If my life were a Disney flick, I'd ask the Genie for one wish: Dad—go poof and disappear.

Ms. Benson smoothens her lilac business skirt down from her hips like she's drying her hands and continues teaching, a mischievous twinkle in her eyes. "Pay attention now. Today's writing lesson focuses on personal narrative. But to spice it up, instead of telling me about you, you will be writing each other's stories. For starters, each of you will need to pair up and interview a classmate. The remainder of today's class will be spent brainstorming a list of questions. And I expect you to approach your write-up as a chapter out of a biography rather than a Q&A format."

Lagan's hand shoots up so fast, it's a wonder he doesn't pull a muscle.

"Yes, Lagan," Ms. Benson says with an adoration-soaked tone.

"It's La-gan!" a few kids chime. Then George, his basketball bud, adds, "As in La la la la, and when the bell rings, we will be gone!" George stands up to give Lagan a chin-raised high-five, and then sits back down.

"Thank you for that phonetic breakdown of La-gan's name, George. I stand corrected." Then she turns to Lagan, eyebrows raised, waiting for his question.

"Well, I was just thinking—" The classic start to so many of Lagan's responses since school started. "Most of us have been together since kindergarten."

"Go on." Ms. Benson lowers her bifocals and looks over the top of them at her manicured fingernails.

"So most of us already know each other." Lagan shrugs, and several kids throw in yeah's with their nods of agreement. Maybe he hopes she'll cancel the assignment.

Ms. Benson emits a teacherly throat clear to quiet down the class. "Which means most of you have no excuse and can get your assignments in on time. As for you, Lagan, can I trust you to work with Talia? Help her to feel welcome and complete this assignment in the process. Yes, why don't you pair up with Talia? But realize that interviewing the new student does not buy you any extra days. Talia, I vouch for this one." Ms. Benson steps forward and pats Lagan's shoulder like he's her son. "Does that work?" Lagan nods once as he beams a smile to the teacher.

Umm? I think she was asking me, but my voice fails me. I suppose Ms. Benson takes that as a yes, too.

Then she addresses the entire class again. "Make time to meet during study hall or lunch or after school in my classroom, if you need to. I'll just be grading papers at my desk. All typed, double-spaced copies are to be placed on my desk at the start of Friday's class, a week from tomorrow. I'll be grading them for content, grammar, and creativity. And I'll bet even those of you who think you know each other will discover something new. Because we're always changing. Always."

Sure. My burns change to blisters. The blisters change to scabs. The scabs to scars. Back to burns again. Is that what you mean by change, Ms. Benson? And what about those of us who don't want to be discovered? After school is not an option, and no one else is jumping up to ask me to be partners. So, Lagan it is.

Seems like this place is no different than the last place I lived. Benton Harbor, a few hours east of Chicago in the Mitten State, was a sea of chocolate while Darien, Illinois, my new home, is a loaf of white bread with a handful of "others." When you're an ethnic cocktail like me, you never know where you belong. Or if you belong at all.

I can read the words behind the stare-downs I get, especially from the girls. Labels they stamp me with that I've heard my whole life: weird, uncool, out there. And then the word they think I can't hear, because they spell it with hand gestures: emo.

If they're thinking I'm emotionally unstable, they should meet my younger brother, Justice. We call him Jesse. Funny thing is, he looks normal with his regular buzz cut, flawless tan skin, and chocolate brown eyes. About the only ordinary detail about me is my average height, but stature doesn't help a person blend into the crowd when the other details scream, "Check me out, I'm a freak!"

My face and hands are a shade of brown lighter than your average Southeast Asian, but not quite light enough to be considered Caucasian. Most people guess I'm Hispanic or Middle Eastern. Once or twice, I've been called an Islander. Not sure which island they were referring to, but I knew they were confused. Not even sure what to call myself since I'm half Indian and half South African. If White Chocolate Reese's Peanut Butter Cup were an option on forms, I'd check that box.

As I doodle different size shaped questions marks on the blank page before me, I instinctively brush under my nose with the top of my pointer finger. My nose is petite on the whole, but my nostrils flare up slightly, making a nose ring out of the question. I leave my hand there as a curtain. Usually, I keep a few strands of my hair pulled over to my mouth—my futile attempt to hide my lips—the part of me that draws the most attention.

No matter how much Chap Stick, lip-gloss, or lipstick I apply, I cannot make my deformed, deeply ridged lips disappear. My bottom lip looks worse than the top, and no respectable cover for lips exists yet. Have to look into that and start a trend. Invent some lip glasses. Call them Lip Shades, for when you can't find the perfect color or get a cold sore, or in my case, your lips always look like your vampire boyfriend prefers lips to necks. If a pair of these puppies could keep a kid from talking too much, teachers might endorse it, and I'd be a billionaire. Run away. Fly to the moon. Take Jesse with me, of course.

Since that's not going to happen today, or ever, I attempt to draw the least amount of attention to myself. But even that seems to backfire in this new school. Between the redhead Hall Cop's eagle eyes and Ms. Benson's assignment, I'm left with little choice the next day. At least it's Friday. Time to eat lunch and face Lagan.

As I walk into the cafeteria after Bio, a parent volunteer offers me a tray. I could have picked one up from the pile myself, just as easily. When I spot a Post-it curling up off the far corner, the plastic tray slips from my fingers, but I manage to grab it before it hits the floor. Relieved, I lift the tray up to the counter and flatten the note to read it.

I'll put your tray away for you. Sitting on the right side at the back table. Saved you a seat. Have lunch with me?

L

So he's taking a day off from being a social butterfly, surrounded by his high-tops-sporting teammates and mathlete buds to sit with me? How did he even know I would show up today? Four words come to mind: get this over with.

Tucking my lower lip under the top and reasoning that one meeting will be enough to finish the English homework, I join Lagan at the rear of the cafeteria. Sort of. I know better than to sit right next to him or even across from him. Instead, I walk over to his table and sit two seats down, on the opposite side.

He blows into his hand and sniffs. "I brushed and flossed this morning if you want to move over. I'm not saving seats for anyone else."

"I'm good." I stare at my tray of food, aware that I haven't thought of one question to ask him.

"Well, okay then." Lagan starts to rise up as he pushes his tray down toward my end of the table.

Startled, I half scream, "W-w-wait!" Catching myself, I pull my sleeves down past my wrists, push his tray back to his old seat, and lower my voice. "I mean, let's just try this. If it's okay?"

Relief washes over me when he sits back down where he started. He doesn't even ask why. Makes me wonder if we'll end up friends someday. I don't have any friends, so one friend...if I keep him on the DL. My family doesn't have to know. Especially Dad. If he ever finds out, well, let's just not go there, because he is not going to find out. Ever.

Lagan speaks first when the awkward moment passes. "Let's start over."

"Okay." I look at the wall in front of me.

"I'm over here." I can see Lagan waving his hands out of the corner of my eye.

"I know." The words leave my lips like molasses. "I see you. I hear you. I'm. Here."

"O-kay." His voice falls flat with an all too familiar sound. Doubt.

I pick up my tray to leave. Better to fail the assignment before disappointment turns to disaster. How do I interview Lagan when I can barely bring myself to talk to him? How else do individuals close the gap between space and silence? People draw near to each other and communicate. Face to face. Eye contact. That is normal. But normal isn't in my cards. I've been dealt a hand that I can't lay down. I step away from the table and turn to face the direction of the conveyor belt where other students are placing their trays.

"Wait." Lagan's voice rises.

"I'm not hungry," I lie.

"Don't leave yet."

But it's too late. I lied to myself too. Somewhere between the Post-it notes and all the times Lagan offered to help me, the new girl, I gave into the hope, perhaps only a crumb's worth, that he might be different. But if he can't handle this, he probably can't handle any of it.

"I'll see you in class." My eyes focus on the red exit sign.

"You forgot something."

That is the first time he tricks me. I stop and turn around to scan the table where I was sitting. Scrawling something in his lap, he reaches over and slaps the spot where my tray lay moments ago. A little yellow Post-it note curls up on the table. Everything inside me tells me to run, but I have been running my whole life. I'm tired. And hungry. Flip-flopping, I return to my spot and sit again.

This note reads:

I'm sorry. I don't understand. This is new. One more chance?

I nod. Then fold up the note and put it in the back pocket of my jeans.

Lagan clears his throat and smiles. "Take two. Or three. Ahh. Who's counting, anyway?"

Inhale. Exhale. Peripheral vision allows me to slow my breathing to match his, my self-prescribed tranquilizer. While we eat in silence, I paint Lagan's features on the canvas of my mind. His earthy brown eyes squint when he smiles. His silky black hair falls to right above his shoulders and a few wisps fall across his forehead, over his left eyebrow. Lagan's skin reminds me of milk chocolate. A tiny black mole on his right cheek dances as he chews. His thinned out goatee draws attention to his oval jawline—a nest for breadcrumbs, which he instinctively wipes away after every few bites. I can see his black Nike high tops extended beyond the cafeteria table that his long lanky legs barely fit beneath. And he raises his dark, thick eyebrows whenever he looks in my direction and smiles, introducing a heart-skipping dimple on his left cheek.

"I'm sorry." I mutter the confession, but it's true. I am sorry. I want to undo the last few minutes too. I don't really know what I want. I just—

"How's the chocolate milk?" he asks, drawing attention away from the past.

That's when I know he's different. And different has potential.

"Fine." A minuscule snort escapes me, and I feel something loosen. "Are you still buying?"

"Most certainly."

Wow. That dimple again. As he walks back to the drinks section of the cafeteria line, I survey the room, always aware that everything can change, for the worse, in a fraction of a second. Nothing but noisy students eating lunches and oblivious monitors walking around. We are safe—for now. When Lagan returns with a carton, he hesitates. Then he places it caddy-corner from me rather than on my tray. I fold my bottom lip inside my top, and wait for him to take his place.

"Thanks." My whispered word falls onto the lunch tray, but Lagan hears it.

He coughs, "YW," into his right fist, and we both giggle.

I reach over and drag the carton closer. I lift it up to open it and find a Sticky Note on the bottom. The guy must keep them in his back pocket. I peel it off and smile. I can see out of the corner of my eye that he is smiling too.

I reread it to myself:

If I ask you yes/no questions, you can answer yes by nodding to your food and no by looking at the exit sign. Is that cool?

I flip the note over and there's more:

And don't worry about me. I'm always talking to myself. No one will suspect a thing!

I resist the urge to bust out laughing when I reread the back. I shake my head and nod to my tray, but before he can ask the first question, the bell rings. Lunch is over. It's a B schedule today, so my next class is not the same as Lagan's. We both stand at the same time. Remembering my manners, I fish a pen out of my book bag, write *ty* on the last Sticky Note, tack it to my tray, and head to gym.

~TWO~

When I walk home that day, I squeeze my backpack to my chest in an attempt to drum down the new voice inside me. Time is ticking. Opening the door, I silently wish for wrong things. Things a teenage girl should not be thinking of. Things I should be imprisoned for.

A family portrait graces the wall across from the front door. I was three, and it's the last picture ever taken of the four of us, because it was the last time Mom was healthy enough to express her wants. And she wanted a memory. One that could stop time, if only for a moment. Mom still had her beautiful, flowing, black hair in the photo.

Dad rarely called her by her name Gita, but on the day the photographer came to our house, I remember Dad sliding the blue and white stoned barrette into her hair, and saying, "A gift for my Gita." The glitter of her matching blue sari fades with each day, like my memories of her, no matter how hard I try to keep them intact. Wish I could say the same for Dad.

Gerard, my father, grew up in South Africa before he crossed the ocean to spend seven years studying political science and law at the University of Michigan. As far as I know, he never went back. But we're allowed to ask about our family history as often as we're allowed to have seconds. Never.

We refers to me and my younger brother, Jesse. He's a year younger and looks a lot more like Mom with skin like caramel, silky straight black hair, and a mouth that curls down ever so subtly around the edges. In the portrait, Jess's two-year-old head has almost as much hair as mine. But things have changed. Once a month, Dad pulls the clippers out and gives him a cookie-cutter buzz. To this day, I wonder if he does it to remind us that Mom is gone—and never coming back.

I lower my eyes to focus on my blue, little girl, daisy-printed dress, which matches Mom's sari. And even though I get my definitive cheekbones, arching eyebrows, and hazelnut eyes from Dad, my mother gifted me my long, straight, chestnut-brown hair; a soft, rounded jaw line; and perfectly shaped feet.

The summer before kindergarten, Mom pushed Jess and me to the beach in a double stroller almost every day after Dad left for work. While my little brother slept on a blanket next to her, Mom would bury my feet in the sand and rehearse her own mixed-up version of "This Little Piggy" as she unearthed each little toe, one at a time. Then she'd scoot around to face me, push the bottoms of our feet together, dig her heels deep into the sand until our big toes aligned, and say with a beaming smile, "Look, we match!" As luck would have it, the only attractive feature I bear remains hidden until I come home, take off my shoes, and put on my flip-flops, or chappals, as I grew up calling them.

Dad, on the other hand, looks like a Hollywood cutout, from head to toe. He's technically Dutch Afrikaner, tall and brawny, with dirty-blond hair that he wears short on top and shaved close on the sides, the consummate professional in his navy blue Armani suit, solid red tie, and polished Rockports. I know it's just a photograph, but I feel like Dad can see right through me, exposing my every thought. Chills race down my arms.

Oh shnap! How long have I been daydreaming? I turn my attention to a precisely creased, half sheet of paper placed on the small wooden table inside the doorway—always waiting for me on top of the etched marching elephants with painted flowers on their backs. Maybe someday the parade of hathis will carry my burdens away. For now, atop the paper, the list, numbered one to ten with Dad's perfectly printed handwriting, beckons me. I look into the mirror above the table before reading it.

A smile slips over my face each time I think about the day, the Sticky Notes, the chocolate milk, and his smile. Lagan—my little secret. I indulge for only a moment longer, and then put on my best poker face before walking upstairs to my brother's room.

Jesse's lying in his bed watching Ellen. Maybe he dropped the remote again. Did Dad not make it home for lunch today to check on him? Standing in the doorway, I knock to announce my arrival.

"Hey, Jess." I pick up the remote and place it back in his right hand. Under his hand really. The accident left Jesse with little lower muscular control. Doctors warned he might never walk again. His arms are his only fully functioning limbs, but without his legs, Jesse has little to no motivation to do anything. And most days he doesn't speak. Maybe the shock never wore off. Maybe he chooses not to. I'll never know.

Number one on the list is the same every day: Check on your brother, make his bed, and give him something to drink.

I don't think twice about it. Pulling out fresh pinstriped sheets from the second drawer, I start my daily routine. After I raise Jesse's hospital bed and scoot his legs over the edge, he guides himself into his wheelchair. As I toss old sheets into the bathroom hamper, I instinctively peek into the shower. Wet scrubs in the shower let me know Dad gave Jesse a shower at lunch. Next I pull on new bed sheets, clear the incense ashes from the night table into the trash, and wheel Jess over to the kitchen, all the while wondering if he can tell something is different. Wondering if I should tell him. Worried that the walls have ears.

As I peel and cut up two apples to throw into a blender with a banana, yogurt, and orange juice, the sound of the front door opening sends a shiver down my spine, and I nearly drop the knife. Every day this week, Dad's been on time. Why today? Why'd he have to come home twenty minutes early today? I lay the knife down like a sword, accepting defeat, my heart pounding to an army drum beat announcing the arrival of the enemy. The army that never shows up to rescue me. Because no one can rescue me.

On autopilot, I retrieve the stainless steel teapot hanging from a ceiling hook, fill it with water, and dial the temperature to high. My hands will not stop shaking. Opening up the canister to retrieve three tea bags, the mugs are clean, but I haven't emptied the dishwasher yet, number four on the list.

I can hear Dad's footsteps walking first to his office where he drops off his briefcase, then to the bathroom near the back door. The faucet turns on. Then off. His hands are clean, a daily reminder that he likes all things clean. Next comes his walk throughout the house, inspecting every detail. My stomach muscles tighten. The list.

The teakettle hisses softly as Dad enters the kitchen. As if on cue, the hiss rises in pitch. Without hesitation, he walks over to me, grabs my left arm, pulls it over the kitchen sink and slams my hand against the tap. I hold on tight, swallow, and bite down on my lower lip. I am not going to cry this time.

"Don't even want to know what you wasted your time on today." Dad speaks calmly, void of any sign of emotion.

There's no "Hi. How are you? How was school?" It's straight to business. The business of destroying me.

"You know the rules." His voice drones, sounding almost bored with the whole proceeding. "If you don't get at least half the list done by the time I walk in the door, I'll give you something to think about for the next time."

The bowl of apples tips on the counter, and several slices fall to the ground. I never finished making Jesse's smoothie.

15

After seeing his fingers tighten their grip on his wheel chair armrests, I turn away. It's not his fault. He's just stuck—in his chair—in this house.

Dad plucks a pen out of his shirt pocket, and as he writes, he speaks, his voice unwavering. "So, we're going to add sweep, mop, and wax kitchen floor to your list."

I hope that he somehow forgets what he is about to do next. I wish foolishly. I am the fool. Dad never forgets.

Examining the thermostat on the kettle, impatience expedites Dad's routine. His map to punish me. Enough to hurt me but never enough to warrant an ambulance. One ER visit was more than enough for all of us.

Like a mad scientist brewing the perfect concoction, Dad adds tap water to the kettle, radiating heat from the metal vessel. He takes one last glance at the gauge, then says, "Don't move."

"Yes, sir." I speak without raising my eyes.

The list on the countertop, numbered one to ten, now eleven, mocks me. I only finished number one. Translation: I earn ten seconds. Ten. Long. Seconds.

"Okay. Straighten your arm and start counting. Slowly, like I taught you." Dad sounds like a dance instructor, except no applause will follow this show.

I will not cry, I tell myself. *I will not cry this time.*

"One thousand..." Dad tilts the teakettle, and hot water splashes and spreads across my lower arm, burning trails down to my wrist. I bite down on my bottom lip, and my fingertips nearly rip the tap off the sink. "And one."

Jesse's fists pound his thighs.

"One thousand..." I bite harder. "And two." I taste blood.

"One thousand..." Nausea rises up my chest. "And three." I swallow my vomit.

"One thousand... " The sound of sizzling confuses me. "And four." It's my skin—cooking.

"One thousand..." I bite my tongue. "And five." More blood in my mouth.

"One thousand..." The colors on the wallpaper blend. "And six." My right knee buckles.

"One thousand..." The ceiling fan spins. "And seven." Or is it my head?

Jesse moans, swinging his head side to side.

"One thousand..." The tiles blur. "And eight." My eyes burn.

"One thousand..." No, not again. "And nine."

My. "One..." Arm. "Thousand..." Is. "And..." On. "TEN!"

Fire!

The dropped kettle clangs into the sink, an exclamation point ringing in the air. Then Dad turns and simply walks out of the kitchen leaving behind two words: "Or else."

I collapse to the ground where I wish I could stay and continue to cry. But there's no time for that. Somehow I manage to crawl to Jesse, hugging my wet, ignited arm. Holding his legs with my good arm, I lay my head on his lap to sob. I hold him, because he won't hold me.

My homework remains untouched till the morning, but I complete the list after I pile on the aloe until my arm is covered with green slime. Then I swallow six Tylenol that I stashed away weeks ago, help Jesse to get into bed, and climb in next to him. I don't want to sleep alone.

All night long. All I know. All I feel. All I see. All I dream. Are five little words: My arm is on fire!

~THREE~

That night the house is on fire in my dreams. Then I wake up, realizing that the house is my arm. Tucking my arm underneath me, I fall asleep again, listening to the sound of Jesse breathing, a song that almost faded to silence last winter.

Shortly after Jesse turned fifteen, he broke the rules. Jesse stood on the roof. The roof of our old house. He was not allowed on the roof. Dad had two rules. Number one: No going on the roof or in his office. Number two: Do as I say. Or else.

When Jesse and I were three and four years old respectively, Jesse couldn't say the word *else*. Instead, he said, "Or elf." If Dad were an elf, Santa would fire him. Santa didn't visit our house on Christmas Eve, anyway. December 25 passed by, just like any other day of the year. Same old. Same cold.

It was a cold night before Christmas, and Jesse stood on the roof. Snow fell. Nothing unusual about that. Benton Harbor lies in the snowy part of the mitten state. Both Jesse and I were born in the bedroom of our harbor town home, in our little house about half a mile from the water where I learned to swim. Mom taught me the doggy paddle, back when she was halfway healthy and occasionally engaged. Jess never got the hang of it, because he loved clinging to mom's neck and riding her back like a superhero cape. Mom was his hero. I loved Mom, but when things got rough, she left. A hero isn't supposed to leave. Not like that.

Before she ever forced Jess to let go and learn to float, Dad put an end to our beach days. "Beach days are for beach bums," he used to say. He hated anything or anyone that suggested laziness. Didn't help that he despised sand entering his palace too.

Those days were long gone. During her last days, Mom slept a lot. And moaned. And cried. Her beautiful, long black hair all gone when she died. She wore a beige woolen cap on her head, a maroon turtleneck, and a tassel-edged red shawl too.

Our lists doubled after Mom's death, and with our homework increasing each year, we both struggled to do it all. That night—the night before Christmas—Dad finished his 8:00 p.m. rounds. My list passed. Jesse's did not. As a junior, I mastered the art of doing my homework while my teachers taught. Jesse didn't multitask well, and sometimes he dropped the ball. This would be the last day he ever ran to catch a ball. He forgot to empty the garbage from the wastebasket under his desk when he took the rest of the trash out. Only one piece of crumpled up paper remained. The point? The basket was not empty.

When I heard the boom of the wastebasket hitting Jesse's bedroom door, I ran upstairs to see if someone had fallen. *Oh crap, Dad saw something unacceptable on his computer screen.*

Earlier that month, Jess convinced Dad that we needed e-mail accounts to keep in touch with teachers and homework partners. As a result, we never had to go to our classmates' houses, a nonexistent option regardless. Dad hesitantly agreed but carefully kept tabs on all our Internet activity. At least we communicated with a few people online, even if we could never go out with them. But we knew to be ultra-careful, always aware of Dad's watchful eye. Jesse and I both remembered to erase our e-mails, delete our histories, and empty the *trash* every few minutes anytime either of us used the computer.

Then one winter afternoon Jess forgot to empty his trashcan. And now, it was too late. As I reached the top of the stairs, Dad left Jesse's room, shaking his head. I held onto the banister until Dad passed me to descend the steps. When I heard his feet step off the bottom stair, I ran to Jesse's room. He knelt by the foot of his bed, his back to the door, and his waste paper basket lay on the floor nearby, mangled and empty. The computer keyboard on his desk looked as irreparable as the trashcan.

"Jesse?" I said his name to let him know I was here. Too late. "I'm sorry."

He didn't say a word. I approached him and placed my arms around his shoulders. I knew not to ask. We had been in this place too many times to know that asking never helped. Asking could not turn back the clock. Diminish the blow. Change things. Asking just made us relive it. And forgetting was already hard enough.

I sat on the bed before I first saw his eyes. Fear didn't fill them anymore. Nor anger. Not even sadness. Instead, a hollow gaze stared past me. Empty caves of lifeless defeat. At the age of fourteen, Jesse had seen enough. Now he stared at the wall, and for the first time ever, I couldn't read him.

We sat there awhile in silence. The sounds of snow pelting his window and the ticking of the wall clock were our only companions. Jesse's revised list lay on the bed, and when I read it, his eyes reflected the words. Madness. Madness walled us in without a fire escape. Dad's precise penmanship made out seven new words that, at first glance, could easily have been mistaken for a grocery list. Instead, it stacked seven words that Jesse could not carry nor accept.

So a little past midnight, when everyone was asleep, Jesse pried open his window and pulled himself up to the roof of the house. Without a hat. Without a scarf. Without a coat. With only one thing crumpled in his left hand. The list.

A nightmare startled me awake, and I dreaded closing my eyes and returning to it. So I wandered to the bathroom, hoping to steal a minute of unnoticed privacy. A frigid draft snatched my naked toes, changing my route, and I headed to my brother's room. When I opened the door, I saw a lumpy mess on his bed and the window wide open, the screen nowhere in sight. I ran over to it and looked out, up, and all around. Then I noticed the fresh footprints on the fire escape. *The roof! No! Not the roof!*

I didn't have time to think as I climbed out and followed the footprints up to the roof where I found Jesse, straddling the highest visible peak. His back faced me as he shivered in his pajamas, his feet, bare and sprinkled with snow.

"Jesse?" I whispered, hoping not to startle him and praying that I didn't wake up Dad with the creaking of my tread.

"Jesse." A little louder this time.

"What?" His back to me, his voice sounded cold, matching the chill in the air.

"Jesse. What are you doing out here? Get back inside. Don't be stupid. You know the rules. And you know Dad's punishment for this one. Whaddya thinking?"

"I'm done thinking." He spoke calmly. Too calmly. "I'm done."

And before I could respond, he stood up, moved to face me, spread his arms open and mouthed the words I'm sorry. Without blinking, Jesse fell back and off the roof.

"Noooooo!" I screamed that one word till I ran out of breath as I scrambled up the roof, slipping and sliding on the snow.

I screamed when I reached the peak and looked over to see his body on the driveway, in front of Dad's car, a puddle growing under his head, and his left leg flipped awkwardly over his body. I screamed when I slid back down to the balcony and scrambled back into Jesse's room. I screamed all the way down the hallway when I ran right into Dad's chest. I pushed him aside and screamed as I stumbled down the steps out the front door. I screamed as I ran out to the driveway and up to my brother. I screamed as I bent down and gathered his limp body into my arms. I screamed and screamed and screamed and looked up to heaven and screamed some more.

I saw Dad on the roof, looking down and shaking his head. Who knows, in disbelief? Possibly confusion? Probably rage. I rocked Jesse back and forth and rubbed his arms, wondering if by any chance this nightmare was playing inside my head and I was still asleep in my bed. That's when I saw it. The paper crumpled up, now loosely held by his limp fingertips. My screaming turned to whimpering as I reached over to retrieve the note. The list. The seven words on Jesse's final list. The seven words that literally pushed him over the edge. The seven words Dad transferred to me, since I did not stop Jesse. The seven words that sentenced us to maximum isolation.

Zero
E-mail
Until
You
Get
It
Right

I tucked the bloody verdict into my robe's side pocket and resumed rocking him.

"Jesse. Jesse. Jesse." My words sputtered out as I wished for the impossible. "Don't leave me, too. We already lost Mom. I can't lose you, too. Jesse. Wake up, Jesse. Wake up. Wake. Up. Please. Jess. Please." I pleaded with anyone, heaven, whatever or whoever would listen.

Dad pummeled out the front door, running toward us while talking frantically into his cell phone. I could hear his words, but he sounded so far away.

"There's been an accident! Come quickly! There's been an accident!" Dad yelled to the 911 dispatcher.

All the sensations around me blended. The snow felt warm. Jesse's body sounded loud. Dad's voice seemed heavy. The blood on my hands felt cold. The snow tasted salty. My eyes felt numb. And the neighbors were falling.

When the ambulance arrived, I rocked Jesse, confused at all the commotion. Why did the neighbors stare at me? The men in white and blue uniforms exited the blinking van and ran toward me. Déjà vu. They wanted to separate us. They wanted to steal my brother from me. The same way they stole Mom from us. Not happening. Not this time. I would hold on tighter this time.

"No!" My crackling voice returned. "I won't let you take him from me! I won't! I won't! I can't."

In the end, the EMT staff pried me away from Jesse's body, offering me a seat near my baby brother in the ambulance. I didn't ask Dad. I just went, and Dad followed in his car. The whole ride over to the hospital, two EMT techs worked on Jesse, putting in lines, pumping meds into his veins, and performing non-stop CPR while I watched, digging my fingernails into my palms.

By the time we arrived at Lakeland Community, the nearest hospital in St. Joe's, Jesse started breathing...barely. Enough to give the team a little hope, and things moved at record speed the second the ambulance reversed into the ER entrance. The back doors swung open, and a team of doctors and nurses appeared, wheeling him away while throwing a plethora of medical words into the air. I only recognized the words surgery and spinal cord.

The EMT driver helped me step down from the truck and escorted me to a couch in the waiting room outside the locked doors of the OR. Dad marched right behind us. He sat down on a different couch and put his face in his hands. We were together, Dad and I. But I felt more alone than I'd ever felt before. First Mom. Now Jesse?

I closed my eyes and hit rewind. My mind replayed the scene over and over again. At times, I caught Jesse by his arm and convinced him not to jump. Other times, I held his hand, and we jumped together. And still other times, I raced up the roof and grabbed his hand, but his weight overcame me. Inevitably, his fingers slipped from mine, and he fell right before my very eyes. Reality exhausted me, so I dreamt of an alternative life. A life absent of chaos and loss and lists. The friggin' list.

I must have blanked out, because when I heard voices, they grew steadily louder like someone turned up the volume. The surgeon spoke with Dad. I wiped my eyelids with the tips of my thumbs and shook my shoulders as I rose up to hear their discussion.

"The situation is difficult." The surgeon—his nametag read Dr. Jenkins—broke the news to Dad. "His arms are remarkably not broken, but the fact of the matter is, he might never walk again, but once we drain the brain hemorrhage and the swelling wanes, he should be able to swallow and speak again. Just depends. Everyone responds differently to trauma."

"What are you saying?" Dad asked as if the doctor spoke a foreign language.

"I'm saying that your son will have to take it slow. Only time will tell what kind of permanent damage both his brain and spinal cord might have endured from the fall. We did the best we could, but the healing process takes time. Just be thankful he's alive, and we'll take it one day at a time."

"Alive?" Dad reverted to his growling self. "You equate a mute paraplegic with being alive?"

"Sir." Dr. Jenkins put a hand on Dad's shoulder.

Dad shook it off.

Dr. Jenkins spoke slowly. He seemed comfortable with Dad's belligerence. "Sir, one day at a time. We encourage families in similar situations to take things one day at a time. We have counselors and social workers available if you need to talk further. I have other cases to attend to. The nurse will be out when your son is stable enough for you and your daughter to visit with him. We are all surprised that he's alive. Very few people survive such head trauma from this type of fall. I'll talk to you more shortly."

And with that, the doc turned and pushed through the doors marked "Hospital Personnel ONLY."

"Bull crap." Dad said to no one in particular. "What kind of nonsense is this? And you're gonna charge me for fixing him up enough to just lay in bed?"

I backed up, repulsed by Dad and shaken by the prognosis, and plopped back down on the couch nearest me. *Never walk again? Might never speak?* My mind whirled in a hundred directions like the flurries outside the window. What did this all mean? Jesse was alive. Barely. But never walk or speak. I hadn't thought of the in between. The stuff that lay between being alive and dead. *In between* stamped Jesse's prognosis as fresh confusion flooded my already cluttered mind.

Dad just stood there and stared at the OR doors. When no nurse arrived, he returned to his spot on the couch. Up to this point, he hadn't said anything to me. Not one word. Not even looked my way. The tension stretched between us like a rubber band pulled to its max. I couldn't think about going home. I closed my eyes to drift back to the last time I spoke to Jesse on the roof, when Dad's voice startled me back to now.

"Get up." Snap! He stood over me, his eyes laced with red. Then he turned and walked out of the waiting room toward the elevators. "We're going home."

Everything inside of me tensed. Like a tiger poised to pounce on Dad, one look at his eyes reminded me who the hunter was and whose hands held the gun. But how could I leave without seeing Jesse? I needed to see my brother and tell him in person that I was here for him. I would take care of him. Help him learn to walk again. Instead, we abandon him? What kind of stupidity was this? But that's just it. The story of my life. And I knew better than to protest, especially in public. I swallowed the angry voices in my head, stood up, and followed Dad to the car.

Like Humpty Dumpty, the surgeons attempted to put Jesse back together again. They even drilled a hole in his head to drain the bleed. I imagined the tube worked somewhat like a straw, sucking out all the awful memories of his yesterdays. Wishful thinking at best.

After two weeks in the ICU, they moved my brother to Acute Rehab where he spent close to three months, relearning how to swallow and maneuver his weight since his legs refused to budge. Dad visited him daily, returning home to report to me like he was sharing Chem lab results: "No change."

I hated Dad for not allowing me to see my baby brother, so I called the hospital as often as I could from the school office during my lunch breaks. The staff seemed to feel sorry for me, the sister whose brother tried to kill himself. So no one asked me why I didn't have a cell phone like most teens, or why couldn't I just use the phone at home.

In that first month after the ambulance took Jesse away, I called every day. But the nurse always told me Jesse was asleep, but doing a little better each day. In February, a female nurse whose voice I soon looked forward to hearing came on the line to answer my questions. Only then did I fully realize that not only might I never again see my brother walk. Would I ever hear his voice again?

Never learned the name of the nurse who took the phone, but I'll always remember her kindness. To help Jesse hear my voice and her patience to tell me what he was thinking. He must have written his responses down for her to read to me. Whatever the case, I never stayed on the phone long. Just long enough to let him know I was thinking about him. And I love him.

April arrived and Dad woke up one morning and announced, "Enough." He was tired of the inconvenience. So he pulled Jesse out of rehab against the doctor's advice, and the ambulance brought Jesse home three months after that night on the roof.

The medical staff assembled a hospital bed in Jesse's room and detailed the home care, rehab proceedings, and mandatory follow-up directions. Dad signed the papers and ushered everyone out. With nothing more than a two-second, "Thank you," Dad locked the door behind them, and before the ambulance left the driveway, I watched in horror as Dad tore the discharge papers to shreds. Like he was punishing the paper since he could no longer punish Jesse.

And once again, my list changed. And the Internet connection—cancelled. So that's how it had been for the last three months, while Jesse made little to no progress. Because Dad never allowed anyone in our house, convinced he could rehab his son on his own, Dad's schedule flexible enough for him to come home for lunch almost daily to shower and change Jesse's scrubs. But Jess didn't progress. Just lay there. And days when I came home and the room didn't smell of incense, Dad's go-to choice for air freshener, Dad didn't make it home. Perhaps a meeting ran over. Or he couldn't be bothered.

Whatever the case, I was strictly instructed to do everything aside from dressing my brother because, "Girls don't look at naked boys. And naked boys don't look at girls. No one looks at you naked. Understood, Talia?" It was not a question.

"Yes, sir." Because that's the best response to Dad's rules. The lawyer makes the laws. Breaks the laws. Then rewrites the laws so he looks innocent. That's how Dad rolls.

So the laws in our house simply rolled over to add Jesse's list to my list. And that was that. Until the school called the house in June, demanding a home tutor visit all summer in order to bring Jesse up to speed academically.

Dad said, "Thanks, but no thanks. We're moving."

"We are?" I asked Dad when he hung up. I guess we were.

Next thing I knew, move we did. Taking Jess's hospital bed, his wheelchair, and our broken hearts to the Chicago burbs just before my senior year kicked off.

Doctors predicted Jesse might never walk again, but his speech should return after the side effects of Traumatic Brain Injury waned. For months, no words left his lips. He does make one sound each and every night. He cries. Each and every night. He looks toward his bedroom window and cries. Eventually, he cries himself to sleep.

~FOUR~

The weekend crawls by, and when I wake up Monday morning with fresh blisters on top of old scars, my arm is red, oozing, and still burning. I goop on the entire tube of A&D ointment, wincing as I spread it over every inch of skin and clumsily wrap gauze from my elbow to my wrist. Then I find a baggy, green sweatshirt to wear that doesn't draw attention to the extra thickness. Every task takes longer than usual. Each time something, anything, contacts my arm, shots of pain fire up to my brain like arrows piercing the bull's eye. Over and over and over again. Twenty minutes remain for me to finish my morning list, and neither Jesse nor I have eaten breakfast.

My lips still sting from teeth bites. My ugly deformed lips. My right fist stops centimeters from smashing the bathroom mirror. That would create extra cleanup and additional chores to pay for a replacement. Time lamenting things I cannot change only blurs my perspective. I need to take care of Jess.

If he doesn't eat now, he won't eat until Dad comes home for lunch. And Dad doesn't always show up. So I quickly shove a bowl of lumpy oatmeal in his lap, apologizing for rushing off. Jess just glances down at my arm, his eyes saying the same two words he said to me that night on the roof. *I'm sorry*.

I tell him, "Don't be. Same old, same cold."

I have to get to school on time. If I'm late, I'll draw unnecessary attention to myself. I side hug Jesse, leaving the remote under his hand and fly out the door with my backpack over the shoulder of my good arm. Lips freshly scabbed, arm on fire, stomach growling, I look forward to only one thing. Lunchtime.

Lunch cannot arrive soon enough. I need distraction and little yellow squares pop up like granted wishes from an invisible genie. A genie named Lagan. Lagan knocks three times before noon with Post-it notes I find during morning classes. In first period, one sits curled up on my desk.

It reads:

Top of the mornin' to ya. Looking forward to 'conversation' today at lunch. NLA-style of course.

I flip the note over, and the back reads:

"Nod/Look Away" in case you forgot.

L

In between classes, I spot one on my locker that says:

Came up with 21 questions. You get two points for every question you answer yes, and no's are three-pointers. When you get to 21, you win...another lunch date with me!

L

After Bio, I follow the smells of pasta and garlic bread to the lunch line. Handed another personalized cafeteria tray by a smiling volunteer, my third Sticky Note of the day reads:

Sitting in my usual spot. Got your tray for u since u looked like u hurt your arm or something. I'll change it up if you don't like. C U now.

L

My gut contracts. I take the Post-it and return the tray. I thought I did a decent job at keeping my pain a secret. Thinking back to the morning, I wonder when Lagan picked up that my arm hurts. I decide I can handle this. I have lied about home my entire life. I have more excuses than pairs of unmatched socks when it comes to Dad. Poker face in place, I walk over to the table next to Lagan's and sit down in front of an untouched tray of food.

"Thanks." I let the whispered word fall in my lap.

"No problemo," Lagan answers, looking away from me.

Out of the corner of my eye, I can see that he hasn't eaten yet either. He lowers his head with his eyes closed momentarily. Then he looks up and picks up his fork.

"Yo, L-Train! Thanks for saving us seats." Two of Lagan's basketball buds approach our table, but Lagan intercepts them before they put their trays down.

"Sorry, dudes. Gotta keep my grades up so I don't get kicked off the team." Lagan pats his math book on the table next to his tray.

"Coach would never drop you. Shoot. You're only the best point-forward Hinsdale has seen in like the last century." The taller of the two fellas tosses in his opinion.

"I'm not worried about the coach. If my parents see my GPA drop, Mom will personally escort me off the court. Not taking my chances. I'll catch you guys at practice. Peace." Lagan nods to the two, and they shrug shoulders before walking away to another table. All the while I'm staring at my tray, being what I do best. Invisible.

I see that he brought me soup, yogurt, juice, and two slices of white bread. Untoasted. *Do you notice my lips too?* Who am I kidding? Who can't tell there's something wrong with me? I dismiss the voices in my head and say to my tray, "I'm ready for question number one. Going for twenty-one. Yes, I am."

"Alrighty then." Lagan smiles, and the sight of that dimple greets me like than an umbrella on a rainy day.

Just hearing his voice transports me far away from the wicked world in which I live most of my minutes. I just hope his questions will keep me here, and Lagan won't snoop around my house of pain.

"Question number one: Is your name really Talia Grace Vanderbilt, Talia meaning 'dew drop from heaven'?"

I nod to my tray, giggling softly to myself.

"Great! Two points."

Two girls approach our table, and Lagan stops. The tall blonde with a hot pink hair extension clipped on her right side stops in front of Lagan and asks, "Is anyone sitting here, Lagin?"

"English assignment, Nadine. Sorry." Lagan shrugs his shoulders.

I glance up and see the other girl, the one with perfectly crimped, shoulder length, brown hair, roll her eyes.

Nadine clears her throat. "That's cool. Let's go, Stace."

I guess the brunette chick is Stacey. They walk past several empty tables before sitting down. Must be nice to be so popular. Can't help but feel a little special that he didn't ditch our sort-of conversation for his fan club.

Lagan shakes his head to himself. "Wanna know something funny?"

Are we still playing the game? Or—

Lagan answers his own question. "With a name like Lagan Kumar Desai, middle name a definite no, and LK, not nearly as cool as TJ or JR. So in third grade, I actually gave my parents the option to change my name to Logan. They didn't go for it."

But you look like a Lagan, not a Logan.

Lagan keeps talking. "Do you ever wish your parents had hyphenated your name? How easy if they had written La-gan, as in, she finished the soup and the soup is now gone, on my birth certificate?"

So the question was…? I look to my left, to the exit sign. Because the soup? Definitely not gone. I carefully spoon a bit into my mouth, failing to pass it past my stinging lips. Ouch!

"Three-pointer! You are a natural. Awesome. Next question: Do you have a favorite color? Let me guess. Green? Since you've worn a different green, long sleeve pretty much since school started."

I nod toward my tray, an unusual combination of warmth and want clouding my senses. Details. He notices details.

"Another two points. Rock and roll! Is your favorite color red since it reminds you of the sunrise?"

Huh? My eyes shift to the exit sign. I just told you my favorite color was green. A smile escapes me. Lagan is creatively sneaking in details about himself. I have to write an intro biography on him too, after all.

"Three more points. We quickly approach twenty-one, ladies and gentlemen. This girl can shoot! Let's continue. Question number five: Does the soup taste good?" He nods his head, predicting an easy yes.

I want to say yes, but the salty droplets inevitably roll over the tender, unhealed slits on my lips. I swallow, not wanting to seem ungrateful, but shift my eyes to the exit sign again. Not even sure why I tell the truth. I wait for Lagan's response or the next question, but he doesn't speak. I look up and over to his seat, thinking the game's over and I've lost. Except Lagan isn't there anymore. He's walking back to the food line, and now he's talking to the cafeteria lady who handed me my tray. She leaves him, then returns promptly and hands him something. He strolls back to our table, and I turn my attention to the soup, picking up a spoonful and pouring it into the bowl. Lagan places an ice-cream cup in between us and sits down.

"Sorry about the soup. I should have known it would hurt your lips. Try the ice cream, and be ready. The next question is coming right up. By the way, I told Vita, the lunch lady, to put it on my tab."

My lips are ugly and he can see them. Instinctively, I pull some hair over my face and reach over to retrieve the ice cream. Peeling the cover and scooping my first nibble, I guess his next question and nod to my spoon before he asks. The icy coldness soothes my lips.

"Okay, so we're up to question number six. But before I ask, let's just tally up the score." He pretends to push buttons on his imaginary calculator in the sky. "The grand total so far is thirteen. Less than ten points to winning. 'On with the game!' the crowd screams. Yes, yes, of course. Time out is over."

I'm beginning to wonder if he forgot that I'm sitting within earshot as he plays sports announcer. He continues after taking a breath. Glad he remembers to breathe.

"Question number six: Is the ice cream yummay in your tummay?" Lagan asks.

I look away, then realize that I meant to nod, so I quickly nod, then finally just whisper the words, "Yes. Thank you." The ice cream is perfect, and my tummay ain't complaining either.

"Fifteen points, ladies and gentleman. We are approaching the home stretch, and there are less than three minutes till the buzzer. Must think quickly." He fidgets and frets. We both know he pre-wrote the script.

"Thank you for clarifying before we move on to the final two questions of the afternoon. Question number seven…" Lagan stops talking.

He cups one hand in the other and reverses. Then his left hand in his right. He repeats this motion, and then finally speaks.

"Someday," he speaks slowly, his voice hoarse but gentle. "Not today. Not soon. When you're ready. When you decide it's the right time. Someday? Will you tell me what happened to your…lips?"

Looking down, panic seizes me. I meant to look away. His words spread like curtains in the space between us, uncovering a window to Lagan's heart. A window he's trying to look through. Into my life.

Of course I would never tell you the deal with my lips.

My eyes well up, and as I gather my things to leave before the bell rings so I can hide in the girls' bathroom, I can see him scribbling a note on a fresh Sticky Note. I plan to skip Gym today with my arm, because wearing my uniform and expose my inch-thick. Gauze covering was never an option. Swatting away tears in defeat, I watch Lagan push clean cafeteria napkins across to me. Then he rests his hand on my tray. He will take it for me. Again.

He doesn't try to stop me this time. Just slips me a little yellow square sheet during this brief interaction. I take the paper and hightail it to the girls' locker room. The moment the cafeteria doors swing behind me, my eyes scan the words on the note.

I just want you to know that, if I could kiss and make them better, I would kiss your lips a thousand times.

Heat spreads across my cheeks.

I flip the note over and a giggle escapes me as I read the rest:

Not romantically. Purely for medicinal purposes, of course. Btw, that last ? was worth 10 pts. whether u answered it or not. So u win! C. U. tom.

L

~FIVE~

I wish Mom were around to talk to. Isn't that what a girl does? Talk to their mothers about boys and crushes and the cloud of butterflies that turn somersaults inside you. *Mom, as much as you called me your sunlight, you were the one who brightened my days. Most of them. I miss you, Mom.*

When I was born, I brought light into our house of darkness. That's what Mom used to say to me when I grew old enough to remember her words. She also said that when I cried as a newborn, it made her cry. She felt sad when I felt sad. She laughed when I laughed. She slept when I slept. Her name means "song," and she sang to me a sweet "gita" or two each time she swayed me to sleep. Everything changed when a year passed and Justice was born.

Mom named me Talia because each day she awoke, like the morning dew, I reminded her that there was a heaven. I hated heaven for taking her from me. If heaven had to choose, why didn't heaven choose Dad? Who was I kidding? Hell probably had first dibs on the man.

Dad chose Jesse's name. Justice. As a lawyer, all he thought about was the law. Dad's kids would know the law, and they would follow it to a T. Or else. That's why we called my little brother Jesse. Every chance we had to forget Dad's tyranny, we did.

Jesse hated his real name. When the teachers would call his name off the attendance list on the first day of school, he wouldn't even respond. Then someone else would say aloud, "He goes by 'Jesse,'" and that would be the first and last time you heard his formal name spoken all year.

On my first day of kindergarten, Dad woke me up two hours before the bus was scheduled to arrive to go over the "Proper Rules of Conduct of a Respectable Daughter in Public." I didn't even know what half of the words he said meant, but I learned to nod and agree at an early age. He lectured me, and soon both of us siblings, each year when school began. We had the gist of his speech down to our own memorized list.

Be on time.

Get good grades.

Socialize with no one.

Come straight home.

In first grade, I asked Dad for the same thing every six-year-old asks for. "Can I have a play date with my friend Melody?"

Dad corrected me on two points. "You do not have time for friends after school, and you do not have time to play. Playing is reserved for lazy people who amount to nothing but welfare- dependent citizens."

I still didn't get it. "Daddy, why is it bad to play when I have plenty of time and hardly any homework?" He sat in his office behind his desk, and his response was my first list. Then he handed it to me, and his words sealed my fate. "Now, Talia, if you have any extra time after you complete your chores, you can have a play date." Having only recently learned to read, the sheer number of words on the page crushed any hope of a semi-normal childhood.

I saw all the other kids run off on with each other's mommies, inviting each other to birthday parties and weekend movies. Maybe their lists were shorter? I put my best tough-girl face on when I rejected their kind invitations. "Sorry, I can't make it." Before long, the kids stopped asking.

At night, under my covers, I cried myself to sleep and dreamt of tea parties and dress-up fun. I always included Jesse in my dreams, because he longed for friends, too. And Mom would be a queen or a fairy or an angel, free of rules and free to fly. When she flew, her long black hair glistened in the sunlight. Mom only broke Dad's laws twice, each incident etched in my mind like a ridge of quicksand around a beautiful castle. I drown each time I try to swim past the memories.

Mom and Dad rarely left the house together, leaving Jess and I alone. Parent-teacher conferences marked one annual exception. Dad prepped her with the same speech every year: "Stick to business. No social comments. Only questions regarding the kids' academic progress."

Mom forgot. Forgetting costs dearly in our house. Somehow, the details will always remain between the walls of my seventh grade math class, but somehow Mom got too involved in Mr. Beakman's story about how he uses math to perfect his shot when he goes deer hunting. All we heard when the fit hit the shan was that Mom asked him if he knew any women who hunted for sport.

They barely reached the house when Dad pushed Mom through the door and up the stairs, simultaneously screaming at her. "You'll pay for each word of disrespect, Gita! You hear me?"

We all heard him. Jesse and I watched from the bottom of the stairs as Mom repeatedly apologized, her words as effective as candy flavored placebo.

"You could get me fired if people start snooping into our lives. That's why we keep people out! Were you planning to invite her teacher over for personal hunting lessons next? What were you gonna do if Mr. Beakman asked to give Talia private shooting lessons? You of all people should know what men do when they're alone with little girls. Or are you thinking of running off to the woods and leaving the children? You just don't get it. So today, I'll make sure you get it and you'll never forget it! You hear?" Who didn't hear his fiery bellow?

Next thing we knew, he shoved Mom into their bedroom and into the closet, latched it, and then a warning echoed through the house. "Now, spend some time thinking about how you can make sure that it never happens again!" Neither Jess nor I knew when Dad had installed a lock on the closet door in their bedroom.

Completed our evening lists without speaking to each other, my brother and I knew to stay clear of the hurricane. I sobbed as I scrubbed down the bathroom floor. I wanted to rescue Mom, but knew, as always, we had to wait it out.

Jesse moved around the house to close the shades and curtains, and I could hear his eleven-year-old fists punching the drapes when he reached my room. When I glanced up from the tile floor to catch Jesse's gaze, two chained rodeo bulls stared back. We heard Mom banging on the closet door, my parents' bedroom across from mine, saying, "I'm sorry. I'm sorry. I'm sorry," over and over and over again.

I went to bed that night hating Dad more than ever. I don't actually know when I fell asleep. I gripped the sheets of my bed and pummeled my pillow in anger, listening to Mom's pleas late into the night. Eyes swollen from weeping, arms weary from punching—I slept. I knew I slept, because I remembered my dreams when I awoke. I dreamt of slaying a dragon, slicing a snake, and beheading a rabid dog.

When my alarm clock sounded, I jumped out of bed, wanting to run to Mom's room to see if she was okay, but Dad hadn't left for work yet. The scent of coffee didn't permeate the air. I didn't hear the morning news on the kitchen TV. Something felt strange. Only after I started my morning routine and read my list on the vanity while brushing my teeth did I understand. Partially. Taped next to my note from Dad, Mom's list stared back at me. Which meant...

Guilt-riddled and heart heavy, I left for school with Jess, but I walked through my day like a zombie. Each time I passed Jesse in the school halls, a glance between us said it all: we only had each other. When the last bell rang, just before walking home, I pulled Jess into a stairwell alcove (away from student traffic), dropped my books, and held onto him for dear life. As I wept hard into my brother's shoulder, the sound of his grinding teeth grated in my ears.

Terrified to face Dad, yet unable to abandon Mom, we marched home, the weight of textbooks on my back feeling heavier than ever. How long did he plan to leave her in there? Always aware of the hourglass, we picked up the pace and ran the last block, resolved to never allow Dad to break our bond. We built a wall around us. No matter how many times Dad knocked down, we vowed to rebuild and rebuild. Right now, we needed to get to Mom and let her know. We'd help her rebuild as soon as Dad let her out. Maybe, just maybe, she was already out. We didn't realize that even when he released her, she would stay stuck inside—trapped in her hopelessness like a fly caught in a web.

When I unlocked the front door, Jesse ran past me, up the stairs, to Mom and Dad's bedroom. I walked into the house, listening for Mom's footsteps somewhere around the house. Nothing. Jesse banged on the closet door. "Mom? Are you in there? Are you all right?"

I darted upstairs to join him. The stench of urine and feces and vomit permeated the room.

"Mom?" I repeated his words. "Mom, are you in there? Mom! Talk to us. Dad's not home yet. Are you okay?"

"Mom!" Jesse pleaded again. "Please talk to us. We just want to know that you're alive. Mom. Please. Say. Something."

Then we heard her faint voice. She said the same two words she had been saying all night. "I'm…sorry."

I started crying again. *What a lie!* She had done nothing wrong. And she sat in jail.

"Mom, I love you. We love you, Mom. We love you," I said at first and then Jesse said the words with me.

"I'm...sorry." Her faint whisper came again.

"I'm sorry too, Mom." I put my lips near the door. "I'm sorry we can't get you out. I'm sorry Dad is so mean. I'm sorry we're too little to fix this. I'm sorry we can't save you."

And that was all we had time for. Our lists called our names while passing minutes taunted us. Dad left Mom in the closet for two days. Two whole days. Two of the longest days of my life. I feared she would die in there. I begged Dad to let her out with all the pleas a twelve-year-old could muster.

I made all kinds of promises to him. From me. From Jess. From Mom. "We'll be perfect, better than perfect for you, if you would just let her out."

Nothing. Not even a hint of bending. Then, on the evening of the second day, I think the stench of bodily fluids overtook him and a number eleven appeared on my list that evening to clean the closest.

Shortly before 8:00 p.m., Dad walked into my room and tossed a key on my desk while I finished my homework. "I'm running out to do groceries. Make sure the house and your mother are cleaned up before I get back."

I sprinted to tell Jesse, and we raced back to Mom's room to unlock the closet. I promised myself that I would not let her see anything negative in my eyes. I knew that my response would either help or hinder her getting into the shower and back on her feet. As I fiddled with the lock, my shaking hands failed to draw out the simple process of turning the key.

For a fleeting moment, I thought Dad tricked us, giving us a key that didn't fit, teasing us with counterfeit hope. Suddenly, a faint click preceded the forceful opening of closet doors, and Mom fell out onto us—the fetor of mom's soiled clothes triggered my gag reflex. I looked away and winced while trying to inhale only from my mouth. Jesse picked up an empty bottle of laxatives near Mom's legs. Dad had his warped ideas on "cleansing us," but this was a new one. And here we stood again, Jess and I, the cleanup crew.

Hearing the second hand clicking on the wall clock like a time bomb, Jess and I frantically went to work, having learned at a young age that tears bore a price tag we simply could not afford. "Or else" there'd be more to cry about than ever. After he helped me half-carry, half-drag Mom to the shower, Jess ran to the supplies closet and ceaselessly gathered, wiped, and wet-vacked all of Mom's insides that spilled out of her over the past two days.

I had never seen Mom naked, but somehow knew as I peeled back her wet, caked-on layers that what lay beneath only scratched the surface of my mother's wounds. The grocery store was less than fifteen minutes away, and each second I stalled moved us one second closer to Dad's return.

I thought if I talked through the process, I'd bring a sliver of dignity to the situation. "Mom, I'm just gonna undress you so that I can help you clean up. Dad'll be back soon, and I need to get you showered, dressed, and in bed."

At first, she sat in the bathtub in a trance-like state, and I felt so ashamed for her, for us, for the situation. As suspected, once I unbuttoned her shirt, her skin exposed multiple bruises from Dad's daily "reminders" of his authority. Much worse than I had imagined, nearly every inch of her body was covered with scabs, cuts, blisters, and bruises. Her body looked sickly, and now I understood why she always wore sleeves and pants. She never wanted me to see this. I couldn't hold back my tears any longer, and as I wiped her down, gently using a washcloth over all her hurts, I bawled over my mother's broken body.

I threw all her clothes into a kitchen trash bag and placed the sack outside the garage to contain the stench. Returning to my mom, sitting on the edge of the bathtub, wrapped in towels, she robotically allowed me to guide her to bed where Jess finished up nearby. He gasped when he saw her legs, black and blue, certain cuts still oozing. Scooping up the cleaning products, he wiped over the closet door, and left the can of Febreze near me as he fumbled on the carpet and out of the room.

Mom stayed quiet, but as I dressed her into clean, cotton pajamas, tears began to slowly slip down her cheeks. I wiped them with my kisses and told Mom, "Everything's gonna be okay," knowing it was a promise I could not keep. I was twelve years old. I did not even know what okay looked like. I tucked her into bed under the covers and Febrezed the room, closet, and hallway until the bottle shook empty, then headed downstairs to join Jesse in the kitchen.

When Dad came home, Jess and I clicked on autopilot, putting the groceries away and holding our tongues, hoping Dad would approve. Back to normal, Dad's version of "normal" was the closest thing to stability we knew, and that was the best we could hope for. But normal didn't return overnight.

Mom had her first nervous breakdown in the closet. I understood this a year later when she had a subsequent breakdown, and the signs resonated unpleasant familiarity. Two months passed before Mom spoke again. Somehow, she found the physical strength to get out of bed the next morning and pick up her list and check it off, one task at a time, as if the last two days had never happened. Her robotic, emotionless activity introduced new terror and confusion. Had Mom crossed over to Dad's side now? Jess and I walked around on eggshells all day long now, whether or not Dad was home. Until one day in May, some two months later.

It was May 12, Dad's birthday. Mom woke up, and like a toy with fresh batteries, she waltzed into the kitchen and cooked up a huge breakfast of pancakes, eggs, and bacon, all before my alarm went off. In the center of the table, a homemade card for Dad leaned against the Cheerios like a paper menu at a restaurant. The cover contained the words *I Love You* scrawled in red lipstick. I imagined they were written with her blood, and I dismissed this as part of Mom's new insanity. Mom's demeanor shifted from somber to chipper, and it felt strangely worse than the silence.

"Good morning, Talia. Good morning, Justice. Come sit for breakfast." My jaw dropped at the choice of her words. One word. "Today is a wonderful day. Do you remember that today is Gerard's birthday? It sure is. We should all be on our best behavior as a gift to your father." *Weren't we always?*

And why was she calling Jesse "Justice?" Yet another suggestion she was on Dad's side? Ugh! What was wrong with her?

"Sit down now. What can I get you? Eggs? Pancakes? Toast? Bacon? Milk? Juice?" And she carried on until we ascended the school bus, and she waved to us like we were leaving for summer camp, wishing us a great day and telling us to do our best in school and shouting that she'd have milk and cookies ready for us when we returned home. All the kids on the bus stared at Jess and me. Nothing unusual about that.

As I looked back at the house, I saw my dad kiss my mom goodbye on the driveway before he opened his car door, got in, and backed out. The bus driver stopped only two blocks from our street while we waited for Joey, who nearly missed his ride as he ran down the hill every single morning. I looked back at Mom, wondering if an alien had invaded her body, because I saw her kiss her fingers and blow on her hand in the direction of Dad's car. I nearly vomited right there in the bus, swallowing to keep breakfast down and turning to face the front of the bus. Life shifted back to a new kind of normal, and I adjusted my heart's rudder to the wind of the season. A wind that blew in temporary peace, intermittent with the usual disappointments and punishments of life as I knew it.

~SIX~

My arm reminds me that the list comes first. I race around after school to get everything done well before Dad reaches home. Jess's eyes shift left and right as he watches me zip back and forth, from room to room. By the time I wheel my brother into the kitchen, his face displays a mix of guilt and disappointment. I don't slow down to chitchat about my day at school, and I know that's unfair. I am his only connection to the real world, and Jesse lives for the stories of teenagers dressed in trendy threads, teachers who make goofy blunders, even assemblies regarding new school policies.

I purposely hold my tongue. I know that Lagan's name is on my mind, and if I open my mouth, I will spill out the news of possibility. The possibility of a friend. I want Jess to know. But I also hate having something he can't have. Guilt drives so much of my life that I waffle between telling him and keeping my life private, knowing he lives vicariously through my life, but fearing I might inadvertently rub it in.

That night on the roof marked Jess's decision to get off the fence. He jumped because Dad said no e-mail. To Jess, no e-mail equated with no friends. Jess did not speak to anyone at school, but he e-mailed friends he met online through video game chat rooms. He preferred friends without faces. If they lived out of state, an explanation of his social bondage deemed unnecessary. Now he cannot communicate with them at all. Not even get online to tell them he disappeared. It was the death of him. Even though, technically, he still breathes. Breathing is about all he does by himself these days, and I bionic legs were free, Dad would have had Jessie fixed and programed before he left the hospital.

The staff that demanded Jesse be tutored failed to note one minor detail. Dad seemed to have friends in every branch of the legal system. I'm sure it didn't hurt that as one of the country's top immigration lawyers, he knew the system. And how to work it. The threat of disruption to our perfectly orchestrated lives, Dad being the conductor, of course, didn't dissipate immediately as it did in the past, and Dad refused to be bullied over to the other end of the stands. Dad wore the bully crown, and he had no plans to share his throne. Next thing I knew, packing topped my evening list, and two weeks before the start of senior year, we loaded our little world into a small U-Haul and drove north three hours to Darien, Illinois.

Dad left all of Mom's clothes in their bedroom, instructing me not to bring any reminders of her. I took only one thing that I am sure he'll never suspect. A strand of her hair. It looks close enough to my hair. I keep it in an overdue library book I never returned—Faulkner's *The Sound and the Fury*. I just flip to page seventy-one when I need Mom. I run my finger along the length of the hair, imagining my fingers running through her locks of blackness. Mementos would only incriminate me.

Like the Sticky Notes from Lagan. I reread them ten or so times and then toss them into the wastebasket on the school grounds before my walk home. I learned the hard way never to keep any letters from friends. The week after Mom died, a kid at my old school named Brad befriended me, perhaps noticing my wet eyes leaking onto my cafeteria tray. Average height, African-American, sporting an army fade, Brad had two goals in life: to be at the top of the Honor Roll and to please his grandmother. He loved to talk about his nana, who was counting on him to get that full-ride linebacker ticket to Michigan State.

One afternoon, Brad asked me to join his friends at their table, carrying my tray over before I could say no. He asked if I needed anything. He genuinely seemed to care. In my weakness, I let him into my world. More accurately, I entered his.

Each day, I found myself drawn to Brad and his crew, the temptation to escape my reality so alluring while surrounded by a group of lively extroverts. Like a magnet pulling north to south, the group's carefree temperament lassoed me in, and for a moment, I pretended to live someone else's life. A life where a mom made warm dinners and tucked me in at night. A life where a dad asked how my day was and kissed my forehead when I had a rough day. A life where a brother rode his bike to the park to play pickup basketball on weeknights after his homework was done. A fabricated life. A normal life. A life not my own.

One day, a few weeks into the charade, Brad wrote me a note and secretly slipped it into my backpack. I never had a chance to read it. When I saw Brad in math class, he wrote a "?" on his notebook and held it up to me after the teacher turned her back to us to chalk problems on the blackboard. I had no idea what he meant. It was in the note. The note I never found.

Later, in the lunch line, Brad asked me directly. "So, whaddya think?"

"About what?" I was clueless.

"My letter. I put it in your backpack. The question I asked you. You did read it? Right?" Brad eyes widened as his voice rose an octave.

"I have no idea what you're talking about. What letter?" I felt bad, but I didn't see any letter in my backpack. A few people were still ahead of us, so I pulled my bag off my shoulder and fished through it for a loose piece of paper. Nothing.

"I'm sorry." I shrugged my shoulders. "It must have fallen out. Why? What'd it say?"

This was the first time I ever heard smooth-talking Brad stutter. "N-n-nothing. M-m-maybe I'll write it again, but this time, I'll put it in your hands. That way you won't lose it."

"Ask me now." What would be so secretive that he had to write me a letter, anyway? Unless...

As Brad looked away from me, muttering, "Forget about it," I suspected that Brad had feelings for me. Maybe he tried to ask me out. Transported back to kindergarten, my mind began to think of all the reasons that I couldn't leave my house. It was only a matter of time when Brad would see through the excuses and conclude that I didn't like him.

"Well, whatever it was that you wanted to ask me, yes! If it includes lemon ice pops." I lied. I would cancel later. For now, I savored the sweet nibble of an undercover crush.

Brad's smile returned, bigger than ever, and we headed to our usual table with our tuna casseroles, applesauce dishes, and fruit-punch juice cartons. While eating lunch together and comparing war stories from morning classes, Brad lightened up further. Before I knew it, he nudged into my shoulder as he joked about how he could make a tastier casserole than today's main entree any day.

"I ain't ashamed to admit that I watch Food Network! Don't hate on a brutha cuz y'all can't cook." Brad proudly claimed his rightful place among guys who were in touch with their domestic side.

The rest of us laughed, and Karie took an unfolded napkin and crowned him "Chef Bradley." Karie's bouncing red curls only megaphoned her personality, and that day, she wore green Nike gear that matched her mint-tinted eyes.

She plopped down next to Brad to interview him like a talk show hostess. "Step-by-step instructions, please." Karie used her thumb for a mike "For us little people out here who don't know the difference between butter and shortening."

The growing volume of our laughter blinded me. That's why I didn't notice. Until I noticed.

Dad showed up at school, carrying a briefcase of anger along with a small, folded-up piece of loose-leaf paper. He spotted me and beelined to our table, waving the note. The note that Brad had written. *Of course.* Dad must have snooped in my bag. I smelt burnt flesh. And I wasn't even on fire yet.

"Which one of you students goes by the name Bradley?" asked Dad in his steady, stern, lawyer voice.

I didn't know whether to run away or scream. I imagined slipping under the table and disappearing through a trap door. As usual, there was no escaping Dad or his collateral damage.

I stood up to leave with Dad, trying to make eye contact with Brad and mouth, "Don't say anything," but it was too late. Dad saw me motion to Brad, walked over to our side of the table, tore up the letter into a hundred pieces, then dropped it onto Brad's tray, all over his food.

"Don't even think about it." He looked directly at Brad, and if his eyes were swords, the fencing tournament was over. Casualties lay all around me. If only death were my reality.

Instead, Dad proceeded to grab my tray with one hand, and with his other hand on my shoulder, he nudged me from behind along the back of the cafeteria to an isolated table. Then he gently placed my tray down and nodded his head to the spot in front of it. This was to be my new seat. At this empty table. Alone.

"And this is where you will sit daily." He looked into my eyes with unwavering authority and spoke just loud enough for me to hear. "By yourself. And for the record, if this boy or any other boy ever tries anything like that again, you will be homeschooled. By me. Am I clear?"

I nodded. "Yes, sir." Aware of the entire cafeteria staring at me. "Crystal."

"Go on. Eat." Dad stood next to me and watched. And what? Hoped the dust from his twister entrance would just settle and life would go on? Same old, same cold?

"Is there a problem, Mr. Vanderbilt?" Joanie, the cafeteria manager, approached from behind Dad, her hands clasped at her waist.

"No ma'am. Leaving now. Have a good day." Like a light switch, Dad's voice softened, and he eased his eagle eye stare when he blinked and smiled at her.

"You too, sir. You too." His tone assured her that everything was fine, so she turned to return to her post by the main cafeteria doors.

When she reached far away enough to be out of earshot, Dad turned to punctuate our meeting. "I'll be checking in on you. Don't test me. Stick to the plan. And put the kettle to boil when I get home tonight. I plan for you never to forget this day. My rules. My words..."

Like a bad commercial I couldn't fast-forward, the stares of students drowned me. What I could tune out was his voice. I already knew the last two words. The scars of "or else" pulsed like surgery wounds on a rainy day. Brad's tiny pursuit of me brought on the first time boiling water rained down on my arm. My personal weather forecast all week, every week simply became, "Rainy with a ninety-five percent chance of...more rain." No surprises there.

The little sunshine I knew for those few weeks teased me like a trip to Southern California. But there was no going back. My friends quickly drifted away from me. Who wouldn't retreat from a girl with a freak dad? And Brad? He avoided my eyes, but he and I both knew there was no point. He never rewrote the letter. I would never know for sure. Dad had complete control of my life, and Brad walked away. It was easier to walk away. I understood. I might have done the same thing had the tables been turned.

And then the tables changed. From the wooden, splintering tabletops of Benton Harbor to the smooth, Windexed laminate tops of Hinsdale North. Table for two had a fresh coat of paint on it. And this girl had to do next to nothing besides never sit right next to someone, keep a watchful eye, and just show up.

~SEVEN~

Leaving Benton Harbor was easy enough. I had no friends. I had no mom. I had nothing to look forward to and nothing to live for. Until now. Until Lagan. Close to two years have passed since a boy, any boy, paid two seconds of attention to me.

Each time that I peel off a Post-it note addressed to me, Dad might emerge from behind my locker. Each time I eat a few seats down from Lagan, Dad could turn up in the cafeteria, just to "check on me." I remain on guard always, and without spelling it out, Lagan adjusts to my pace, even when my heart crawls slower than a limping snail. And yet, over several weeks, the small doses of nods and exchanges amount to something I experience for the first time. Ever. Friendship. A friend.

The whole thing makes no sense. But Lagan, no matter how many roadblocks I construct, continues to press on. Maybe he likes a challenge. Or maybe he actually wants this. Each time I answer no, I wonder what makes him return to me. To the possibility of me, that is.

"Do you have a cell phone?" He interrupts me during American History with a fresh set of questions, no assignment pending.

"No." I don't bother looking up from my text to answer.

Ms. Rose flips through a Time magazine at her desk.

"Do you have an e-mail address?" Lagan asks his second question.

"No."

"Fax machine?"

"Nope."

"Internet access?"

"Nada."

"Are you allowed to get snail mail?"

"Not unless it's my report card."

"Do you want to go to the movies?"

Wouldn't that be fun! "Yes. But no thanks."

"Are you allowed to go out with friends?"

Pause. *Do you have to make me say it?* "No."

Then a breakthrough. Sort of.

"Are you allowed to go to the library?"

I think about this. For most of my school projects, Dad purchased extensive encyclopedia software. If I can think of something I need for school that isn't covered, the library has potential. Still seems risky, though. Dad would probably accompany me and stay until I checked books out. "Maybe."

"Is your dad a cop?"

"No." More like an armed felon hiding under a fancy suit, I want to say. "He's a lawyer. Immigration Law."

"Close enough. Maybe it's the whole overprotective dad thing?" Lagan's voice strains as if he's reaching for the sugar on the top shelf. Problem is, poisonous pellets fill the sugar tin. And he has no clue.

"Something like that." Actually, I don't know that I have ever thought it through. It is all I know. I learned at an early age not to question Dad. I don't know if I have ever asked myself why Dad does what he does. Does he take home all his pent up frustrations from work, perhaps from representing overseas clients who are never awake during Central Standard Time? Mom told us once that she met Dad at work, but the story ended there. Maybe Dad missed Mom and took it out on us? My eyebrows must have burrowed into each other, showing my dislike of the question.

"Sorry for asking." Lagan looks genuinely sorry, his averted eyes accompanying his lowered voice.

"No. It's just. I don't have a good explanation. It's just my life, I guess."

***

These are better days—we have graduated from nodding to cafeteria trays. I still discern where and when I'll risk real conversations. Unforeseen opportunities arise in English Lit circles, Science Lab, during assemblies, and occasionally in study hall in the school library, if we secure two side-by-side cubicles.

I love how Lagan creatively tells me about himself while asking me about me. During a team math competition, he quickly moves his chair next to mine. He has no intention of winning. He has every intention of digging deeper.

After knocking a geometry proof out, he scrawls, Chocolate or Vanilla? on the scratch paper.

I circle Vanilla and write the words of course underneath.

He puts a question mark after my words.

I scribble back, Everyone loves chocolate. Vanilla seems lonely. I prefer to represent the underdog. I shrug to let him know it might not make sense, but it makes sense to me. He changes my period to an explanation point. He either approves or he's excited. Doesn't take much, apparently.

After the second question, Comedy or Suspense? appears from beneath his writing hand, I have to think back to the last time I saw a movie. It was with Mom. The Fisher King. A nineties flick starring a comedian Mom used to love.

I cross out ~~suspense~~ and write romantic in front of comedy.

He smirks and writes, CIA Suspense like the Bourne Trilogy, but I like those too. Shhh. don't tell anyone. Have a rep to uphold. Don't want the guys to know I'm into chick flicks, and then proceeds to black out the words ~~chick flicks~~ as he surveys the room suspiciously.

By the time I answer ten questions, all the teams have handed in their contest sheets. We're last, but I don't care. We have a few fun facts to walk away with.

I prefer spring. He likes autumn.

He plays basketball. I can run. Pretty fast if I need to.

He plays the guitar. Writes his own music, apparently. I play a mean vacuum.

I can bake from scratch. He has mastered mac and cheese from the box.

He chooses bacon over sausage any day. I prefer bacon, too. But turkey. He's all for the pig's contribution to the best scents to radiate from a kitchen.

He loves music: to sing it, dance to it, or just listen to it all day long. So would I if I had time. Not sure about the dancing thing, though.

He owns an iPod. I listen to the radio of my alarm clock.

I read fiction. He doesn't like to read. Well, there's one book he reads every day. A little weird, but okay.

I investigate further that day during lunch. "What's it called?"

"What's what called?" Lagan needs to work on his short-term memory is what I'm thinking.

"The one book you read?" Duh!

"Oh that. It's nothing. Just a little book on life and war. You probably wouldn't get into it."

"Try me. I don't mind a story on war. Who's the hero?" Heck, any war story that isn't my own would be a nice diversion.

"Heroes. Plural. That would be you. And me. And the gardener."

Speak for yourself. I'm nobody's hero. I roll my eyes and say, "Whatever. So what's the gardener's name? Does he fight with a spade or a rake? Do you even know the difference between a weed and a flower?"

Lagan holds his hand over his heart and throws his head back before saying with theatrical gusto, "Ouch! Feeling my heartbeat slowing to..a..."—he falls off his stool— "stop."

"Now if I ROFLOL, the school newspaper will report a cafeteria poisoning. That might get us a better menu. Hmm? Now there's food for...What were we talking about?"

Back upright with his lower lip slightly jutting, I wonder if he'll ever get used to a girl who is not easily impressed.

He answers my question. The next day at lunch, he hands me a book.

"*The Beautiful Fight* by Blank," I read aloud. "Sounds violent." Besides, how can there be anything beautiful about fighting? "Who's Blank? Is he a one-name wonder like Madonna or Sting?"

"Haha. Blank is where you fill in your name. Because you're part of the story. Wanna borrow it? I put Sticky Notes to mark my favorite parts." He slides it over to my side of the cafeteria table.

"With all my free time..." I'm pretty certain that between Dad's lists and homework, I'll never get to it. I pick up the book and check the Post-it notes. They're blank, like the author name. "Okay, on one condition."

"Oh, I forgot to mention," Lagan says, "I don't need it back anytime soon. I have a second copy. Keep it. Or not."

"Yeah. That's what I was gonna ask." How did you know? I don't do well with deadlines. And sounds like that's the case, so... "Thanks. I think."

I turn over the average-sized book that has a plant budding from the earth with a brilliant red sunrise in the backdrop. Pretty. On closer examination, that's no plant. It's a sword, the sun's rays creating a brilliant metallic luster when they hit the emerging weapon.

When I get home, I carefully move Mom's precious strand to Lagan's book. Now I have two people to think about each time I open this book. Whether I read it or not is TBD.

~EIGHT~

The date is February 7. We've been playing these games for five months, and Lagan still has no clue regarding the hell I return to each day after school. I shake my head, Etch –A Sketch-style, and soak in Lagan's latest innovation to enter my head and heart. He names our conversation over lunch today, "Face-to-Face," giving me two Sticky Notes during math class—one with a happy face and one with a sad face—with instructions to bring them to lunch with me.

Basically, I put one face on each side of my tray: on the left sits the happy face, and on the right, the sad one.

"If the word I say makes you happy, put your hand on the happy face. If it makes you sad, cover the sad face." Lagan smiles, and I nod. Simple enough.

I pick up a spoon heaping with applesauce. My lips are well scabbed over for a change, so they don't sting as I eat today. I swallow a second spoonful and wait for the first word.

Lagan clears his throat and looks up at the ceiling. "Blueberries."

I move my left hand over the happy face. I prefer raspberries, but blueberries are a close second.

After looking side to side, Lagan says his second word: "Swimming."

I put my hand back on the smiley face. Swimming reminds me of Mom. Plus I love that the world becomes silent under water. I think of the beach near our Benton Harbor home. The last time I swam was over five years ago, when Jess wasn't bedbound. I have no idea when I'll swim again, but if given a choice, I'd choose the life of a fish any day.

"Reading." Lagan's next word pulls me to the surface of my shallow dive into the past.

Another easy one—happy face covered again. Although I do hate reading one thing: the lists with Dad's perfectly legible cursive letters. Curse those lists. Curse Dad.

"Homework," Lagan says, reining me back.

I think I surprise him when I cover the smiley face again. For me, homework means that many fewer minutes I spend doing housework.

Lagan raises an eyebrow and then shrugs his shoulders.

"Home." Like a log falling on the tracks, Lagan derails my train of thought.

I expect a curveball at some point, but I don't expect to hallucinate. I see the etch of the sad face on the Sticky Note turn into Dad's head with a finger raised to his lips, warning me to give nothing away. Instinctively, I flip the Post-it note over and put my hand over it. I hide Dad's face when I come out of hiding. I'm not exactly sure why I choose to cover the sad face, knowing that Lagan might suspect something. The fact that he never pushes me for details helps. He just allows me to peel back my heart, one thin layer at a time.

I keep the frowning, face covered, when I hear Lagan's next word: "Jesse." I look at my hand on top of the sad face as I realize that I feel both when it comes to Jess. I flip the sad face upright again, cover it, and move my other hand. Now both the faces are covered. Lagan knows I have a brother at home named Jesse. But he has no idea why he isn't attending school. Or the fact that Jess is the sole reason that I can't run away.

Wanting to run away now, I decide that detective Lagan had collected enough clues for today. I look at the clock on the wall. I pull my hands into my lap, and then start organizing the garbage on my tray. The lunch bell won't ring for another ten minutes. I stare at the simple round faces. One happy. One sad. Life in 2-D appeals to me. I would trade my reality for this alternative any day.

"No more words," I say. I'm done. I have no more to give.

We eat in silence as the minutes pass.

Aware that the bell will ring any moment, I rise from the table.

Lagan rises too. "Last two, I promise."

"No."

"Lagan," he says the first. His name.

I look up and scan the room. Deep breath. I look back at Lagan, into those dark brown, almond-shaped eyes, perhaps for the first time, and smile. My hand slips over the happy face and the bell sounds.

He smiles back and reaches over, placing his hand on top of mine. "Say your name."

My heart pounds a mile a minute. It's time to go. Like a glacier in the middle of June, I'm frozen, yet melting.

"Please." Lagan's hand wraps a little tighter around mine. "Say your name."

"Umm. Uh. Okay." I stutter, trying to find my voice. "Talia."

Lagan slides my hand off the happy face with his hand. And moves his hand to cover it. Smile stretched wide, he picks up the yellow Post-it, holds it to his chest, and taps a playful heartbeat over the note. Over his heart.

I shake my head, look up to the ceiling, and half expect a ton of confetti to rain down. Warmth spreads over my face. As usual, Lagan takes my tray for me in exchange for a Sticky Note before we head out of the cafeteria. This one has just one word on it: Like.

I am still blushing when I look up to see Lagan's back walking away. Luckily, blushing isn't too dangerous for this bronze-toned teen girl. A blush feels like a spreading heat wave without the rosy cheeks. If this is what it feels like to be struck by lightning, I've been struck twice in less than a minute. First his hand on mine, then his animated exit. I rub the back of my hand where his hand rested and raise it to my healing lips. Yes. I draw an imaginary check mark in the air. Definite like.

I fingertip tap into my palm, my imaginary iPhone, to post an update: "Met a boy that makes me smile. Sure do hope he stays awhile." Not wanting to get ahead of myself, I alter my relationship status from *Single* to *It's complicated*.

~NINE~

Walking home, my mind hurdles back and forth between two bridges, the gap between them so wide, each leap reminds me that failure to return to the correct side in time will cost me. Yet, for the first time ever, risk appeals to me. Perhaps this little taste of happiness is worth the fall from Dad's grace that threatens my every breath. I inhale deeply and jump.

Lagan's smile.

Jump back.

Boiling water on my arm.

Vault forward.

Lagan's hand on mine.

Return.

Broken glass cuts.

Bound forward again.

Lagan's eyes looking right into mine.

Retreat.

Mom's empty eyes staring at the ceiling.

Lagan's Romeo exit.

Jesse's legs that never move.

Lagan holding the smiley face to his heart.

My heart breaking.

No version of reality allows me to have this—him—Lagan, for more than a moment. Graduation lies only four months away. I turned in all the college applications that Dad allowed. All to schools that I can commute to. Out of state is out of the question. Dad's goal for me for college seems to be for me to take over his business some day. He has no clue that I love to write. That I want to be a writer. Write stories where I can hide my past in between the lines of worlds my imagination paints, most often in my dreams. The last thing I want is to have anything to do with Dad or his practice, but that's not something I need to worry about now. I'm just relieved that he's letting me apply.

I know Lagan applied to schools in the city and in California. If he decides to stay local, we could find a way to secretly meet, and then he'll propose, and we'll elope, and then, and then... Who am I kidding, anyway? This thing, this, this— what is this anyway? Similar to dreaming while I roam about wide-awake, except that waking up will be painfully real when June comes around.

My mind seesaws with every step closer to the house, wondering if it's worth it. At the same time, I am in so deep, I don't know how to rewind. Even if I reason to myself that Lagan is too huge a risk and I need to stop, retract, and forget about him, my heart begs for more like a newborn searches for her mother's breast. I long for time with Lagan like I used to pine for my mom to stroke my head as I fell asleep. I don't know how I'll keep my joy a secret from Dad. I do know one thing. It's time to tell Jesse.

I enter the house and find Jess asleep with the TV running. I continue to complete the remainder of my circuit, mentally editing the words before I tell my brother. I have my eureka moment while unloading the dishwasher, as I see my reflection in a Corning Ware platter. I finish organizing the last of the silverware and race to Jesse's room to take care of his needs. He's awake now.

"Jess, I have a new story for you." I hear my voice chirping the words.

Jesse turns off the TV with the remote and lifts his face toward me.

I begin my tale. "It's about this girl at school that I've been watching. She's really interesting to watch, so I've been sort of spying on her, eavesdropping, and just living vicariously while following her around from a distance. I actually think she's a little nutty. Maybe that's what draws me to her. Maybe someday we'll be friends. I think we'd get along. For now, she's fun to watch, and she gives me fresh material. Helps me stay distracted."

Jess's eyes light up with anticipation. It has been awhile since I made time to talk to him. We both need this. I sweep up the incense ashes, move Jess to his wheelchair, and change his sheets. All the while, I tell him about a girl named "Katrina." A girl who finds Post-it notes everywhere. A girl who eats lunch with a guy named Logan every day, but never sits close enough to make anyone think she joined this guy for lunch. A girl who smiles and giggles to herself, tucking the reasons for her joy into her books. A girl who seems to be falling in love with this boy whom she eats with day after day.

Jess holds onto each and every word, telling me with his eyes that at times he is confused. Other times, he is happy for this girl. Still other times, he looks down, sorrowful over the girl's self-imposed limitations—to love and be loved. When I am about to tell him not to feel sad—it's just the story of a stranger after all—Jess lifts his hand and points in my direction. Then his lips form the word *you* just as the front door slams shut.

Dad is home. The list is done. The air is full of new information, and Jess looks at me, not needing an answer. He already knows. And I know that he knows. As Dad makes his rounds up and around the house, I make a two second motion of secrecy to Jess by putting my forefinger to my lips. Jess nods, and we lock the story into our imaginary vault.

Shutting my mind off from my world of fresh possibility and reentering my hazardous home life, I wonder if this is what jet lag feels like. While I'm awake, I want to sleep. While I sleep, I want to be awake. I sleepwalk through my evening chores, and I spend all night replaying every interaction ever shared with Lagan, from the very first Post-it note, to all his creative games and witty conversations. To today. And his hand. Resting on mine. When my alarm buzzes, I awake more tired than ever. I have no choice. I cannot be found out. I have to maintain my facade—at least until Dad leaves for work.

He must have had an early meeting, because I smell coffee that I haven't made. I look at the clock terrified that I overslept. It reads 6:30 a.m. Whew.

As I clean up, dress for school, and head down to Jess's room to help him with his morning routine, I find Dad is gone, but he left a note by Jess's bed:

Early start today. Make sure you get to school on time. I'll be home late tonight. Last second business trip to Vegas. Big case I have to attend to. Taking the red eye back. Don't wait up. Don't forget, I'll be double-checking EVERYTHING.

Dad

Wow. A chance to breathe, for once. I debate skipping around the house and throwing the sheets up in the air. But my instinct keeps my excitement at bay. I have no reason to trust Dad. What does "late" mean? He could be trying to trap me since a little over a month has passed since my last punishment. The memories of Mom remind me to never let my guard down.

Doesn't mean I can't imagine breaking the rules. Even if I don't follow through. Invite Lagan over for milk and cookies. Introduce him to Jesse. Slow dance with him around the kitchen. I'm bound to miss the bus if I keep daydreaming. Hello? Shaking off my digressions, I race through my remaining tasks.

Each time I do anything for Jess or pass his room, he smiles at me. He has smiled more today than I've seen him smile since when Mom was alive. He is happy for this girl—for me—and it feels nice. I wonder if he's ever been in love?

Never thought to ask my baby brother. We both know how critical it is to keep everything confidential. Even a hint of unusual behavior will arouse suspicion. And suspicion in our house translates to guilty as charged. No trial. No jury. Straight to life in prison. Makes the electric chair sound appealing.

Instead, Warden Dad despises my middle name, Grace. I'll never know how Mom pulled that one off. I never asked her. In Dad's world, no probation or early release for good behavior in sight, leaving me no choice but to press on.

I grab my bag and head for the front door, almost forgetting one last thing. Dropping my pack to return to Jesse's room to hug him goodbye, I see he isn't watching TV. Instead, he managed to pull his sheets off himself and is trying to lift his legs. A little above the bed. One at a time. My bottom lip quivers as it hits me. He's rehabbing himself. A tear escapes. He's trying. Really trying to live again.

I ease away so he won't register my sight of him. As I race out the door, I yell, "Bye Jess," and resolve to help him regain his strength. And maybe someday, even walk again.

~TEN~

When I finish my Chem quiz quickly and pull out a blank sheet of paper to doodle on while the minutes pass, I steal glances at Lagan as I draw a sketch of the ocean. Waves I can relate to. I often dream of swimming across the Pacific to Japan. Or the Atlantic to England. Starting over as a refugee.

Today my picture looks different. There are two stick figures instead of one. Two swimmers—moving toward each other—dodging riptides, sharks, and exhaustion. Will they reach each other? Only time will tell.

Lagan walks past my desk to the front of the class to turn in his paper. On his way back, I slide my folded drawing to the edge of the table. He slows his pace when he nears. I smile to myself and slip the paper off, watching it sail to the ground. Lagan picks it up, and instead of returning it, he puts a different paper on my desk.

He coined this "TGE" for The Great Exchange. It's our way of sharing with each other how we feel at the start of the day. No words allowed. After I know he is well past me, back in his seat, I unfold his paper and gasp in disbelief.

The ocean. There are two swimmers. Swimming toward each other. The sun is rising in his sketch. I remember how he mentioned that his favorite color is red. Something about the color of the sunrise. There are no sharks in his picture. However, one detail makes me wince. There are storm clouds, but they aren't in the sky. Instead, they rage in the water with lightning bolts darting to and fro. And the kicker, they only surround one of the swimmers. The female swimmer. Me.

I take my pencil and flip it to the eraser side. I try to erase the clouds. My fury at my life rises, and I rip through the picture. I rip his picture.

What do you want from me? I can only give what I can give, what I can afford, without Dad finding out. Who am I kidding? Graduation is around the corner. Four months away. I only have four months of Lagan left. It's not enough. But what choice do I have? I can't live for the future.

Too many dreams of make-believe futures have been shattered. I know better than to hold too tightly to my dreams. I lost the dreams I thought were plausible. Mom used to put flowers in my hair on my wedding day. Jesse used to run along the beach with me, flying kites on a breezy summer evening. Dad used to disappear. Nowhere to be found. Missing. No access to Jess or me.

Like sand slipping through my clasped hands, my dreams only leave me wanting. Then, when despair morphs to rage, the sand solidifies into broken glass. My hands now clasp foolishly, full of shards where hope bleeds from me, one broken promise at a time.

With bloody hands, my rage craves revenge. Last night, I dreamt of taking a knife to Dad's throat. I awoke to find myself standing in the kitchen with a butter knife between my tightly squeezed fingers. Terrified of what I was capable of, I knew I needed to distract my mind before I returned to bed and laid my head down on my pillow.

That's when I first opened it, *The Beautiful Fight*, the book that Lagan marked with blank Post-its. I skimmed one story, carefully replacing the yellow Sticky Note before nodding off to sleep.

In the story I read, a woman had been bleeding for twelve years. My lips have been bleeding for more than a decade. The woman in the story wanted help, but she didn't want anyone to know her business. She was afraid to ask out loud. I can relate to that. She had spent her every penny on doctors, but to no avail. Her bleeding persisted. *I feel spent.* Thinking about Mom and Jess, and how I still bleed, and no one arrives to rescue me. No cure I can afford seems to exist.

The woman in the story did something strange, but it doesn't seem so strange to me. People do strange things when they're desperate. Desperation drove her to search for help in an odd place. A garden of all places. Greenery surrounded a large crowd that followed a gardener. Then the woman reached forward, into the crowd, and stole. Just a touch. Of the gardener's back. And just like that, she stopped bleeding.

All night, I dreamt that I was the woman, following the crowd, pressing forward, and hoping to reach forward and just brush his shoulder. The crowd faded in my dream, and all I could see was the cloth in front of me. But, just as I lunged forward, an axe fell in front of my grasp, just missing my wrist.

Turning my head to see where he was, I saw him inches away from me, removing his hood. He'd been walking in the crowd the whole time, watching me. Dad stood still, hood back, holding the axe to the ground, staring right at me, shaking his head no. *Not now. Not ever. Don't even think about it.*

The crowd moved on without me. As did the gardener, his back blurring with the distance. Dream over.

The bell rings, startling me from my excursion from now. I crumple up the drawing, gather my things, and shuffle quickly out of class—alone. Lagan runs up behind me, but I ignore him. Just when I've resolved that I can handle this, I can't. I am better off alone. *Can't you see that?* I am the personification of complicated. And no one wants complicated.

I know it's not fair, but life isn't fair. Fair is for fairy tales. I live on the other side of the tracks. Where the king hurts the princess, and the prince never arrives in time. The dragon burns down the castle. The queen stopped breathing a long time ago. And no one lives happily ever after.

So much for starting my day with anticipation. Just like that, the frigid breeze of my reality blows out the candle. I promise to back away. To detach my heart strings, one at a time. I need to get used to the fact that forever is for other girls. The ones whose fathers teach them how to dance as they get ready for prom. The only prom I'll ever attend will occur in my room. By myself, wearing the single pretty black dress I own from Mom's funeral. I'll dance with my shadow. Even Jess can't dance with me.

Thinking of Jesse, I recall seeing him lift his legs in the morning. *That's it.* I'll focus on my brother. Today is the perfect day to start. I'll rush home, finish my chores quickly, then spend the rest of the evening until Dad returns, helping Jess with his physical therapy. Thankful for my baby brother, I vow to do whatever it takes to get Jess back on his feet.

Keeping my eyes on my feet as I move to my next class, I note that Lagan no longer follows me. Good. Maybe he's used to my roller-coaster temperament. Or maybe he's decided to finally leave me alone. I drift from class to class, creating a new schedule in my head to work with Jess. Each time Lagan slips me a Sticky Note, I throw it into the trash without reading it. I know this hurts him, but I have to cut this off. I'm used to bleeding. He'll get over me. Brad did. And so will he.

As I take my lunch to the girl's locker room, I plop down on the bench and wonder which one of Lagan's many friends will keep him company today. My appetite disappears with my reflection as I close my eyes to the yellow bathroom tile that surrounds me. I hate who I've become. Now Lagan will have to pick the sad face if I say my name. I'd pick the sad face, too. For everything.

I think about the picture Lagan drew. Why does it make me so angry? What is it about the clouds that make me cave into despair? Maybe because the clouds sit so close to me, I sense Lagan suggesting that it's all my fault. I'm the reason that we can't get close. Closer. The clouds are my problems. My roadblocks. My no's. I have listed more than enough for the both of us. Meanwhile, Lagan swims free, basking in the sun.

Indecisive should be my middle name. I flip-flop back and forth until I'm reminded of the bleeding woman in Lagan's book. At some point, she had to come out of hiding. She had to remove the *I'm fine* mask. Terrified to admit to too much, I debate asking Lagan about the clouds. Up to now, I have never shared any concrete details regarding Dad. I don't want sympathy. That never solves anything. And changes nothing.

How can I forget the first time that Lagan took a risk and tried asking? About my lips? Something inside of me wants to tell him. A little. Just so he might understand that I don't choose these clouds that hold me captive. To know that if I could remove the clouds, I would. I really would. But how? How can I tell him without saying it? Without writing it down? Without leaving evidence?

My whole life I have imagined this moment when I would tell someone the truth. The truth of the madness that I live every day. I imagine what it will be like to invite someone into my world. Even just for a moment. To not be alone. And then it hits me. Dad's in Vegas today. Who knows what time his red eye lands? Should I? Do I dare?

No one besides Dad's high-rolling clients has ever stepped into our home, and even then, those visits are rare and late at night, usually after we've turned in for bed. Like a pendulum, I swing from the extreme of ending the friendship to inviting Lagan to see for himself. Maybe this will be the deciding factor. If he sees with his own eyes what I come home to each day, he might realize that I am too much for him. I decide not to decide for him.

What if Dad shows up? My mind has played this game a million times. Falling off the tightrope into the unknown. Crossing wobbly bridges, knowing too well that alligators snip at my heels. What difference does it make? I'm drowning anyway. May as well go down with a little fight. No regrets.

Something like that. When I recall Jess lifting his legs, an unfamiliar desire to dance stirs inside me.

I quickly throw the rest of my lunch away, realizing that I only have five minutes before the lunch bell will sound. Phrasing and rephrasing the question in my head, I race against the clock as blood pulses in my ears, and my heart pounds two feet in front of me. I close my eyes to get a grip and run right into Lagan's chest.

"Looking for someone?" Lagan asks, half-smiling.

"Face-to-face. Was this your idea or mine?" I'm so glad he's here.

"You hated my picture." Lagan cuts to the chase.

"No." I start to lie. "It's just that the clouds. Why so many? And around just me?" Bodies bump us left and right as students head to lockers for afternoon books.

"The clouds." Lagan inhales. "The clouds were really hard for me to draw."

"What do you mean?" I ask as we move down the hallway, toward my locker, elbows touching, more and more kids filing in.

"The clouds are your hurts. Even though the ocean is full of water, you can't hide your sadness from me. I see you're sad. I just don't know why. I want to reach you, but your sadness keeps me away. Without knowing where the clouds are coming from, I have no way of knowing how to move past them. Like it's always cloudy in your world. Your eyes. No matter how often I steal a smile from your lips, it's still raining in your eyes." Lagan pauses, then he finishes. "I'm sorry."

How many times has Lagan apologized to me since I met him? It's not his fault. None of this. *My life is not your fault.* I take a deep breath and say two words that I have never said to another soul: "Come over."

"Today?" Lagan's eyebrows furrow toward each other with understandable skepticism.

"Yes. After school. For an hour." I know this chance might never come again.

"Are you sure?" He puts his hand on my arm as he looks into my eyes.

When I nod yes, he pulls closer and whispers into my ear, "Should I wear a tie?"

"Only if you're worried about impressing my brother." I giggle, and we part for our afternoon classes. I smile through the rest of my day, and when the last bell rings, my smile turns to pressed lips, attempting to keep out an intruder. Doubt. It's time.

~ELEVEN~

I find a Post-it on my locker when I return to get my textbooks.

> Meet U outside by the gym doors. If U change yur mind, no biggie. Still want 2 have lunch with U tom.
>
> L

Just like Lagan, always giving me an out. I pack my books quickly, clip my lock, and head out the back doors. Walking around to the side of the school, I spot Lagan's tall, lanky figure leaning against the school's renovated brick. Shades and black winter cap pulled over his ears, his head bops to some tune on his iPod as he dribbles his basketball. He catches me looking toward him, and picks up his dribble, pulls one ear bud out, and saunters in my direction—smiling—perhaps relieved that I didn't bail.

During the trek home, I can hear the basketball hit the pavement behind me, a sound that simultaneously gives me anxiety and joy. Picking up my pace when we reach past two blocks away from school property, I focus my mind on Jesse to keep my mind from dwelling on the possibilities of Dad's rage. Not sure how Jess will feel about me bringing Lagan home.

The image of an army of white blood cells rushing to guard the entryway into our cancer cell floods my mind. Which makes Lagan a rookie covert-ops agent, entering a realm of terror beyond his skills of training. No one has prepped him.

He has no map. Land mines lie all around, and my feet continue to step forward—back into my world.

Not even twenty-four hours have passed since I told my brother about Lagan. I hope Jess is still in a good mood. And if Jess says no, I'll just send Lagan away. *Keep it simple* is my mantra for this anything-but-simple experiment.

When we reach a block from my house, I turn to look back. Lagan's still dribbling, approximately three sidewalk squares behind me. He smiles, raising his eyebrows above his shades. That dimple always manages to surge my pulsing heart.

I turn to face forward. Take a deep breath. Then another. I have to say something as a head's up. A little background info, just so Lagan won't totally be caught off guard.

After inhaling once more, I start to explain. "My brother..."

"Yes." Lagan lets me know from behind that he can hear me.

"My brother." I start over. "He doesn't talk."

"Okay." Lagan waits.

"Or walk."

Lagan picks up his dribble. "Oh."

Another deep breath.

"Or much of anything. He needs a lot of help." I finish, the house now in sight. "I need to spend a few minutes helping him when we first get there."

"Okay," Lagan says and resumes dribbling. "Should I wait outside? I could wait outside."

"Yeah. That's a good idea. I'll come out to get you in a few."

We're home. I look down the stone path to my front door. I scan the driveway like a car could magically appear that isn't there. Then my eyes roam the street and all around. No sight of Dad.

I look directly at Lagan and quickly instruct, "You can wait in the backyard. There's a bench. I'll see you soon."

With that, I run to the front entrance, unlock it, and shut the door behind me.

"Jess! Jess, I'm home." Grabbing the list, I race up to Jess's room to tell him the news.

Except that Jess is not in his room. What? My heart sinks. Where is he?

"Jess! Jess!" I scream. *Where are you?*

Our house is not that big. I run through the other bedrooms, back down to the kitchen. Nope. I run to the living room. Not there either. From bathroom to bathroom and still no luck. Then I see the door on Dad's office partially ajar, and I slow my pace. We're not allowed in Dad's office. It's up there with the roof rule.

"Jessie!" I find my brother lying down on his chest, to the side of Dad's computer desk.

"Jess?" I kneel to look into his eyes. "Jess? What are you doing? How did you get here?"

Jess's eyes shift back and forth to his elbows. They are scraped up and dried blood speckles a few of the sea green tiles. He dragged himself? But then my eyes see it. The bottom drawer is pulled out and something silver glitters in the light. A gun. *What the?* A real gun!

"Jesse!" Heat surges into my ears. "What were you thinking?"

I slam the drawer shut and start shaking Jesse's shoulders.

I keep screaming. "Jesse, I don't care what you were thinking, okay. Promise me!"

I need to lower my voice and calm down. I hate being screamed at. I hate the sound of my voice screaming more.

I repeat more calmly, looking Jesse right in his eyes. "Promise me that you'll never leave me."

Jesse looks away.

I cup his face and turn it back toward mine.

"Promise me." I am not taking no for an answer. "Promise me now. I cannot do this alone. I need you."

Jesse exhales and says one word: "Okay." Then he looks away again. I feel bad for yelling at him. Sheesh. I totally forget that Lagan is waiting out back. I need to clean up this mess first. Story of my life.

"Let's get you in your chair." I force a smile. "I'll be right back."

I walk back to Jess's room, and as I gather some wet washcloths to clean up the blood, I imagine my life without my brother. The thought sends shivers down my neck. Flashbacks from the roof reel in my mind, as I realize that Jesse is not safe left alone. Today the gun. Tomorrow a knife. Again and again, I am reminded that I have no control of the future. But I have to try. I will not give up without a fight.

I wheel his chair back to the den, and after cleaning up Jess, wiping down the floor, and restoring Dad's office, we move to the kitchen. I really hope that Dad sticks to his note and returns home late. It's time to tell Jesse.

"Jesse, I'm going to forget about what happened today," I lie. *I will never forget this.* I gather some fruit out of the fridge to make a salad. "I have something to tell you."

Jesse looks up at me now, his mouth curving at the edges to make a small smile.

"Well, not exactly a something. More like a someone. There's someone I want you to meet." I watch closely for any sign of resistance.

Jess shrugs his shoulders, so I continue talking. "He's out back. His name is Lagan. Yes. The same Logan I told you about last night."

Jess nods. This could not be a worse moment to introduce a stranger into our house. Moments after discovering my brother's second suicide attempt, I change the topic. Forcing us both to move on, move past, and move into another person's world.

Yet, I don't want to send Lagan away. I know that this opportunity might never... And just maybe, Jess and Lagan would become friends, and... I am getting ahead of myself. First things first.

"Do you want to meet him?" I need his permission.

Jess stares down at his lap. I keep cutting and peeling. Peeling and cutting. The words *forget it, another time* are on the tip of my tongue when Jess raises his head and nods yes.

I put the knife down, wipe my hands on a paper towel, and rush past my little brother. "I'll be right back."

Glancing at the wall clock as I first race to the front door, I decide this will be a short visit. In and out. The driveway still lies empty, and Dad's car isn't rolling down our street. I hightail it to the back door and fling it open, finding Lagan just where I suggested. Sitting on the bench, dribbling his ball, he seems so focused as the ball moves smoothly back and forth between his hands. I think I startle him when I call out, because he jumps up, letting the ball roll away, and then looks left and right. He points to himself with both thumbs.

"Yes, you." I laugh, all too aware that this is no laughing matter.

Lagan gathers his book bag and ball, and when he stands a foot away, he gives me another chance to pull a u-ey. "Sure about this?"

"Not really, but come in. For a sec." I grab his free hand, and direct Lagan to the kitchen. He adjusts the grip and now our fingers entwine. My heart takes flight at the sight and feel of our kissing palms. As Lagan looks around, my eyes linger on our hands. Mine in his. His in mine. We fit.

Not two minutes pass when my house of cards collapses before we reach the kitchen opening. I hear a car door slam shut and wiggle my hand loose to run to the front door to check the peephole, my heart sinking like quicksand. As I peer out and gulp relief by the bucket, my stomach remains on the floor.

"Just the mailman," I say as I look back down the hallway. Lagan stands frozen, unsure of what just occurred. I traipse back to him, shaking my head, my heart's decibels returning slowly to their original pace, to stay alert-mode, rather than panic-mode. "Sorry. I thought my dad came home."

"Okay." Lagan nods, putting his bag and ball down. His eyes seem to ask, "Is there more?"

I take a deep breath, not sure how much to peel back, my hands still shaking from the false alarm. "And that would be bad." That's enough. For now.

"Let's go." With my hand on his back, I direct him toward the kitchen, shifting gears, still aware of the ticking clock. "I want you to meet my brother."

Lagan doesn't budge. Instead, he reaches for my hand and pulls me to himself in an unexpected embrace, my emotions ricocheting like a copper ball bouncing through a pinball machine. His whispers tiptoe across the top of my head. "It's okay. Slow down. You don't have to say anything. Just know that I'm here. I'm here for you."

I swallow as my arms slowly rise and circle his waist. I have never known the strong arms of any man holding me. His squeeze pulls me in closer still, and my arms don't want to let go. His heartbeat pounds against mine, and I am transported. To safety. Warmth. His heat forms a shield around me, and I burrow my head into his chest, searching for a place to hide. A place I know I can't stay. Tears begin to slip down my cheeks, and my simple plan—of a simple meeting—simply unfolds.

Time stops, and if touch launches, I'm somewhere in the clouds, flying above storms. All the while, Lagan's hold blankets me as I inhale the sweet scent of peppermint-flavored Trident each time he exhales. My breathing steadies just as the chime of the grandfather clock in the living room jump-starts me back to earth. I loosen my hold and look up into Lagan's eyes.

"I…" My voice falters. I clear my throat and start again. "You…umm. You should meet Jesse. And then you should probably go."

Lagan nods okay.

I purposely avoid holding his hand, still dizzy from the hug, and I swallow a spoonful of fear for the umpteenth time today as we enter the kitchen. Jess's back is to us until we circle around to him, and the fruit salad sits on the granite countertop, untouched.

"Jesse." I put my arm around my little brother. "This is Lagan."

Jesse manages a smile, but I see my reflection in his eyes. It rains in Jess's eyes too, and I begin to understand what Lagan means by the clouds. Lagan crosses in front of me to move closer to Jess and puts his hand on Jess's arm.

"Hey. Great to meet you." Lagan pats my little brother's shoulder and grips his arms in a typical guy-to-guy greeting.

Jesse nods, a small smile emerging.

"Man, check out those guns!" Lagan describes Jesse's bulging upper arm, and I'm cringing inside at the mention of the word.

Somehow I hadn't paid attention.

"You make me want to get my butt to the gym ASAP."

And we all laugh. Well, Lagan and I. Jess smiles.

"Speaking of...." Lagan makes his exit. "I have basketball practice in twenty minutes, so I have to jet."

Eyeing the fruit on the counter, Lagan reaches over and pops a strawberry in his mouth and mumbles, "Bye, guys! Thanks. Gotta go. See you 'round."

He beams us a smile, makes a beeline for the back door, and lets himself out, locking the door behind him. I pull at the door to make sure and then return to the front door again, still on edge. I watch Lagan's back disappear down the street, dribbling away, the driveway still empty. Exhale.

As I return to the kitchen, I remind myself about my vow to help Jess. This will be our first day of rehab together. Passing the spot where Lagan held me, I can't help but stop, put my right hand on the wall, and search for a pulse. After rewriting the memory on my mind, I swagger to the kitchen, excited for new beginnings and avoided land mines.

Jesse waits for me, but today will be different—no cakewalking—literally.

"Lift your left foot," I say, pulling a stool up to face my brother.

He shakes his head no.

"I didn't ask you if you wanted to." I'm putting on my tough-love hat. I want to see Jesse rise. And run again. Walking comes first. Strengthening his legs before that.

Jesse inhales a deep breath, then lifts his leg. An inch maybe.

I grab an unpeeled apple and say, "Hit my hand." My open palm holds the fruit a few inches above his foot.

Jesse raises his leg again, tapping my hand softly.

"Higher." I nod, coaxing him with my smile.

Then Jess, gripping firmly to the sides of his wheelchair, lifts his foot again, the contact with my hand sending the apple flying.

I bust out laughing. "Again." I grab another apple. And he does. And I jump off my stool to avoid getting sideswiped by an aerodynamic Macintosh. Now both of us are laughing. I think we're both enjoying the mess that there is no hurry to clean up.

"Hold on. I have an idea."

I leave and return from the garage with a large Ziploc bag filled with sand secured into a second bag to avoid even one grain from escaping onto Dad's pristine kitchen floor. I sit down to face Jess and slowly raise one of Jesse's leg. Putting the bag of sand on top of his ankle, I help him do leg lifts in sets of ten, allowing him to use his own strength as far as he can go.

His legs raise the weight, but not without the strain of clenched teeth. Walking is out of the question, for now. I don't want Jesse to quit by pushing him too hard, too soon. He does a few sets on each leg until beads of sweat form on his brow. I ignore his gritting teeth and heavy breathing, because I have to think of the goal. Feeling sorry for himself, he almost ended his life today. Together, we have to keep at it. Together.

When Jess grips my arm, his mouth forming the word *enough*, I pause.

"One last set." I start over, knowing the sooner I push him, the sooner he'll get there. During the final set, I ask him what he thinks of Lagan. Distraction always helps me. He smiles wider than ever before. I take that as a like. Status update in order: *My little brother just gave a thumbs up.*

***

Dad doesn't return home till the next morning a little after six. I couldn't sleep, so I woke up before my alarm was set to ring at six. With last night's chores done, the house in order, and our secrets safely filed away under never happened, I sit at the kitchen table, eating oatmeal and reading Shakespeare when Dad waltzes in with a stranger, perhaps a client or an associate. Instinctively, I lower my head and hide my face behind Othello. Saturday morning chores await, but I have time. And Jess still sleeps.

"Geri!" Dad's overweight, balding friend sounds like a Texas cowboy. "You never told me your daughter was so darn perty. Now you'd get a killing if you offered her serv—"

"Shut up, Jed." Dad turns to me. "Go to your room. And close your door. NOW!"

As I inch my way up the stairs, I hear the two exchange a few more words before my right foot lifts off the top step. A conversation that freezes me in my tracks.

"I pay you the big macaroons for clearing the paperwork on the pertiest girls. Don't get all wild buck and kicking, because I can tell a perty one when I see one." Fat baldy again with the comments.

Creep.

"I already told you that she's..." I sense Dad pausing, as if he's searching for the right word. "Jeez, Jed, I don't owe you a thing. So don't EVER ask again. You hear me? Now let's get down to business. Tea?"

Hmm? What a joke! Dad actually sounded protective, sort of. But protecting me from what? And I couldn't care less. Dad's business has always been his business. The less I know, the less space in my mind I have to waste on him. I rinse my mouth after flossing, sit at my desk, and open up *Othello*, noting that even Iago seems less scary to hang out with than Dad. Or any of his slimy friends.

The words blur as I recall last night's events. Sleep didn't find me at all as I listened for the sound of Jesse rustling his sheets in the next room, his breathing a bittersweet song in my ears. Goosebumps cover my arms as my mind conjures images of Jesse's scratched knees and the silver of Dad's gun.

I finally cave as my head lowers to the desk. The rough pages of *Othello* don't make the most comfortable pillow under my cheek, but exhaustion makes it easy to not care. I close my eyes, gifting myself a few moments in another room. The hallway where Lagan first held me. As I drift away from morning shores, my senses awaken and I'm falling. Falling into strong arms, breathing in sweet peppermint, and swimming through clouds.

~TWELVE~

Lagan gives me my first Post-it notepad on Monday, an entire stack of empty, attached sheets. It's sea green to match the color of my eyes, he tells me.

"I want it back." His eyes squint some kind of wonderful, and I instinctively swallow.

I want to be back too. In your arms. Whenever it's convenient, of course.

He's looking at me glassy-eyed. Which means I didn't speak my thoughts. *Thank God!* Swallow. Breathe.

"The notepad." Lagan must sense my absence when he explains the obvious.

"Okay." My flight is over. I'm all ears...and heart too, after his brief home visit.

"With your thoughts on each page." Lagan gives specific instructions. I should focus now. "And if you feel unsure or unable to write, just give me blank ones. Knowing you're returning each sheet to me is enough."

"So you want me to write? Anything in particular?"

"Monday's theme is childhood wish list. In as little as one word or as many as you can fit on the tiny Sticky Note, share what you missed. If you could have had anything as part of your little girl years, what would you have wanted to own, know, or experience?"

Sounds like an English class assignment. Since the brief visit home last Friday, in a sense I gave Lagan the green light to

84

enter my world, and let's just say that his gas tank is full and his GPS programmed to discover me, from the inside out. One word at a time.

Monday's green notes fill with words that are fun and easy to write at first. But with each word, a memory of Mom resurfaces. All that she gave to Jess and me. All that she wanted to give. All that she couldn't give. Talk about a sneak attack from the back window into my heart. I feel like a deflated balloon by the time lunch arrives. I hand over my completed notepad by placing it on the table between us, not bothering to peel them off one sheet at a time.

Lagan slides the tiny gift back to himself with the suspicion of a drug deal. He rolls over a Chap Stick with a label that reads Natural Lime-scented with Aloe and Beeswax.

"Wappy Walentine's Week." He smirks and waits a beat. "That's code for..."

"I know." I cut him off. "I might be a little out of touch, but everyone knows what February 14 means."

I hesitate, and then indulge since my radar reads clear. "Are you asking me to be your...Walentine?"

Lagan chuckles, but his laughing ceases instantaneously. He's flipping through my words on the green Sticky Notes. His dimple disappears under downcast eyes.

I must have left... "Wait." I reach over to retrieve the Post-it pad. "I think I put something down I meant to cross out."

But it's too late. He's already read it. The one I meant to tear up and flush down the toilet. Darn it. Lagan takes the notepad and puts it into his book bag under the table. Silence lingers between us for a bit. He's forming his words carefully. I'm rehearsing a lie. He knows too much. How could I have been so careless?

During the last ten minutes of American Government, Mr. Mason gave all the students free time in order to practice AP questions. Less than six weeks remain till the exam, and he wants us all to rock it. We all pulled out our heavy prep books, and I positioned mine in front of me like a shield. Then I went to town, knocking out the green Sticky Notes in a matter of a few minutes. It was almost too easy to compile a childhood wish list. Such few pleasant memories existed that the words spewed out of me like a leaky faucet no pipe wrench could shut.

Dolls. Tea Parties. Play Dates. Princess dress-up clothes. I flipped four pages and kept writing.

Crayola markers. Teddy Bears. Disneyland. Pretty shoes. And on and on I listed. No reservations. Wishes I had never before voiced. Nor breathed. Stored up inside, under my cobweb-covered heart, labeled "Oh well."

Presents. Christmas trees. Chocolate Easter bunnies. Ice cream with rainbow sprinkles.

Cartoons. Swings. Slides. Monkey bars.

Friends. Fun. Field trips. Cotton Candy.

And before I knew what my pen transferred from my vault, phrases of sadness seeped out from under my locked closet of lost time.

The *Happy* in Happy Birthday. The *Good* in Good Morning. The Sweet in Sweet dreams.

And that's when I let the words that altered Lagan's smile slip out of my heart—onto a Post-it note.

The *Love* in I Love You.

I hesitated as soon as my pen lifted from the page. I choked on my spit as if the words were bile. It would take more than a mint to mask this bitterness. I started to tear the page out when I thought to myself, Let me just finish writing. I'll come back to it. The words were still flowing, and I wanted to get them all out as if washing utensils. I just wanted the sink to be empty. Then I'd throw away the chipped mug. The one I dropped while daydreaming. In the business of evidence elimination, I got promoted to CEO when Mom passed away and Jess sailed off the roof.

Cartwheels. Ballet slippers. Flowers in my hair. Flowers anywhere.

Tag. Red Light, Green Light. Hopscotch. Hide and seek.

No more green sheets. Shivers ran down my spine as I stared at the last three words. In our house, Dad familiarized us with a different version of hide and seek. We hide nothing. And we seek only his approval. And yet we hide everything. If Dad ever discovered my true thoughts, dreams, or intentions, I would be thrown into maximum security, locking shut the one window I've been permitted to look out. School. The bell rang and I tucked my green Post-it pad into my back pocket. If Dad showed up, it would be easy enough to drop behind me. No name. No trace.

I wait now, sitting caddy corner from Lagan, holding my breath. A million scenarios zip through my mind. If Lagan doesn't think I'm some sort of freak yet, he has no reason to doubt now. My appetite wanes. My whims of being someone's walentine vanish. My...

"Can I ask you a question?" Lagan interrupts my downward spiral.

"If I have the choice not to answer, ask away."

One trip to the house has changed nothing of consequence in my mind. My life of fear is as present as the empty tables behind me. My future without Lagan remains as sure as the cafeteria tray in front of me.

"Okay." Lagan begins after a long pause. "Actually, it's more of an observation than a question. I already have my answer, I think."

Confused as to where this line of conversation is headed, I nod slowly and wait silently.

"I notice..."

Lagan's tone is serious when he continues, void of the thespian animation I've grown accustomed to. I don't know if I have any energy left today for serious. I sigh and hold on to both sides of my tray, fighting the urge to run away, both mentally and physically. By now, Lagan has to have noticed that this—me—I'm not worth it.

Lagan starts again. "I notice that although your name suggests the delicacy of a dew drop, you remind me more of a waterfall. A powerful, roaring, rippling rapid that is rarely, perhaps never, visited. Because, well, because before anyone reaches you, there are a ton of downed trees. But lucky for you..." Lagan's right eyebrow raises and his dimple reappears, "I never sign up for easy. I prefer Frost's road less travelled."

I look at him with a *come again* blank stare before saying, "Now that you know what my names means, I think it's only fair if you tell me about yours. I heard once that if you really want to know about a person, find out about their middle name. What did you say it was again?"

"Kumar." Lagan's smile turns down at the corners, and his eyes dart off to the side, like he might be avoiding mine. "My middle name is Kumar. And it means..." Lagan clears his throat and lowers his voice to barely a whisper, "Prince."

As in Prince Charming? That's so goofy. And precious. At the same time. "Your mom took one look in your eyes and knew, huh?"

"Well, all jokes aside about Indian parents and how they name their kids, I want you to know something. There's something I need you to know." Lagan's eyes darken with the shadow of his lashes. "I might not wear a crown or own a sword, but I don't give up easily."

"So should I knight you or something?" He has never met a dragon like Dad. *You have no idea what you're saying.*

The intensity in Lagan's voice lightens while his gaze remains fixed on me. "How 'bout I knight you. Once Talia, dew drop from heaven, now Glaciera, frozen waterfall from Alaska."

It's my turn to laugh out loud.

"Hmm?" Lagan strokes his chin as if seriously considering his goofy suggestion. "I rather like that. Glaciera. Frozen yet moving. Slowly. If only I knew how to melt through to...?" Lagan's dimple disappears again as he strokes his goatee and gives me his best detective stare.

"Funny you mention that." I throw out a line. "You have. You do. Melt me." *Whoa. Did I just say that?* Looking at the clock, my ears swell with heat. Bell, ring already. My heart's done enough spilling for one day.

Lagan's dimple returns. As I rise to escape, my words still lingering in the air, and his hand reaches over and covers mine.

"Were you gonna ask me something?" I attempt to ignore the obvious. His hand on mine. More melting. Hello?

"Will you go to—"

"I can't." I finish his sentence and make to leave. I am sure he knows the answer before he asks.

He insists. "Wait, let me finish."

I sit down again. He has thirty seconds to change my mind. From running away. Far away.

"Will you come to my graduation party?"

"You know I can't go anywhere." I shake my head and look off to the exit doors. "Why do you even bother asking?"

"It's just that there's someone I want you to meet. Her name is Rani. You two really need to meet. She's my cousin, and we've been best friends since we were kids. I can't believe I haven't even told her about you yet. Maybe if you meet first? Anyway, maybe you could show up. Just for a bit. Like how you asked me to stop by your house. Just for a second."

I still shake my head no, thinking only one word: impossible. When he says two words that give me goose bumps. "Sneak out."

If he only knew the consequences of such a risk. "I'll try," I lie.

I just want this conversation to be over. Dream, go poof already. Cuz that's about all his request will ever amount to. Another daydream to file away in my shuffled playlist of distractions.

The bell rings. His hand moves off of mine. Another day. Another dance with fire.

~THIRTEEN~

With graduation a little over three months away, the high school buzzes with end-of-the-year planning, and most seniors who have received their college letters have checked out academically and show up to primarily socialize. I'm not one of those. I have received a few college letters. Each envelope skinny, and everyone knows what that means.

I don't get it. My GPA is 3.9. My record clean. My teacher recommendations raving. Why hasn't any college said yes yet?

I have an appointment during third period today with my guidance counselor, a Mr. Donatelli, whom I have avoided long enough. The word counselor suggests advice, support, and a person you can confide in—three things that warrant the guillotine in my house.

The only other time I saw Mr. D. was when my gym teacher forced me to pay him a visit when I refused to take my long sleeve shirt off from under my gym uniform.

"You hiding something under there, Talia?" A girl named Katie snickered in the locker room, egging on the other girls to break out in catty laughter.

I'd played this game before. I simply pulled up the sleeve on my good arm. But Miss Robinson insisted. "Go to guidance and come back to class when you have a note."

Mr. Donatelli didn't ask me many questions, really. I knew the routine. "Call my Dad. He'll explain why I have to wear long sleeves."

After a two-minute conversation, Donatelli scrawled a few words on a pink slip, slid the paper over to me, and said nonchalantly, "Return to class."

I walked back to gym class staring at the same excuse I had read over the years: Cultural Customs—Excused. That was back in October. We're halfway through February now.

According to the school policy, even if a senior never heeds his or her guidance counselor's suggestions, each senior must review his or her academic file on the appointed date in order to assure all ducks are in order and no careless details ignored causing delays in processing of diplomas...blah, blah, blah. I read the student handbook, and whoever composed this has a serious problem with run-on sentences. It could have simply said: *Meet your counselor once or you don't graduate.* That's about as many words most seniors can process these days, between their lack of sleep and hangovers.

I hear the stories in every class. "Hey, did you hear so and so hooked up with the geek from Calc at so-and-so's party last night? Anything can happen! It's senioritis till June, baby! Senior-frickin-itis!"

I secretly wish I could participate in Senior Skip Day, the one day when every senior meets at the beach on Lake Michigan, the Millennium Park Bean, or the Ferris wheel at Navy Pier to begin celebrating graduation. Anywhere but school. I'll be one of two or three rejects (the others will be seniors who wake up and forgot to check their calendars) who walks from class to class to stare at a blank whiteboard for thirty-nine minute intervals.

Most teachers take off, too. At least mentally. Which helps, since I plan to catch up on my sleep and a few assignments. No plans to engage in any personal interviews as to why my dad won't allow me to skip school, even when the incident won't show up on your permanent record, the one liberty seniors get in the name of tradition. The system lets this one day slide. Just this one.

Anyway, Senior Skip Day is sometime in May. Today is Thursday, February 13, and third period is my designated time slot to meet with Mr. Donatelli. I stick a lilac-colored Post-it on Lagan's locker to tell him I won't be in math class. He's been handing me different colors all week.

Tuesday's were pink for Mom. I filled that one up with all the words I knew Mom to be. And all the words I knew she would have been had she had the liberty to be who she wanted to be. Wednesday was blue for Jesse. Those were easy to fill out too. I love Jess so much, and finally observing his strength growing each day has renewed a sense of hope that neither of us has felt in a long time. Perhaps never.

Today is lilac for me. For today's me. What do I wish for me? Today? At first I consider writing the word "freedom" on the cover and putting ditto marks on all the subsequent sheets. Then I think of a different way to say the same thing. A way to tell Lagan how much I want him to stay a part of my world today—every day—without freaking him out. I hope.

I write in code. Not the kind that takes a genius to figure out. Just a very long run-on sentence. With one word per little square sheet, I carefully print the words: I. Yes. Dew. Drop. From. Above. Have. Dropped. Fallen. Actually. Is. Falling. In. To. Deep. Waters. With. You. Who. Have. Found. After. Searching. For. Days. And. Weeks. A. Way. To. Swim. Through. The. Clouds. To. Reach. Me.

"Talia Vanderbilt?" A voice startles me, nearly knocking me off the bench. "Mr. Donatelli will see you now."

I place my Sticky notepad in my sweatshirt pocket, tuck my pen into my bag, and follow the short, stocky woman with bifocals and a pen that holds a makeshift bun in place, back into the office cubicles separated by thin partial dividers. No room for secrets here. Perhaps the principal has a real office with four walls and a door. The guidance counselor, an average-sized, blond, white male in his thirties, wearing a deep purple button down and a pink, pin-striped tie, points to a chair opposite his desk with his pen and continues perusing a file with my name across the side of it. Maybe the pink tie is for Valentine's Day. But that's tomorrow. Then again, perhaps he's celebrating all week too.

"Well, well, Talia," he says, still turning pages over in the open manila folder. "It appears that you have been very thorough. All your graduation requirements are complete, and your record is impeccable."

"Thanks." I don't know what else to say.

"There's just one thing."

Isn't there always? Sigh. "Yes?" I try to tame my eyes to keep them from rolling.

"Talia?" He finally looks up at me. "Have you ever participated in any extracurricular activities?"

"No."

"Clubs?"

"No."

"Sports?"

"Nope."

"After school job?"

"No, sir."

"Volunteered anywhere?"

"Not unless raking my neighbor's leaves counts?" The ones that blow onto our yard, of course.

Mr. Donatelli chuckles, a nervous kind of laugh. "Not quite. More like volunteering at a hospital? Shelter? Elderly home?"

"Umm. Never had the chance to." I slip a hint without thinking.

"What do you mean exactly? Do you have any particular explanation for your complete absence of participation other than at the academic level?" Mr. Donatelli's voice sounds almost accusatory. He holds up the copies of my rejection letters from colleges. "Do you realize that colleges are looking for much more than a stellar GPA these days? They seek well-rounded applicants. Students who do more than just crack their books open and perform well on tests."

"Thank you for your time, Mr. Donatelli." I have my speech rehearsed and memorized. "I'll look into everything you have mentioned. Thank you again."

I rise to leave, hugging my book bag in a futile attempt to still my pounding heart.

"Please sit down, Talia." Donatelli begins at the start of my file again and shuffles through several papers before pulling a single sheet out.

I lower myself back into the chair. The clock reads 11:22 a.m. Technically, he still has eight minutes to remind me of the obvious. I have nothing that makes me shine, and I probably will not get into college.

"I see that Loyola has not replied yet." He holds the paper up like I can read it from where I sit.

Regardless, that is my dream school. If breathing counted for something, Loyola's admission board might give me the time of day. "I don't really expect to get a favorable response from LU, sir." My eyes shift back to the clock. "I just applied there since the school is close enough to commute to. I don't plan to live on campus."

"Actually," Donatelli carries on, "there's a note here in your file saying you are a finalist in their essay contest, and the English Department is considering offering you a scholarship. Of course, they still require evidence of at least one extracurricular."

I feel like I'm listening to someone else's life story. "I'm sorry, Mr. Donatelli. There must be some mistake. I never entered any writing contest."

Mr. Donatelli slides the paper over to my side of the table to read for myself. "No one formally enters the Loyola Essay contest. Each applicant's personal statement automatically qualifies as an entry, and the English Department chooses the top ten as finalists from which three are chosen nationally to receive substantial scholarships upon entry of freshman year. Granted, the student must maintain a certain..."

His voice drones on regarding the history of the contest and how no one from Hinsdale North has ever won. All the while I skim the letter. The impossible escape lay in my lap. Talia Grace Vanderbilt—Finalist. Essay titled: "Addicted to Thinking." The typed, eight-by-eleven sheet with Loyola's logo above lists all my information. Shock, sandwiched between terror and cynicism, cements my fingers to the page and my bottom to the seat. Not to mention my tongue to the roof of my mouth.

"Didn't you receive a copy of this letter at home?" he asks. "Perhaps it got lost in the mail. Let me call them over there at LU and request an official copy be sent to your house, and I'll make a copy for you to bring home and discuss with your father."

Bubble of possibility pops. Crash landing back to reality. Of course. Dad saw the words *pending one extracurricular activity* and probably ripped the letter into shreds and didn't think to even tell me about it.

When Mr. Donatelli puts the receiver down on his desk, he hasn't hung up yet.

"Dr. Deans, the English Department head, wants to ask you a few questions."

He hands me the phone, and I hear a woman's voice asking for me to identify myself.

"Yes." I clear my throat to find my voice. "Yes. This is Talia Grace Vanderbilt."

"Hello, Talia," the voice on the other end says confidently. "My name is Professor Katherine Deans. And I am pleased to inform you that your chances to be chosen as one of the top three of this year's ten essay finalists are really good. You are a very gifted writer, young lady. We in the department have all read your personal statement and are in agreement. We would like you to join us for your undergraduate studies. Perhaps even consider working part-time in our Writing Center to help other students with their assignments? We would be delighted to have you enroll in our Creative Writing Program, if you choose to accept our package, pending one small condition."

"Yes." I finally interject since I hear a pause, my mind still spinning off its axis.

"Talia," Professor Deans details the condition, "We need proof that you have participated in at least one alternative activity in addition to your academics. We cannot officially mail you a decision regarding admission prior to the completion of your application. If you can establish a minimum six-month volunteer position with a reputable organization by the end of this week, we trust you will complete your commitment, and we will begin processing your admission. Immediately following, we will enclose your financial aid package with which I believe you will be very pleased."

I need a pen. I motion script in the air with my free hand to Mr. Donatelli. I am thinking ten steps ahead. Dad doesn't know anything about this yet. Translation: Time. Hope. A dream not shot down. Yet.

Mr. Donatelli reaches across the desk, handing me a black ballpoint. "Professor Deans, should I call you once I've researched my options and made a decision? Okay. I'll get in touch with you no later than next Friday. And, Professor Deans, thank you. Thank you very much."

Deep breath, then I hand Mr. Donatelli the phone to hang up. He takes the receiver without removing his eyes from his computer screen. Several sheets slide out of his printer, which he hands to me immediately.

The bell rings. Lunchtime. I stand to shake Mr. Donatelli's hand. He smiles. "Take a look through these volunteer opportunities and consider one that interests you ASAP. I would hate to see you lose this chance of a lifetime. And if you need me to call your father..."

I shake my head as I turn to leave. "Thanks. You've already done plenty. Thank you, though. It's up to me now."

Ball in my court, papers folded in my hands, I float to the cafeteria to play one-on-one with my thoughts for a few moments longer. I reach into my sweatshirt pocket to make sure it's still there. Can't forget about my lilac Post-it book confession. Bet casserole surprise is on the menu today.

~FOURTEEN~

"What is that you're reading?"

I recognize the voice instantly, and my heart sinks faster than an Olympic diver in the pool of despair. As I raise my head to look into the eyes of my father I think of two things that must remain out of sight for me to live: the lilac Post-it notepad in my pocket and Lagan. *Where are you?*

"D-d-d-d-ad." I stutter, shifting my cafeteria tray as if worried the imperfect alignment with my body constitutes a failure in Dad's books. "What a surprise! What are you doing here? Is everything okay? Is Jesse okay?"

I Frisbee questions to Dad to mask my relief of avoided bombs and my anxiety over simmering grenades. The burning wick shortens every second Lagan nears the cafeteria. Where is he?

"Justice is fine," Dad says, still standing. "I was on my way to stop by the house on my lunch break when a Mr. Donatelli calls me on my cell."

Didn't I tell that man not to call my father?

"He tells me you have a scholarship to Loyola, because you won a writing contest. When did you enter a writing contest? And when were you going to tell me about this?" His voice begins to crescendo.

"Dad." I need some air. "Do you want to talk outside? I can sign out early from school. We can discuss this while driving home."

"I have a client I'm meeting in twenty minutes. You have the next three to explain this, and we'll discuss it further when I get home tonight."

"Okay." I swallow. Still no sign of Lagan as I scan the cafeteria.

"Are you waiting for someone?" I avert my eyes back to him immediately.

"No." I shake my head as the lilac sheets burn inside my pocket. "I was just checking the clock. Umm? The letter. Loyola. Basically..."

And I explained the happenings of the last hour inside Mr. Donatelli's office, finishing by offering over the sheets of volunteer options to Dad, who has been nodding the entire time.

"Keep them." He sounds amazingly calm. "We'll discuss this in the evening. In the meantime, cross out the options of any hospital or clinic. Too many snoopy people work in those places. That garden place sounds like it might work, but I'll check it out thoroughly before deciding. Make a call and set up a time for us to visit the place and review the time commitment and security of the grounds."

He looks at his Blackberry and turns to leave. "I have to run. Get your list done and then make the calls. And, Talia, if this works out, you're gonna save this ol' man a ton of money." Do I detect a smile forming at the corners of his mouth?

With that, I watch Dad's back exit the cafeteria, and the first word on the lilac notepad has grown dark and thick, the ink now combined with the sweat from my palm, which held onto it for dear life every second Dad stood across from me. Always watching. Always testing. I don't know when the shaking began, but I can barely hold the paper straight as I force myself to read the printed description entitled, "Volunteer opportunity: Calling all Green Thumbs."

"Are you cold?" Lagan asks when he sits down in his usual near but far seat on the opposite side.

Startled for the third time today, I vow to stop reading in social settings. At this rate, I'll die of a heart attack before any ploy of Dad's destroys me. Sheesh.

"Where have you been?" The bell will sound any minute.

"I thought I told you. Didn't you get my response on your locker?" My mind is spinning. Did Dad walk by my locker on his way out? I'll know soon enough. Walking on eggshells almost sounds inviting when you've spent your entire life walking on broken glass. *Annie Lennox, call me up. I'll give you something to sing about.* Mom loved that song.

"I had a meeting," Lagan continues when I don't respond. "With Mr. Donatelli? My guidance counselor?"

Coincidence? Or? "Oh. Good guy that Donatelli fellow."

"You know him?" Lagan laughs. "Sounds like you two are friends or something."

"You sound jealous." I egg him on. "You know he's old enough to be my d..."

I stop right there. I stop joking. I stop breathing. I need to rein in my words. And my distance. Inhale. Heart start beating again already.

Lagan tries to pick up where I dropped it: "You were gonna say your—"

"Forget I said anything. How was your meeting?"

"Fine." Lagan lets me slide—away from uncomfortable—again.

"All set to graduate?" I smile, thankful to move on.

"All systems go," Lagan chimes. "How 'bout you?"

"Pretty much." Looking up at the clock, I realize there isn't enough time to explain everything. And before I can suggest we talk more later, the bell rings and lunch is over.

"Hey, do you want to meet in the computer lab after Gym? We can tell Mrs. Tyler that we're doing online research for our final papers. She'll give us hall passes. We just have to check back with a bunch of printouts to prove we found some resources. We can always read them on our own after school."

Did you read my mind? "Uh? Umm. Okay." I hesitantly agree. I am itching to tell him about my morning's weather forecast. From sunny to thunderstorms, to cloudy to near tornado, to the sun returning. Like I'm Mount Denali, creating my own weather system relative to Dad's proximity. From Glaciera to Montania. My name inventory increases. Alaska might just be my future calling.

"Awesome." Lagan rises and puts one hand out with an open palm. "Now hand it over."

I almost forgot. I wonder if I should explain. No time. I pull out the lilac sticky pad, place it on the table, and head to Gym. I turn back just before exiting the cafe to see if Lagan has left, but he's sitting there flipping through the sheets very quickly. He looks up and catches me glancing his way. All smiles, he nods his head with approval. I swallow, smile back, and then turn to sprint to the girls' locker room. Top of the hour weather update: Sunny with a ninety percent chance of love in the air.

~FIFTEEN~

My volunteer position at the Chicago Botanical Gardens, located only miles north of Evanston, materializes within twelve hours, shuttling me into an unlikely future with the speed of time travel. Back to a future I never dared to dream. Every possible glitch is zapped by one word: money. My dad agrees, because he will save money. The director at the garden arranges for my training before I hang up, because the gardens need immediate attention, and my help will cost them no money. Professor Deans informs me that my acceptance letter is in the mail, and I will be pleased to save plenty of money.

Lagan is the only person, besides myself, who could care less about the financial consequences. He calls my newfound opportunity a modern-day miracle. A way for us to see each other outside of our customary, twenty-six-minute lunch period. Somewhere other than class or the cafeteria. He schemes aloud, "Don't mind me if I stop by between homework and basketball practices."

I just listen at first. I allow myself a few laps in his romance-washed imagination. Risk of reality sets in, and I see Dad appear at the side of the pool. I quickly drown, and that's that.

Lagan catches my lowering eyes. "Of course. I'll be extremely careful not to tell anyone about where I'm going or whom I'm visiting. And I'll only come by if and when you want me to. I'm not going to sign up, either. It's obvious what we're avoiding. Your dad isn't gonna come to work with you, is he?"

His question forces the wobbling walls of my cave to collapse. The word dad hangs in the air like a fully loaded gun. Pointed at me. Trigger cocked. I feel nauseated. If I had a lemon ice pop for each time the word dad tsunamied my peace, my tongue would be one frozen yellow iceberg. The name Glaciera seems more appropriate by the day.

"My dad..." I clear the frog from my throat and decide once again if I'm going to hide under a pile of rubble or push through with the truth. "My dad will do whatever it takes to control me."

I speak as if talking about someone I know. But I expect nothing. Lagan can't rescue me, even if he understands. As of late, really since I met this guy, I find myself asking the same question over and over again. What have I got to lose? So little remains of me, that any more loss is like a kick in the shins compared to all that Dad has already stolen from me: Mom, Jess's legs, my childhood, Jess's voice.

Lagan looks to the right. Off into the distance. Processing a clearer package of me cannot be easy. But I never asked him to. He's the one who came knocking on the door of my life that has always had caution tape running across every inch.

I fidget in my seat, but the bell won't ring for ten minutes. With my hands gripped to my tray, I digest the fact that no Sticky Note can cover my time bomb reality. Wanting to save Lagan from failing to solve my life, a math equation that's not his problem, I stand to leave. He doesn't stop me. I move slowly, holding onto a grain of sand that maybe, somehow, he'll suggest otherwise. Give me a reason to sit down. Reach out to me with his strong grip. Calm my racing heart with his smile that always lifts me out of the quicksand. A Sticky Note. Anything. But nope, nothing. He stares at his tray, speechless.

I don't bother saying bye. A gush of sadness threatens to escape as I move away from the table. I say goodbye to my dreams. Of Lagan—of us—in my heart. I say farewell to the only person who has ever waltzed into my thorn-infested life and asked me to dance with possibility. My life has known nothing but goodbyes, and none of them have been good. I move out of the cafeteria doors and all the sounds around me fade.

I think I hear Lagan's voice. *Come back! Don't leave! I need you as much as you need me. Come back!*

I turn my head to reply, but Lagan's eyes stay fixed on his untouched lunch. Sigh. I contrived Lagan's voice in my head, the only place happily ever after could exist. The space between us expands like paint spilled over, widening as the clock ticks away. Separated now, by more than a sea of cafeteria tables, a single tear escapes down my cheek and slips past my lips, reminding me of the salty taste of my bitter past, present…and future.

I hug my books and head to the nurse's office. There's a wait. Not that it matters. Time is one thing I have plenty of at this moment. When the last bell rings, that's when time becomes my enemy. For now, I watch my whimsical fairy tale shut close, the final page ripped out.

While sitting on the chair outside the room, next to two others, I recognize the girl next in line. She's from my gym class. She gives me a once-over, huffs, and rolls her eyes. The boy on the other side has his head slouched back, his baseball hat covers half his face, and his foot lightly taps the floor. The iPod must be tucked inside his pocket, the wire from one ear bud barely detectable as my eyes trace it behind his ear, down his neck, into his shirt.

Following suit, I put my backpack under my seat, and lay my head in my hands. If I sleep, I might be able to escape the dam breaking that crackles within as I exhale without a single friend in the world again. An unexpected friend shows up when my mind drifts away. The woman who bled for twelve years. She's inviting me to come alongside her. Maybe she's not done telling me her story.

She holds my hand and pulls me along, and my once cemented feet loosen, permitting me to watch her journey. Her pace quickens as the sun begins to set in the garden and the crowd thickens with others carrying burdens alongside their broken hearts. I still don't get it. Why is she here? She's fine now. Her bleeding stopped.

When we're inches from the gardener, she lets go of my hand and reaches for his back. A gentle brush of her fingertips, like a single paint stroke down a canvas, and he notices. And turns. And begins to search for her. For the woman who stole a touch.

We stop in our tracks. The crowd stops too. Ridicule and complaints fill the air. So many wall him in, it could have been anyone. Why does it matter? And then I hear her whisper in my ear, "It matters to me. He's looking. For me."

My hands drenched, I hear the nurse calling my name. My plan to tell her I have a headache is no longer a lie. My head pounds as if circus elephants have taken up residency between my ears, but she has no patience for my drama. I can't remove myself from the seat. Defeat nailed me here two bells ago.

"Talia?" The nurse repeats my name. "Talia, either come into my office or go back to class."

I still can't move. Where's that cape from Harry Potter when I need it? The option to disappear vanished the night Jesse jumped off the roof. How's that for a story, Nurse Eva?

The nurse meant what she said. She must deal with this all the time. Students who just park themselves outside her door in order to skip class without being marked up. She's already back in her room, filling out paperwork. If I want to receive a pass into last period, I have to move out of this seat, into her office, state a legitimate complaint, and qualify as sick enough to warrant missing my previous two classes.

I wipe my wet hands on my jeans, and as I lift my arm to wipe my face on my sleeve, Kleenex finds itself in my hand. Warm fingertips from behind wipe the damp hair from my eyes.

"Thought I'd find you here."

Lagan's voice pulls a wooden block out from the bottom row of my heart, and before he has a chance to place it on top, I stand up, face him, and crumble into his arms—a whole bigger mess than Jenga. I see the nurse glance up from her desk. Shake her head. Then return to her paperwork. Drama. Nothing new. If only she knew the details. No one. Not even Lagan. Knows the details.

Saturated Kleenex disintegrates with the second and third dam break. Lagan moves me back into my seat and leaves to talk to the nurse. She glances over at me. Then writes something down and hands a pink slip to Lagan.

"Let's go." Lagan lifts me. Fresh Kleenex replaces the shreds in my hands. He reaches below to retrieve my book bag, and we head out the back doors of the school. The afternoon sun forces my eyes to squint as I let the warmth of the spring day dry my face. School lets out in about twenty minutes.

Lagan holds my hand and walks me over to the elementary school, two blocks down from our schoolyard. The younger kids don't finish for another hour. We near the playground as I watch my left foot step in front of my right. Not sure why I'm letting him lead me, Lagan backs me onto a swing seat with a gentle but firm lift and cups my hands around each chain. He leans into me and our foreheads touch.

"Swings." He whispers the word like a memory. "This was on your list."

And before I have a chance to protest, Lagan moves behind me and pushes me once. Twice. And then pushes so hard, he runs under me and screams one word: "Underdog!"

I am the underdog.

I am flying. And I am screaming. I am so high my feet sail toward the dangling branches of the nearest maple, my toes brushing the bottom leaves. My screaming ceases as I allow myself to taste the wind against my cheeks. I imagine jumping off, sailing into the clouds, somersaulting into the sun.

Then I hear a sound I don't recognize. It's a sound I haven't heard in so long. Someone is laughing. I can feel my stomach shaking. She's laughing louder. Guffawing with all of her might. She is free to laugh. For once in her life, she is free to know joy. If only for a moment. She is free.

My lips close. The laughing ceases. The swing slows. A school bell sounds in the near distance. My toes skid on the dirt below. Lagan stands in front of me and catches me as I slide off the swing. The sweet scent of peppermint hits me as my face nearly collides with Lagan's. I am in his arms, and I am shaking like a leaf. I need to move. Back away. Head home. The list. Jesse. D...

"I accept you." Lagan says these three words as if he's known his whole life, and he's just letting me know. In case I still don't believe him.

"I have to go." I ignore him. I can't afford to add to my list right now. I turn to run home, and he catches my arm.

"Wait."

Every second is one second closer to boiling water. Bleeding lips. Jesse crying. I need to go.

"I just want you to know..." Lagan wants to talk. I am already moving away. Backward. I can still see his face as he squeezes one last thought past the caution tape. "I accept you. No matter how little of you I can have. I accept you."

I turn to sprint, and after running a hundred or so yards, I reply over my shoulder, shaking my head and smiling, " You're crazy!" Then I face forward to pick up speed in order to make up time.

"You're right!" I can hear Lagan screaming. "I am crazy! About you—Talia Grace Vanderbilt! Crae-crae, I tell ya!"

~SIXTEEN~

During the last weeks of March, Dad accompanies me from college to home, to the garden, back home several times on the 'L' and buses in order to gauge when to expect me on my volunteer days. Always in the business of control, Dad surprises me when he allows me to navigate the train system alone from Loyola's campus and walk the final mile to Chicago Botanical Gardens for my orientation.

It's Saturday, March 20, and based on travel times, I agree to four-hour shifts a few times a week to fulfill my six-month contract. Never having done more than take the bus back and forth to school, I feel the thrill of accomplishment before I even pick up a rake. Or do they call it a spade?

Jason, the grounds director, hands me a rake-like thingy and a roll of twine, then tours me around the garden, pointing out the heaviest traffic zones that require weekly maintenance. Jason reminds me of a shorter version of Liam Hemsworth. I guess the shaggy, full head of hair look is in again. Then he guides me to my special project area, which will be my focus during most of my four-hour shift.

We cross a sea of green as we approach a weeping willow, and I stop in my tracks, stunned. Like the clouds rolling away to make way for the sun, I know without a doubt that I'm in this place for a reason bigger than landscaping. So many branches drag their fading leaves on the earth below, and like the girl who hides her deepest hurts behind chapped lips, under the canopy of the willow lies the bark of the trunk, peeling and inaccessible to the sun. So many limbs lie half or fully shattered, hidden from the eye of any distant viewer, that the garden staff considered uprooting her or letting her die slowly. Most onlookers will never see the irreparable damages underneath her branches. Most will never know of her damaged heart, weighed down by the tornadoes in past days. Storms that have left her wanting to sleep and weep no more.

Jason leaves me after instructing how to make reasonably sized piles of debris. I listen silently, all the while merging with my surroundings. I am the weeping willow. And I'm not alone. Someone I never expected showed up today: the gardener from *The Beautiful Fight*. He's here to tell me something.

I lay my rake down and pull on my gardening gloves. Then I reach down and begin gathering a pile of branches scattered all about the tree, and with each drop of a limb, I find myself laying my hurts at the invisible feet of the gardener. And instead of rejecting, resisting, judging, or wincing. I sense his invisible hands asking for more. Of me. All of me. Every broken branch. Every hurtful memory. Every lost moment. Every vanished dream.

I don't know exactly why, especially why now, but I want to try again. I'm the bleeding woman and I want to reach for him. Someone I cannot see. Do not know for sure exists.

I cannot do this alone. I want like I have never known want before. I want to be wanted.

Like a puzzle with only the edge pieces fixed in place, I see only part of the picture. I have time to put this puzzle together, one piece after the other, and if the completed picture doesn't sit well, I'll just collapse it and go back to same old, same cold.

I'm lost in thought as I gather and tie, rake and bundle. When Jason returns to check on me, his smile affirms that I won't be fired. At least not today. He turns to visit his other new volunteers, and I'm reminded of my question that I forgot to ask him earlier.

"Jason?"

He turns to listen, but only slows down his pace.

"Speak." He walks backwards now. "I have to still check on a few more zones. Can it wait?"

"I just... What time does the garden close at night?"

"Shortly after sunset." And with that, he races off and out of sight behind bushes of hydrangeas, purple and blue.

That explains why the wood plank with hours etched into it only displays opening hours. It hangs at the end of the parking lot by the entrance gate. But this is a garden, absent of walls or doors or locks. I like this place more and more. A plan births in my head of a rendezvous with a friend.

Lagan wanted to meet me here on my first day and pose as a casual visitor in the garden. Disguised with sunglasses, hat and wig, he suggested. I told him no. I asked him to wait. In time. I needed time. I need time. To adjust to this nibble of freedom I've never known before. And, of course, to assess Dad's radar for this rare allowance. Give it a month. Give me a month. By then, I will know how safe we will be if we meet here in the garden after hours.

The first month, by myself, working under and around the weeping willow, the gardener meets me. Like he is waiting for me there each day. Little by little, he pours hope into the crevices of my broken lips and heart. And little by little, for the first time in my life, my dreams change.

The majority of my off-road daydreaming while weeding and grafting leads me to Lagan. Recklessly, I veer toward an imaginary future of wedding bells, kisses, and babies. Of pretty lips, flowing gowns, and flowers in my hair. Of dancing toe-to-toe, sailing oceans, and watching sunsets.

Laboring under a blue canopy unleashes a momentum I cannot contain, because no one can hear my thoughts in the garden. And Dad hasn't shown up since the first week, when

he arrived unannounced every other shift just to "check in."
The dirt under my fingernails and tan on my face seems
assurance enough that I clearly work during my shifts. He isn't
a fan of dirt of any sort. The simple fact that flowers grow in
dirt deters his return. Making me love the dirt all the more.

A month into the job, and I am in love with mud.
Springtime in Chicago blooms all around me, the broken
willow blossoms soft tiny yellow petals on her healthier
branches, and the scent of lilacs fills the air. But it's the earth
that beckons me. During each of my twenty-minute breaks, I
sit on the floor under the willow, burying my fingers into the
ground. The aroma of the moist black soil caffeinates my
senses. My gardening boots and socks set nearby, I spread the
dirt over my legs, working my way up from my toes to my
ankles to my knees. And as I massage the dark grains into my
skin, I'm back on the beach at Benton Harbor. The dirt
transforms into sand. Lost in my world of sand castles and
seashell hunting, I don't hear the approaching footsteps.

"Starting an earth therapy clinic?" Lagan's voice startles
me.

I shake off the dirt quickly.

"Sorry, I didn't mean to sneak up on you."

"How long have you been standing there watching me?" I
ask while frantically putting my socks and shoes on. "

"Oh..." Lagan looks up to his right. "Like ten minutes."
My jaw drops.

"Kidding. More like thirty seconds. But I have to admit,
I've never seen you so...so..."

"Chillax?" I rescue his search for the perfect word.

"Yes." Lagan approves of my choice.

"What are you doing here? How did you know I worked
today?"

"I missed you." Lagan makes a goofy, pouting face.

"I just saw you yesterday in school."

"Exactly." He points his index finger upward and continues. "Twelve hours away from you feel like two hundred. So I took a chance and biked over here, hoping that you might be working today. If wrong, I'd have a long bike ride back to work off my disappointment. Instead, I have a picture of you, more beautiful than I've ever seen you, to think about as I pedal back."

My giggle turns to laughter as I rise and slap my hands together to shake off the excess dirt. "Did you say beautiful?" I can't stop laughing. "Are we on the same planet?"

"You have laughed more in these few minutes than the entire time I've known you."

I shake my head, impossible, but even as I look down at my legs covered with dark brown specks, I know he's right. I realize he doesn't know. I haven't told him.

"Are you jealous?" I tease.

"Only if some guy is the reason for the smile on your face." Lagan speaks steadily without smiling.

"Not exactly."

Lagan's eyebrows raise and he backs up to lean against a thick branch that has rooted into the ground.

Taking a deep breath, he snorts a nervous chuckle. "Okay. What's his name?"

I debate prolonging the torture. Never seen Lagan squirm before. Satisfied, I erase any doubt in his mind with two words.

"The gardener."

"What about the gardener?" Lagan's wrinkled forehead smoothens out.

"He's the reason I'm smiling." I put it simply.

Lagan's grin reaches for his ears, and then turns to a playful frown. "So, I guess you don't need me anymore?"

How do I answer that? "Isn't it obvious that...I like you." I surprise myself when I speak these three little words.

Dimple in full effect, he moves closer to me and makes a funny request. "Can you say that again?"

"Seriously?" *You're lucky I said it once.*

"Please. This time I'll empty my mind so I can hear every sound, syllable, and word pronounced. I just want to hear it one more time, so I can remember how you say it. And to know for sure that you did say it. Come on! Cut this guy a break and grant him one tiny wish."

His face inches closer to mine, only his clasped hands in a childish begging gesture linger between us. I can feel his breath on my face. Sweet peppermint intoxication.

I take a deep breath. Another. Then another. I turn to look through the branches to the green expanse between the main gardens and us. No one. Nothing but manicured emerald blades sparkling in the sun. I turn back. Lagan's eyes are waiting.

"I. Like. You." I blink. And then look down at my boots.

"So...." Lagan tries to cash in while the jackpot cha-chings with unusual generosity. "You'll come to my graduation party?"

My heart sinks. I fall backward to plop down on a nearby limb, Lagan's request anchoring me back to my reality. A reality with a dad that forbids normalcy. I'm a little ticked that he keeps asking. I don't answer.

"Just try." He fills the silence. "If you can, just try. Okay?"

"Okay." I can accept that. My version of trying, of course. "I'll try."

***

May begins and the days whirl by. Within weeks, Lagan and I will no longer see each other daily. Summer vacation will start. My hours at the garden will increase. Lagan will leave for his summer internship overseas. Something about a water well-digging project in some remote village. He plans to study International Justice and dreams of the day he can represent those without a voice. Becoming a lawyer is just a means to give him access to his ultimate dreams: to change the world, for the better. Impending change threatens and entices me. Perhaps a month will be enough to get over him. To say goodbye. To adjust back to life alone. Just Jesse and me again.

**

"My break is over." I remind us both one Saturday afternoon in May when Lagan turns up at the garden during my first short rest. Dad happens to be working today, but I can't guarantee that will be the case every time Lagan decides to pop in. I tell him he has to stop with the spontaneous visits. If we get caught... "Plus, I have work to do."

"Of course." He makes to leave. "Hey, when is your next break?"

"I have a thirty minute break for lunch in two hours. Around 12:30. Why?" I know exactly why.

"No reason. I'll let you get back." He leans into my space and whispers in my ear. "Can I take you out to lunch?"

"You know I can't leave the grounds." I make a fist and playfully punch his arm nearest me. Which moves him back. *Breathe.* Now I can breathe again.

"Who said anything about leaving?" He shrugs his shoulders. "This here is as out as out gets. I'm talking simple, private dining under a weeping willow that needs a new name."

"New name?" I lower my fist. Did we just change the subject?

"Definitely. How about 'Waterfall Willow'? Weeping is just too sad for the new, happy you that I've only seen under here. Under this..." He motions around us with his arms. "This broken mess of a tree."

I nod, tickled by Lagan's naming quirk. "Waterfall Willow it is."

"Okay then." He makes to really leave this time and finishes his thought as he spreads branches to exit. "I'll meet you under the waterfall for lunch. I'll bring the food. If you bring your smile?"

If I agree, I know I am inviting him. Back here. Again and again. Opening up a gate with the posts that read unknown and risk all over them.

"Say yes." Lagan slowly stretches out an open palm toward me.

I swallow. Knowing I gave up choice when I repeated the three words *I like you* the first time Lagan and I stood here under the willow.

I pick up my rake as I silently promise myself to be super careful. "I'll see you at lunchtime." Avoiding his eyes, I wonder if Lagan can hear my heart pounding in this quiet place.

"Yes, you will." Lagan rides off across the field. I watch him bike away leisurely as I rake slowly at first, when he halts, and turns around to yell one last thing. Go figure. "Oh, and don't worry! I'll bring a bunch of paper towels!"

"Thanks!" I shout back, just as he turns and disappears past the field.

I rake and rake until my arms ache all over. All the while thinking of two firsts and a last.

The first time a boy asked me on a date.

The first time I ever told a boy that I like him.

And the last time I rake under a weeping willow.

~SEVENTEEN~

Half expecting him to pull out his bow and arrow, Jason arrives five minutes before my lunch break to dismiss me. *Okay, Gale.* I haven't seen the movie, but there are *Hunger Games* posters in half the girls' lockers at school. I'm sure the book is better.

"Get yourself cleaned up and get some grub." Jason takes the trash bag from my hands and tells me the work will be right here waiting for me after lunch.

"Okay." My tired body agrees easily. "Is it okay to eat out here?"

"Eat wherever you like." Jason shrugs. "Just remember to throw out your trash."

I walk back toward the closest ladies room to wash up, and I can't help but laugh when I see the mirror above the sink. I look like a three-year-old with smudge marks up and down. I am one muddy mess. I grab a handful of paper towels, wet them, and go to work giving myself a sponge bath of sorts. Too bad I don't have a hairbrush. My wet fingertips will have to do. Pleased with the results of warm water, I move close to the mirror to examine my lips. As I run two fingers along the scabs, I silently vow not to kiss anyone until my lips are healed. Fully. Not even certain that Lagan is thinking along those lines, I giggle to myself as I mosey on back to the weeping—I mean waterfall—willow.

I see Lagan's bike from a distance. Of course he'd come back. Still have to get used to this guy who keeps his word. The sun peeks above, burning my cheeks, forehead, and eyelids. Sheesh. I forgot my shades in the restroom. I debate running back to retrieve them. Then decide three extra minutes with Lagan warrant a little squinting. I'll get them later.

Lagan empties a medium-sized paper bag as I enter the welcoming shade of the willow.

"Hey!" I announce my arrival. "What's cooking?"

"You forgot to say, 'good-looking.'" Lagan turns his palms open like he's waiting to catch a beach ball. "You know... 'What's cookin', good lookin'?'"

Not following, so I just say, "Sure," and leave it at that.

I sit down on a nearby nice-sized branch to survey the spread atop the brown paper bag. Saran-wrapped croissants filled with cold cuts. Two clear plastic tins: one with fruit salad and the other with sliced cucumbers. He also brought two iced coffees. *Yum.*

I like this place. Sitting closer. Sharing words. Face-to-face. "Thanks for bringing lunch."

"Thank you." Lagan looks over his sunglasses to correct me. "For letting me come back with lunch. And, of course, for bringing your smile. Sit here." He points to the spot next to him. "Dig in."

We munch for a bit in silence under our waterfall willow away from the world.

"Can I ask you a question?" Lagan pops his last bite in. I haven't made it through half my sandwich. "What is it about the gardener that makes you smile?" Lagan is all about my smile these days.

I want to show him rather than tell him. So I pop the cucumber container open and munch away at four slices. Lagan stares at me, but waits patiently. When I'm done, I lay my four reshaped cucumber slices down on the paper bag. Each piece is now a light-green, wet letter.

L I S T

Lagan's eyes sadden as I explain how my whole life I've had lists from Dad that I fearfully complete with the clock ticking like a horse rider's switch. I don't want to stay in this place of sadness. We no longer dine under a weeping willow, after all. I rearrange the cucumber slices. Now they spell a new word.

S T I L

"I know there's an L missing." I move us from weeping to a waterfall. "This is what the gardener tells me he wants to give me in exchange. He has no lists for me to complete. When I'm still, he moves me. Well, more like he moves me out of the way. The part of me that forgot how to search for...hmmm?" I'm searching for the right word. "Hope. It's all very new. But...I like this place. This place of still. More and more." A sweet calm runs over me. Still.

Lagan's hands reach to cup my chin. As I blink, tiny droplets escape, roll down my cheeks, and disappear into his palms. Just a waterfall kinda day.

"You better eat up." Lagan starts to gather up and organize the spoils after wiping my tears. "It's already one. Only fifteen minutes before our date is over!"

"So this is our first date?" I want to hear him affirm it. "What does that make us? Are we...," and I'm not sure I want to finish my thought.

"Eat up, I said." Lagan ignores me. He's munching on cucumbers now. Facing slightly away so I can't see what he's spelling with the slices.

I scarf down the yumilicious sandwich, washing down every bite with big gulps of watery ice coffee. I pick at the fruit salad while looking around the grounds, determining realistic goals for the remainder of my shift. If I can bag my piles and tie heavier branches that hang too low back upward, the weaker ones will support their weight with the strength of stronger more stable branches nearby.

It's 1:15 p.m. Lunch break is over. I rise up and Lagan hands me the container of cucumbers while gathering up the rest of the garbage.

His instructions surprise me. "Read this after I'm gone, okay?"

"K." I can't help but giggle. This is a first. I initiate a non-verbal communication game, and Lagan plays along.

"Best get back home before my mom starts wondering if I biked to Alaska. See ya Monday."

I'm holding a rake in one hand and a plastic box of munched cucumber letters in the other.

"How will I know the order of the letters?" I panic. What if it's a puzzle I can't solve?

He leans forward and hugs me carefully, so as not to knock the contents out of my hands.

A smile. A wave. And off he disappears, his tires leaving a temporary crease in his grassy trail.

I lean the rake against a branch and open up the container. There are only three cucumber slices in there. Two letters and one shape: I ♥ U.

~EIGHTEEN~

Monday arrives not soon enough. I anxiously count down the minutes till lunchtime to tell Lagan that I ate his cucumber slices up. That they were yummy. That he can't take the letters back. The letter. Really. The letter to me telling me that he hearts me.

We still sit seats apart. The end of the school year has enough days that I'm not willing to risk being pulled out of school and missing precious time with my prince. Gosh. That sounds so girly. I still have to watch myself. Limiting my smiles around Jesse. Don't want to gloat. Keeping my poker face on when Dad is around.

Saturday streamed into Sunday, like any normal weekend. Chores. More chores. Homework. More work. And broken eggshells everywhere as Jess and I tiptoed around Dad's cancerous anger. Well, I walked. Jess just lays there, a charade that has to be getting old. Then Sunday evening brought about the most unusual moment. As I carefully walked past Dad's office to make my way up to bed, I could have sworn I heard a muffled sound, coming from his desk. I know that sound like I know the back of dad's hand. He was crying.

I witnessed a similar incident a couple years back, but I dismissed it as a fluke. After Mom passed away and Jesse's fall, when packing our house up became top priority, I approached Dad in his office to ask whether to save or donate several books from his college days. He looked through them quickly, and after removing one from the stack, told me to toss the rest in the donation bin. I left the room to continue sorting when I realized I forgot to ask him about some jackets I found in the basement closet. As I turned the corner toward the den, I stopped in my tracks. Dad gazed at the saved book and turned page after page, one at a time. His eyes looked more tenderly at the words than I'd ever seen him look at anything or anyone. I nearly choked as I gulped back disbelief when I saw Dad's hand wipe a tear from his cheek. He was crying? Over a skinny book called *The Foundling*?

I didn't think to pay attention to the author's name, but I looked up the word in a dictionary that night before I went to bed. Webster's defined foundling as "an abandoned infant, a stray, an outcast." I will never know if the tears were for Mom or for himself. That day marked the first and last time I ever saw my father cry. Until yesterday. Last night. But I just moved from a weeping to a waterfall willow. I can't allow myself to dwell on Dad. I'd rather sleep and dream of days past and days to come, with a boy who says, "I heart you!"

School staff shortens lunch fifteen minutes early for a Monday afternoon assembly. Seniors shuffle into the auditorium, Lagan walking behind me. We both feel shafted. The talk is titled "Power Hour" by Principal Jenners. She wants seniors to powerfully transition from high school to their next stages in life, whether that includes college or employment. About ninety-five per cent of us will attend some type of continued education. That's what the stats suggest. Lagan comes prepared with two pens and Sticky notepads. He hands me one and writes me the first message.

Cucumber slice for your thoughts?

I write back:

You know we can't eat in here.

He responds:

Lol. Just wanted to know what you thought of my cucumber message, actually?

I scribble:

Oh that! Refresh my brain. What letters did you munch out?

He shakes his head and smiles. He scans the aisle, making sure the roaming teachers don't catch him ignoring the talk. No one near our row, he scrawls:

There were only three letters. Do you really need me to write it? Again?

I write:

Funny you ask! Three letters is all I'm asking ;)!

I look up to see if he's reading over my shoulder. I know a guy who asked me to repeat three words not too long ago.

Lagan chuckles quietly. Busted.

His next note reads:

Okay. I'll be happy to rewrite my three letters. If you'll tell me which way you read them?

"Fair enough," I say, nearly under my breath.

Lagan rips off the last three sheets to expose a clean sheet, and in crinkly bubble letters, he draws three cucumber-wanna-be letters. The two letters I and U and a heart.

I smile. Big. Then scrawl quickly:

Does the order really matter?

He shakes his head no as he shrugs his shoulders. My smile tells him I approved. And I approve. Now. Here.

When can I see you again at the garden?

Lagan moves from mush to business.

I write honestly:

I don't know.

He scribbles:

How often are you there?

He wants a date. Something to look forward to. I understand. All my life, I've wanted to know when, for sure, I would be safe and when I could begin to live.

I scrawl:

Let me look into Dad's schedule and get back to you. Okay?

Then I blacken out each word completely. Not taking any chances.

***

When I arrive home, I check in on Jesse and complete the checklist at record speed. Since Jesse's muscles have gained strength daily, he's been less and less of a burden on me, making my list shorter. I tear up each time I come home and see him doing leg exercises on his own. His legs have also developed flexibility, and I see his quads have nearly doubled in the last month. How he hides from Dad daily by lying in bed or sitting in the wheelchair is dually disturbing and calming. Dad wants predictability. So that is what we give him.

I find Jesse feeding himself fruit with a fork at the kitchen counter while sitting in his wheelchair. I must ask him something, carefully.

"Jess? Do you know if Dad keeps his monthly work calendar anywhere specific? I've watched him type appointments into his Blackberry, but does he have his schedule anywhere else? Maybe in his den somewhere?"

"Why?" Jesse has been saying simple, one-syllable words clearly, too.

"I..." How do I explain without revealing too much? I don't want to get Jesse in trouble for knowing too much. "I just want to know which nights he works late so I can plan my work hours. Request late days when he won't be around to be mad that I work late. That way I can start to make money when my volunteer hours are done and save up faster for…for…I don't know. For a rainy day."

"Check. His. Comp. U. Ter." Jess's broken words breathe criminal suggestions.

Dad's computer is strictly off limits. I nod to Jess. We simultaneously glance at the microwave clock. Dad could be home as early as ten minutes. Or late. Later. He has been inconsistent lately. Apparently the practice is growing, and the increased overseas client load falls on his shoulders. We overhear him on his business line in the evenings more and more. That's what happens with the time change across the ocean. I make a quick decision and head to the den. Jess will cover me, when or if Dad comes home early.

Dad has yet to lock his den. But the desk and shelves and even the chair remain in meticulous order like a floor model. Perfect. I memorize the angles of the chair. The laptop. Even the door's openness. Everything must return as is. I hope I can pull this off.

As I reach for his chair to sit down, I half expect to be shocked at the touch. I'm aware of every passing second by the clock tick-tocking faintly on his desk. I wipe my sweaty palms on my jeans and pull out the keyboard on top. As the screen comes to life, I realize that I need a password. Duh. Of course it wouldn't be that easy.

I try *Gita*, Mom's name. Doesn't work. Then I try my name. Nothing. I have one last shot before I get locked out. Running my fingers through my hair, I ask myself, what one word sums up Dad. I can think of several, but one stands out: control. It seems too obvious. Too easy. But I imagine him sitting behind the desk, daily reminding himself that he is in CONTROL. I choose all capitals with the shift key locked in place. As I press the enter key, imagining the computer will spit the saliva of rejection in my face, my heart sinks as the screen goes blank. Suddenly, the open prompt sounds, and several icons line the right a screensaver of a renovated stone castle with a white stretch limo parked in front. A tall, curved wall of stone-embedded bricks surrounds the expansive green grounds edges, like a scene taken out of somewhere in Europe.

Probably a daily reminder that Dad is king of his castle, but I don't have time to worry about that.

I quickly scan the icons to see if one might suggest a schedule. There's an iCal app in the bottom left corner. That would be too easy. I click on it, having to start somewhere. Shocked when the month of May pops up, my eyes fill with notes entered in almost every box. Meetings, appointments, client names, time durations. A lot of hotel names in major cities. New York comes up a lot. And L.A. and Las Vegas, too. Interspersed with several female names. Immigration cases up the ying-yang, I'm guessing. Details galore paint my eyes like dollar signs. Jackpot! I quickly scan the weeks, looking for repetition. But do not find any. In fact, there are also blocks on the board with blank spaces. Which indicate that Dad either doesn't write everything down or he could pop up out of nowhere at any moment.

I shake my head in disbelief and disappointment. I almost shut everything down, when my right hand scrolls up to the arrow. Sure. I guess it makes sense to check the next month. But it looks the same. All over the place. Nothing consistent weekly. I skim quickly to see if I see any repeating names. A few do appear on May and June. I scan July and August as well, a sleuth without a clue. One overseas appointment with a client from Mumbai appears about mid-month on each of the spreadsheets. Dad works late when international business partners visit. Hmm. "8:00 p.m. Meeting with John Brown" appears on the...May 17. Then on...June 17.

Wait. Is it possible? Yes! July 17 and August 17 too! Jackpot, for shizzle. It's time to cash in and skedaddle before my snooping gets me in boiling water, literally. I close out of each month, and then out of iCal. Then I put the computer back to sleep before carefully placing Dad's keyboard under the sliding middle drawer after wiping the keys down with my sleeve. As I move away to examine the angle of his chair, I twist it slightly to the left, making a perfect right angle between the seat and the front of the desk. I second guess my memory and pull it out a centimeter. Then push it back. My heart pounds against my chest so loudly, I might have a heart attack over this one centimeter until Dad sits down in his chair. I wipe the top of the chair with my shirt to erase my fingerprints. Almost done.

"Hello?" Dad's voice calls when he opens the door.

I move quickly to the door. Too quickly. My swinging arm knocks a stack of letters off Dad's desk. Before I can rearrange the stack, definitely out of order, I see Dad's shiny black leather shoes tapping in the doorway. My streak of luck runs out. My hands shake as I think a mile a minute as to how I will explain my entering his sacred domain. Like it even matters. The scent of burnt flesh pushes out the aroma of moist earth like a bully not waiting in line to use the playground slide. Except that he not only pushes me out of line. He pushes me off the slide—to my death—once again.

"Dad." I choke on my first word. When the coughing ceases, I say, "I'm sorry."

He doesn't flinch. "I'll see you in the kitchen."

"Can I explain?" I beg, not sure why I feel the need to try.

"In order to explain? Not following you, Talia." He speaks while reading his newspaper as if nothing unusual is happening. "If you think you'll get out of your due punishment, you're simply wasting my time. And yours."

I take a deep breath and squeeze my holding hands to steady the shaking. I rise, place the pile of letters back where they started, and look Dad in the eyes and say in my best brave voice, "I needed to find Loyola's acceptance letter from Professor Deans. Mr. Donatelli reminded me that it was imperative that I call her and thank her personally, as well as send her a formal thank you letter. I didn't know if you would get home before she leaves her office at five, so I thought…"

"That's where you're wrong, Talia!" Dad screams out his words, and I start shaking like a flickering strip of paper in a spinning fan. "You did not think! Get out of my sight! Get to the kitchen. Put the teakettle on. Ten seconds for disobeying. Ten more for foolishly wasting my time with your pathetic excuse. I'll give you a reason or two to never try that stupid idea again."

"Y-y-yes, D-d-d-dad." I move past him, careful not to brush his side. Jesse pounds his thigh. He didn't warn me in time. He heard the car. His voice wouldn't project loud enough. I couldn't hear him silently screaming. Fear seized his vocal chords, and now I reach for the kettle.

I instinctively put two fingers on my lips. Almost healed. I rip off a tiny scab to punch back. To taste blood. I don't care anymore. I accept that I will never have beautiful lips. The tears puddle along the edges of my eyes, and I swat them away before they stain trail marks on my face. The water overflows out of the kettle, jabbing me with a reminder that only one thing floods my life: loss. I gambled. And I lost. Again.

I turn off the tap and bump into Jesse who has wheeled up behind me. After I turn on the burner and drop the kettle on top, I collapse into Jesse's arms for fifteen seconds of surrender. His arms hold me tightly. And before I can own the strength, he pushes me away and moves back to his spot by the counter. I double over the sink, the tremor in my hands unstoppable, even by gripping the granite top. The kettle whistles so soon. Even the hot water seems to taunt me today. I hear Dad's footsteps enter the kitchen, and his cell phone ring tone alarms all of us. Dad stops in mid-stride to take the call.

"Who is this? Ah, yes, Professor Deans from Loyola. Yes, we received the acceptance letter and financial package. Yes, we are very pleased with it. Talia? Yes, she's doing fine. Yes. Yes. She's..."

About to have her arm burned for her own good.

"She's right here. Yes. She started her volunteer hours at the Botanical Gardens. She's working very hard over there.

Yes. As a matter of fact, she was about to call you herself to thank you for everything. Here, let me pass her the phone."

Dad has the phone covered with his other hand when he approaches me. "Keep it short and sweet. Professor Deans from Loyola."

I take the phone and thank Professor Deans, hoping she can't hear the fear in my stutter. I press end and return the phone to Dad's palm.

He has three teacups on the counter. He pulls three tea bags out of the canister and asks nonchalantly, "Tea anyone?"

Seriously? I don't know if he's playing a different kind of mind game. Quench the prisoner's thirst before kicking her in the guts to make her choke on her spit? I look at Dad blankly and put my arm across the kitchen sink. Proceed, please. *The sooner you burn me, the sooner I can start healing.* My whole body resumes shaking as I wait. And in the reflection of the tap metal, I see my eyes. And they're not the same. It's raining. But there's a small glint of something I never saw before. Like a single ray of the sun breaking through. Just a sliver. Just enough to form a tiny rainbow.

Dad stands next to me now with three cups of steaming water. Not the kettle. Blood pulses in my deafened ears, beating with the thudding of my heart, as he explains. "Since Professor Deans actually called and affirmed your reason for being in my office, your punishment has been reduced to three cups of boiling water. No counting necessary."

And the pouring begins. The cups pour over my arms and my teeth bite instinctively and rip fresh ridges into my lips. One cup. Two. Then three. It's over. My skin bubbles. But it's over. My flesh stinks. But it's over. My arm stings down to my bone. Wound upon wound upon wound, my arm reads a timeline of hurt. But it's over. For now.

Dad refills the three cups and asks again, "Tea anyone?"

"No, thank you." I choke to get out the words. "May I be excused?"

"Sure." Dad carries on. Same old, same cold. "Just hurry back and start dinner. We have a lot to celebrate. Talia's going to college. Your father got a raise. Jesse…well, Jesse is breathing."

I stumble out of the kitchen and run to the upstairs bathroom. As I quickly fish through the medicine cabinet for the burn cream and gauze, my right hand trembles, and I drop the tube. The remaining ointment only covers a quarter of my forearm. The aloe ran out after the last incident, and Dad never replenished it. I read somewhere that toothpaste works. Toothpaste it is. I fish out the Colgate from the first drawer and spread the entire tube over my burnt arm. The numbing covers the pulsing throbs like a thin blanket during a winter storm. If only I could stick my arm in a snow bank and leave it there. After wrapping my goop-covered arm lightly with gauze, what choice do I have except to return to the kitchen?

Dad sits with his back to Jesse at the dining table. I see the ingredients for lasagna lined on the countertop nearest the stove. The last time we had lasagna, Mom baked a cake, too. We followed the steps on the bottom of the box. Remembering Mom's hands atop my little girl hands, the noodles slipped from my tiny fingers, so Mom essentially held them for me. When you're four-years-old, you think you're still holding stuff when an adult holds your hands around the item. Now I know I didn't hold the noodles at all. Mom held me and my whole world together back then. Whenever her world wasn't being ripped to shreds.

Jesse's eyes spell murder as he pierces Dad's back with invisible knives. Afraid to alert Dad, I silently pick up a cutting board and chop up onions and tomatoes with my right hand, standing between Jesse's face and Dad's view. As my hands move systematically, my burnt arm curses me alongside an unfamiliar word. *Hope.* The number seventeen. The seventeenth of each month.

Four hours later, everyone fed, kitchen cleaned, and lights out, I lay in bed, recapping the day. My mind is a Sticky Note. Lagan scrawls I heart U. Over and over again.

I cannot fall asleep for the life of me, my throbbing skin prevents my eyelids from closing. I can no longer lay here. Even the flipping of pages reignites the stinging. I listen for Dad's snoring and make my way quietly back downstairs to the kitchen for a cup of water. Gulping it down, I open up the freezer to search for an ice pack. Two. We have two! Taking both and sliding them in between the gauze and my pajama sleeve, after a few minutes, relief seeps in. My arm is frozen, and I cannot feel. I know that I can't fall asleep with the ice packs. They will defrost, and the burning sensation will return leaving me with wet sheets and awakened anger.

I don't know why, but I walk back to Dad's office and stand at the door and reenact in my head how I clumsily tried to exit. How I failed to notice the stack of letters on the corner of his desk. How I didn't watch my personal space and failed to escape. How I failed.

I shake my head, and as I stare at the letters in mixed up order as I had left them, I realize that Dad never returned to his office to organize them. He would never know which order I left them in either. Before I can stop myself, like a magnet that has no power over the pull, my feet move swiftly, my hand takes the stack of letters, and I quickly place them one by one back on the desk, after reading the senders' names. I just want to read the acceptance letter myself. See my name on Loyola letterhead. Feel my future in my hands.

Utility bill. Mortgage bill. Another bill. Business mail. Credit card statement. More business mail. Then I read a name that stops my dealing fingers. "Amit Shah." The return address is Kolkata, India, and the plethora of colorful stamps suggests that it cost a pretty penny to deliver.

The name sounds so familiar. Like it's been filed somewhere deep in my memory, and I just have to remember who he is. I don't have the luxury to think while standing here—guilty as charged if Dad catches me returning to the place of my destruction. I make a split second decision to peruse the already opened letter and return to my room in no more than three minutes. My fingers carefully remove the letter written on blue-lined stationery, and I read as fast as my eyes can move.

[Amit Shah asked me, a teacher at the district school, to write this letter for him. His wife has been our faithful household help for years. This is the least I could do in return. Please accept this letter on their behalf.]

Dear Gerard-Sir,

We were recently told that Gita died several years ago by a neighbor who has some connections with a family friend living in Michigan. Why did you not tell about our daughter's death? Doesn't her death clear all her debts to you? We only hoped that she might see a better life in America. We're still in shock that we'll never see her again.

In all the ten years since she left us, we only received two letters from her, which our teacher friend read to us. In the first, she told us that she gave birth to a daughter. The second told us she had a son. That is all we know. We are devastated to hear the news and still cannot believe our precious Gita is really gone. Never to step foot again in the country of her birth.

We forgive you. We simply desire to contact our grandchildren and perhaps bring them to India one day for a visit. We hoped one day our Gita would return to see the room we built for her, run in the fields of rice paddies like she did as a child, and break bread with us. Since that dream is dead, we can at least hope to give our grandchildren a comfortable place to lay their heads when they visit India. Please do not discard this letter. Stamps are still very expensive for us, and we cannot afford to write often. Please tell our grandkids that we want to see them. They're all we have left of Gita. Please, we beg you, tell the kids about us and give them our love.

Thank you,
Amit Shah
P.S. Gita's mother sends her best.

My mind is whirling in all sorts of directions. When did Mom ever have a job? And Dad was her boss? I mean, he controls this house. There is no question about that, but this letter mentions debts and an employer. Before I can entertain the remaining hundred and one questions that well up inside me, I refold the letter and carefully funnel it back into its envelope. I then stick the letter back in the middle of the stack and reshuffle the letters to restore order and disorder.

I stumble on the first step as I begin my tiptoed ascent back to my room. My burnt arm hits the railing as I catch myself from tasting the wooden stairwell. Without thinking, I bite extra hard on my lower lip to contain the squeal of pain that threatens escape. The taste of fresh blood mixes with new information with the strength of a cocktail that threatens a new kind of intoxication. I am drunk on the possibility of possibility.

As I falter up the remaining steps, I hold my throbbing arm against my chest. The numbness wore off so quickly, and I silently curse the ice packs for teasing me. They are soft, cool bags of mush now. I lay the blue packs on the bathroom counter top and adjust the tautness of the damp gauze. The choking tightness around my forearm reduces the stinging, ever so slightly. If only I could choke my father in his sleep for keeping my grandparents from me. From us.

I glance at the clock. It reads 2:15 a.m. I pull the covers over my head and wonder what it's like. To be lied to. Taken from your parents. Told you'd have a better life. Only to find out you're in debt like a slave. Oh Mommy! If your parents ever knew what happened? So many things about Dad make sense now. But so much does not. What kind of immigration lawyer is he after all? Who is he representing, and what did he hire Mom for?

I fall asleep with a divided heart. My mind swirls as I imagine a secret rendezvous in the garden. May 17 can't come soon enough. Then I shift to the letter, wondering what it must have been like for Mom to leave her parents, unaware she'd never see them again.

I know now why the name Amit Shah sounded so familiar. Mommy said his name in her sleep during those last days. When I'd ask her about the name, she just shook her head and stared off toward the window. I know now that she was looking back. To her childhood. The time when she had a mom and dad. Perhaps a dad that could have protected her from all her hurts. From her cruel husband. From all the madness. A dad named Amit Shah.

I fall asleep asking questions about my mom and about my grandparents. About a past I have no connection to. And a future I have no control over.

I fall asleep thankful. For cucumber letters, the information on Dad's monthly schedule, and grandparents who are alive. I do not remember who held my hand as I walked into dreamland. I do remember thinking, *Oh God, my arm is still burning!*

~NINETEEN~

At night, I dream of Mom and her life before Jess and I arrived. A thousand nights. A thousand different jobs. One moment a nurse, like Nightingale. The next a writer of sorrowful tales. Then suddenly a hairdresser. And with the turn of her back, a dancer with her hair tossing here and there as she twirled. Then another turn and suddenly Mom wears velvet purple robe like a queen, tucking lilacs in her hair, then tossing the rest in the air, letting them fall anywhere. A palace blooming with freedom. And finally, she becomes what I knew her least as—a teacher. Showing me how to braid my hair, paint my nails, and walk in heels. Things I never learned. Mom never had the time to teach me the little things. Whatever life lessons we learned from her came from watching her. And somehow, in this topsy-turvy, mental whirlwind, I journey to my little girl years, my eyes still closed.

When I was in third grade, one day shortly after winter break, my teacher Miss Cook got engaged. Few of us students knew what that meant. To acknowledge the importance of the occasion, Miss Cook gave us a night off of homework. We all giggled as she seemed momentarily lost in her gaze of her pretty, little, pale hand, too tiny for the sparkly diamond sitting atop her ring finger.

"I'm getting married, girls and boys!" Adding doubles and reading circles could wait. She spent much of the lesson time spewing details that were beyond my scope of experience or understanding. But I listened. Watched, really. I'd never seen her so radiant, speaking so fast at times, I wondered if she forgot that she stood surrounded by a room full of antsy eight-year-olds. Some of the boys appeared to fall asleep with their heads on their desks while Miss Cook's voice jabbered on.

"The wedding is at the end of August, two weeks before the school year starts. My wedding colors are honeydew green and salmon pink. I'm going to look for salmon bridesmaids' dresses with honeydew buttons down the back. And the girls will all carry single long-stemmed, light pink roses, and I'll hold a pretty bouquet of pink flowers with plenty of light green trim. And the groomsmen will have matching bow ties, and we'll dance the night away, and..." She stopped to take a breath. "And when you see me next school year, my name will change. I will no longer be Miss Cook. Next September, when you see me in school, please call me Mrs. Drakowski."

Dra-what? We all looked around at each other until Joey, one of the few boys who paid attention, raised his hand to ask, "Can we just call you Mrs. D.?"

She smiled and nodded yes. Her eyes looked so dreamy. I bet if he had asked, "Can we call you Mrs. Dracula," she would have smiled and nodded yes.

After school, I raced home a few steps ahead of Jesse to tell Mom about being engaged. Even back then we had our chores and lists, but with a homework pass, I had a fleeting hour void of times tables and cursive letters. I made sure to still bring my reading book home. Dad didn't know that I had no homework. I had a better plan for my stolen time.

The smell of dhal and rice greeted my senses the moment we stepped inside. I guess we were having Indian food tonight. Yuck! I wanted to have mac and cheese like the other kids in my school. Or pizza. Or chicken nuggets.

I immediately made up my mind not to let tonight's menu ruin my time with my mother. After carefully lining my shoes in the closet in their assigned spot, I ran to find Mom in the kitchen drying dishes. She put the last of the teacups behind the glass cupboard when I caught her in a squeezing hug from behind, as my backpack fell to the floor with a thud.

"Mommy! You'll never guess what I learned today?"

"Math? How to read? More math?" Jesse came up from behind panting. Did his sarcasm have anything to do with the fact that I ignored his plea to "wait up" the whole way home? I continued to ignore him.

"Jesse. Talia. Clean up and finish your homework. Then get at least half your chores done before dinner. Chop-chop." Mom spoke toward the kitchen window. Always on the lookout for Dad's impending and dreaded arrival.

"Mommy, can I tell you a secret?" I whispered into her waist now that she had turned to face me. My hands clasped around her tiny waist, praying she might agree to deviate. Just this once.

"Jesse, run along." Jesse released an emphatic huff and shuffled up the staircase to his room.

I moved away from Mom to sit at the kitchen table. "What is it, Talia? You know your Dad does not—"

"Mommy, sit down. I know Dad's rules. Just sit and listen for a minute. I have some big news and then some bigger news."

"Homework first T! You know the—"

"Mommy, that's what I'm trying to tell you! I have no homework tonight. Mrs. D., I mean Miss Cook, gave us a homework pass, just for today!"

"Well, why didn't you say so?"

"Mommy!"

"Okay. If that's the big news, tell me the bigger news, and then get your chores finished."

"Mommy, Miss Cook got engaged!"

"That's nice."

"Mommy! Because she's engaged, she's getting married, and she'll wear a long white dress, and there will be flowers, and dancing and, and, and..." I sounded like my teacher. "And her name will change. We have to call her Mrs. D. in September."

"That's nice Talia. If that's all you wanted to tell me—"

"Mom, there's more." I took a deep breath. "I want to get married. Someday. Not now of course. But I want a ring. I want to wear a pretty dress. I want to dance with a nice man who loves me and carry a large bouquet of purple lilacs. I love the smell of lilacs."

Mom stared off to the kitchen window silently.

"What is it, Mommy?" Why wasn't she happy? Laughing? This was exciting news after all.

"Baby T, you should go and clean your room now."

"Did you even hear a word I said, Mommy? Mom? Weren't you excited when Daddy gave you a diamond? When you picked your colors? Didn't you wear a pretty, long, white dress?" Come to think of it, I never saw any pictures of my parents' wedding. I guess I never thought to ask.

"Mommy, can you show me a picture of your wedding? Please! I want to see your dress."

Mom gulped like she had just swallowed a golf ball. "I don't have any."

"Why not?"

Instead of answering my question, Mom rose from the table, removed her apron, and hung it over the door handle, grabbed my right hand, and said, "Come on! I don't have any wedding photos, but there is something I can show you. I have one picture of myself when I was younger that I can show you. But you have to promise me that you'll never breathe a word of this to your father. Or even Jesse. Can you do that? Can you keep a secret?"

"Let's pinky promise, Mommy! Kids at school do it all the time. You just do like this..." I wound my pinky around hers and then continued. "I promise to keep your secret if you keep mine. I don't want Dad to know that I want to get married. I just don't think he w—"

"Needs to know." Mom finished my sentence and rubbed her chin atop our entwined fingers. "Pinky promise, it is."

Then we raced up to her room. I followed on her heels. Jess looked busy in his room as we scurried past. Perfect.

Mom closed her bedroom door behind me when I stepped in. Then she knelt down by her bed to remove the corner of her sheet nearest her pillow. After which she unzipped the mattress cover just a tad. She reached into the space between the mattress and box spring until her arm disappeared. What was under there?

"He doesn't trust me with anything." Mom lowered her voice like she didn't want the walls to hear. "I don't even know where he keeps all our birth certificates, passports, and such, but there's one thing I saved. Your dad has no idea I have this. Here it is." Mom pulled her arm back, her hand holding a thin, faded magazine.

"Quickly. Come sit next to me on the bed. I'll show this to you, and then I have to hide it again before your dad comes home."

She flipped it open too fast for me to read the cover. From the pictures, it reminded me of the kind of magazine you found by the grocery check out. The colors were faded and there were very few words on each page, just numbers under each lady's photograph. The woman on the first page was a young Indian model wearing a poppy red sari and lots of gold jewelry—even a dainty chain ran from her nose to her ear. Her heavy black eyeliner created a dark and mysterious gaze.

Mom began flipping the pages carefully, and gorgeous women who looked similar to my mother plastered the fragile paper, wearing bright colors, sitting on sandy beaches, lying on intricate rugs, and poised in complicated dance positions.

"Mommy?" I needed to ask a question. "Is the picture of your wedding dress in here?"

"Not exactly. Hold on. Here it is." Mom smoothed the page open and leaned back for me to take in the picture her hand rested over.

"It's you! Mommy! You were a model?" I didn't wait for an answer. Now my hand caressed the page of a young teenager dressed up like she was invited to attend a fancy dinner at a royal palace. "Mommy, you're beautiful! Where's this blue dress? I mean sari. Do you still have it? Do you still have all these sparkly blue and silver bracelets?"

"They're called bangles."

"Do you still have this pink lipstick? I've never seen you wear it. And these sparkly silver high heels with rhinestones? Where are they? How old were you, Mom?"

I read the digits $500 underneath her photo in my head. "Mom, did your sari cost $500? That's so much money!" My eyes squinted to read the small blackened word under the price, still faintly visible through the ink. "Es-cort. Mommy, what's an escort?"

Mom shook her head and moved her hand to cover the word. "I thought I... That's nothing. They just spelled the word skirt wrong. Yeah. That's all that is. A mistake. They made a mistake."

"Mommy?" Why did she sound so unsure? "Why would they charge $500 for a skirt? Unless there were rubies hidden underneath it. Because there's nothing fancy about a sari skirt."

"Yes, Baby T. The jewels lay under the skirt." Mommy exhaled a long sigh.

Then she moved to close the magazine, but my hand bookmarked the spot. "Wait. Can I look at it just a moment longer? I want to remember you as this beautiful queen. In case I never get to see this again, just let me look at it for a few more seconds."

Reluctantly, Mom opened it back up and said, "Okay. But only for two seconds."

"I bet this is why Daddy fell in love with you! Did he buy you these fancy clothes? Did Daddy marry you because you looked beautiful in this picture, Mommy?"

Mom took another deep breath, and her silence made me turn from the picture of her to gaze up into her face. Tears began to gather at the ridges of her eyes. "Yes, sweet T. Something like that. Your dad bought me—I mean, brought me—to live out his American dream. He told me I fit perfectly into his plan, so he married me. But..." Her voice faltered. "But there was nothing fancy about it..."

And with that, the magazine collapsed shut. Vacation over. Time to file the past away. We scooted off the bed, and Mom carefully returned her secret back beneath the mattress while I stood guard at the bedroom door.

Mom's words made no sense to me. I lay down to sleep that night thinking of a beautiful, older Mommy dressed in sky blue, wearing silver, her long hair glistening in the sun. How did you find her, Daddy? And why didn't you buy her the sari? Wouldn't you want her to wear something pretty for your wedding day?

I made a childish vow to find a sari like that when my day came. Forget white. I would wear a sky blue sari and silver bangles on my wedding day. Mommy would walk me down the aisle, wearing a matching sari. I began dreaming of my husband that night. I had never thought to name him. Until tonight. His name shall be Lagan Kumar. Remembering how Lagan told me what his middle name means, I giggle to myself. Prince Lagan, it is.

~TWENTY~

Tuesday morning, I don't notice my burnt arm until I finish brushing my teeth and the hand towel grazes it as I wipe my dampened face. It doesn't sting. I partially unwrap my arm. It still looks bubbled, blistered, and discolored. But it doesn't burn anymore. As if my arm is infused with anesthesia or maybe my brain is? Am I awake or still dreaming? I pinch my good arm to make sure. *Ouch!* Odd.

Running through my morning tasks, I stop whenever the wall, the sheets, the counters, or anything, makes contact with my forearm—the burnt arm—and it feels fine. Numb really, like it fell asleep, but without any pins and needles. I find a loose, green, long-sleeve shirt to throw over my lighter green tank and call out to Jess to say goodbye.

He doesn't respond, so I drop my pack at the door and run by his room to make sure he hears me. He's not lying in bed or sitting in his chair. He's standing! Holding one side of the bed railing and one side of his chair. His arms shake like vibrating harp strings. I hold my breath as I watch from the doorway. He's trying to walk. Jess is trying to walk! My brain screams silently as I run up behind him and nearly knock him forward, squeezing him with all my might.

"Jesse! You're gonna walk again. I just know it. You are so gonna walk again!"

"Your. Arm?"

I let go, and he moves to sit down in his wheelchair.

"I have to run, or else I'll miss the bus." I have to give him another hug. So I do. He looks at my arm in surprise. "Oh. My arm is fine. What can I say? Bye. Love you. See you after school."

"Okay." I can hear Jess speak as I leave the room and race to the front door.

"Byeeeee!" I yell through the house as I lock the front door and sprint for my bus stop. Doesn't help that I'm wearing extra layers on this hot May afternoon. Remembering the letter, I bet the temperature in India this time of year has even the cows sweating. I board the half-empty bus and find a seat, relieved that I made it and thinking of how I'll tell Jesse about the letter.

On the ride over, I think about the pleas of my faraway grandfather. The rice fields. Mom not seeing her parents for over a decade. And the shock they must have felt when they found out she died. When no one came to Mom's funeral, Jess and I just assumed that we had no relatives. To think there were family members, two people out there, who actually wanted us. The thought of living in a small hut on a rice farm with homemade bread sounded like a resort compared to all I've ever known home to be.

When I enter school, the hallways seem less busy as I walk over to my homeroom and slip into an empty classroom. The bell rings, and Ms. Miller looks up from her magazine and rolls her eyes.

"Of course you would show up. One always does." She talks into the magazine she's reading, and then she looks up at me with an odd expression, like I'm a green cat. "Did you forget to check your calendar, dear?"

"Excuse me?" I stop organizing study cards for AP History to field her question.

"Senior Skip Day." She's back in her magazine. She flips a page and keeps talking. "It's today. You are a senior, right?"

"Oh that." Sheesh.

"You want to take a walk around the parking lot?" She genuinely wishes I weren't here. "You know you don't get marked absent today. It's your one freebie. Sure there isn't any place you'd rather be?" She looks up again, and if eyes could push, I'd be halfway out the door.

I rise and look out the window, wondering where I should camp out for the next seven hours. Shuffling out of homeroom, back into the barren hallway, I wonder what Lagan is doing today. Returning to my locker without a plan, I unload my textbooks. Maybe I'll find a free computer in the Library and Google rice farms in India. Try researching my grandparents' names online to see if I can find any additional information. So many details missing from the letter I shouldn't have read. Then I'll leisurely wait around the cafeteria with hopes that Lagan might show up for lunch. Slim chance, but worth the effort. Regardless, I have nowhere to go.

I open my locker and an envelope falls out, landing on my feet. I recognize Lagan's handwriting on the outside. Wow! What special occasion would warrant this upgrade from a Sticky Note? Only one way to find out. I slip the note into my daily planner, shelve all my texts, and sail toward the library in search of a secluded cubicle. I rip open the envelope like it's Christmas—my first Christmas card—in the spring.

Talia,

Some people make wishes when they see a falling star or when they blow a birthday candle out. Not I. I never make wishes. Until now. I wished for one thing. I wished under our waterfall willow that you would trust me. I will not make a promise I cannot keep to you.

Today is an almost perfectly safe day for us to spend the day together. Are you game? I'm waiting for you outside in the parking lot in my dad's old, white Honda Civic. Dad lets me borrow the car once in a while, when my bike or the 'L' can't get me where I need to go. To cover your tracks in case there's a "situation" and you need to be back in school ASAP, I bribed the secretary in the main office with homemade brownies my cousin Rani helped me make. Ms. Right in the attendance office promises to call me on my cell, and I'll have you back to school in under five minutes—plenty of time for anyone looking for you to not suspect a thing. Soooo... now that we have your only reason for saying no to me covered, will I see you in a few? The car's running, and I miss you already. Hurry.

    Smitten like a mitten,

    L

    I shake my head no while my legs beg to differ and propel me toward the back doors that lead to the student parking lot. I'll just say hi and let him know I can't. That way I can at least see his face. The lot is less than a quarter full, making the white Civic easy to spot. Lagan wears shades and a navy blue sport jacket, looking like an undercover CIA agent. I open up the passenger door to sit in order to explain my rehearsed excuse. The one I practiced on the walk over here.

    "Hi, I'm sorry—"

    "Hold on." Lagan cuts me off, and places shades on my face and a checkered yellow and green sunhat on my head. "Go on. What were you saying?"

    I'm looking at that dimple, and I can't say it. I bail on myself and rethink my plan.

    "I..." *How about a compromise?* "I'll come with you. But I want to be back in time for lunch. Just to be on the safe side."

    "Done." And before I can change my mind, we're driving out of the parking lot down side streets, listening to "Let Me Love You" by Ne-Yo on the stereo. Lagan's voice singing the lyrics tickles more than my ears as the warmth of the morning sun washes over my face through the windshield. He flips the sun visor down and then back up. I smile, because he gets me.

    "Umm? You forgot to mention where we're going?" I interrupt his concert.

    "The mall." Lagan grins while checking his rearview mirror.

    "I..." I feel a need to explain why my wardrobe is so outdated. "I've...never shopped at the mall."

"We're not shopping, exactly."

"Okay." I need more information to calm my jitters that threaten earthquakes every inch we travel away from school grounds. "Why are you all dressed up, by the way?"

He laughs. "This ol' thang? Why? Do you like it?"

"Sure. If you're planning to cook in it." What's cookin', good... A raised eyebrow tells me this time he's the one who doesn't get it. "Forget it." I twirl my hair and count the passing cars. Anything to box the rising anxiety in me. We seem so far from school property now.

"We're here." Lagan shifts the gear into park and circles from his door to my door before I unbuckle.

"Thanks." Warmth rushes to my cheeks as he opens the door for me.

"Can I hold your hand?" Lagan stretches his palm to me. "Wouldn't want to lose you in this huge structure where the sights and scents might lure you away from me."

"I suppose. Purely for the sake of safety. Of course." I collapse my hand into his, making sure my burnt arm is on the outside of us. It still feels frozen, but in case the sensations return, I don't want Lagan to catch me freaking out.

Lagan's warm, long fingers envelope my tiny hand, and I silently wish he could hide me entirely. We walk into the mall through the kitchen department of Ikea and the sight of teacups sends a shiver down my neck. I check my watch to monitor our prompt return. Lagan catches me fidgeting with my wrist and squeezes my hand, perhaps trying to assure me everything's going to be fine. What was that about a promise he cannot keep?

"Are we having fun yet?" He steers our path to the food court area, then we zigzag our way past shoppers for Red Mango.

In minutes, cold vanilla yumminess tickles my taste buds and soothes my lips. We stroll past more busy display windows until we enter Forever 21. I'm looking at my watch constantly. Over an hour remains before the first lunch bell sounds.

"Would you try on a dress for me, just for fun, even if only for..." Lagan glances down at his cell phone. "Sixty-four minutes and thirty-two seconds? Thirty-one seconds? Well, now thirty seconds?" Lagan's eyes plea childishly. "Don't keep me waiting. I'm losing time by the second here!"

I love the kid in him. I don't understand why he'd want me to try on a dress, but if I'm Cinderella, that makes him Gus, the fairy Godmother, and the Prince all rolled up in one. Goodness, and I thought Cinderella had her work cut out for her.

"It depends on the dress." I'm aware of the ever-present conditions that outline my reality like a picture frame I cannot escape from. "Long sleeve is about the only thing that'll work for me."

"Summer fashion trends make your stipulations a little tricky, but I think I...." Lagan doesn't finish his sentence. Instead, he moves to the racks where prom dresses sparkle with sequins and satin. My insides tighten. Dad would never allow me to attend prom, let alone the mall. Lagan's eyes spot me, probably making sure I haven't run away.

"Here."

Lagan hands me three different satin dresses—purple, and pink and royal blue. The light pink reminds me of the color of roses my mom loved. I like the simplicity of the lilac one, although it looks a tad large. The floor-length, chiffon, blue gown is strapless with tiny rhinestone outline on its sweetheart neckline. I'm flattered, but shake my head no.

"I'm not finished." Lagan pushes the dresses into my arms and nudges me toward the dressing room. "I'm going to find you a summer sweater and black tights or stockings or whatever you girls call that stuff. I just have to pay for the panty hose first. Some stuff they don't just let you try on. Good thing I have a sister and a cousin who edumacated me in girls' clothes. Rani taught me how tights are a must if a girl doesn't feel like shaving her legs."

I burst out laughing. The whole scenario is suddenly comical to me. But I am impressed that Lagan contrived a way to cover every inch of me and still give me an opportunity to wear a dress that doesn't say eighteenth century all over it. I comply and enter change room number five to squeeze into the first dress. Pink is not my color. I quickly move to the second one, which transforms me into a purple hippo with skinny legs. No to the no!

Goldilocks better be on my side today, because there's only one dress left. Just then a knock and two items being thrown over the top of the changing room startle me. Skin toned hose and a dainty white bolero.

"Thanks."

"Come out soon." Lagan sounds as excited as my mom when she used to dress me up for kindergarten. "I'm waiting near the cash register."

I slip into the last dress. *It fits!* I survey myself, and apart from my scarred arms and bony legs, beautiful almost describes the sight I see. My plain black flats that I wear to school every day don't match, but the blue gown's a tad long, covering them. I pull tights on and allow my arms to snuggle into the soft cotton of the sweater, extra carefully with my injured arm. The material runs over my scars like chinchilla fur. How can it not hurt? Closing my eyes momentarily, I whisper, "Thank you."

I take one last look at myself, and for a split second, I imagine Mom in her blue sari, standing next to me, smiling. I step outside, ready to remind Lagan that I'm only trying this get-up on for a minute. Lagan leans over the counter as he discusses something with the cash register lady, so he doesn't see me until I'm two feet away. Then he stops in mid-speech. His jaw drops. The woman behind the credit card machine smiles, nods, and slides a small shopping bag toward Lagan, although his eyes have not budged.

"May I do the honors?" Lagan asks as he closes the gap. "You look...stunning! Just one small touch, if you'll let me?"

He reaches into the bag on the counter and turns back to me. After gently pushing my hair behind my ears, Lagan slips a sparkly silver headband over my hair.

"Are you sure?" I ask, nervous about drawing more attention to myself.

"Positive!" Lagan won't stop staring at me. "You're my prom queen, and I don't need a prom to announce it."

"You're hilarious." I swallow, still aware of the ticking clock. "Okay. Now that you got what you wanted, can I change back into my clothes?"

"In four minutes and thirty-seven seconds," Lagan says as he motions to the sales rep with two fingers in the air.

She bends down to fiddle with something on a lower shelf, and the music in the store suddenly stops. Then it starts again. This time slightly louder. And slower. It's this year's prom theme song: Savage Garden's "Truly, Madly, Deeply."

"Can I have this dance?" Lagan reaches for my hand, guiding me to an opening in the racks.

"Umm." I am as certain as I am uncertain. This boy is definitely crazy. And I am terribly unsure as to how this will all turn out.

"Thanks." Lagan answers for me. "I'll lead if you let me."

And he pulls me closer to him, putting my hand on his shoulder and cupping the other into his. I've never slow-danced before, and I feel frozen in time. But we're moving, Lagan's hand on my back gently helping me to thaw as the music plays sweetly all around us. Traffic stops around us, and a few shoppers cease shuffling through racks to watch our stumbling feet and giggle-filled twirls.

Then as the song begins to crescendo into the chorus, Lagan pulls me closer still, and I can feel his lips brushing softly across my forehead, from one side to the other, ever so slowly. I close my eyes and allow myself to soak under a waterfall of a thousand peppermint kisses. Is this what heaven is like?

My head lowers into Lagan's shoulder and something sweeter than the musical notes propels our bodies to move perfectly in sync. I open my eyes to make sure my feet are still on solid ground. Not waltzing on water. On the last twirl, I catch a glimpse of myself in a floor-length mirror. The crown headpiece glitters and reflects back into my eyes. Mom always wanted pretty things in her hair. *I am a princess today, Mommy.* If only for a moment. *My prince came for me.* If only for a moment.

~TWENTY-ONE~

The music fades and Lagan clasps my hands into his. Leaning forward, he plants a very soft peck on my forehead. I'm not even sure you'd call it a kiss. *You are my dream, my wish, my fantasy, Lagan.* I'm over the top and I do what I do best when I can't handle it. I back away, shaking my hands from his, afraid to want more. More of what I know I cannot have.

"Wait!" Lagan says, as I push through racks, incapable of retracing my steps to the fitting room.

Fear disorients me. I'm so afraid to get caught, afraid of what all this means, and afraid to believe Lagan's words, especially the word queen. Most of all, I'm afraid to feel. I've never held on to anything I loved. I turn to find Lagan on my heels, and as I see myself in his eyes, I don't fit. I crowd out his happiness and bring clouds, storms, and unrest. I retrieve the band of illusion from my hair and clumsily shove it toward Lagan. I want to say, "Thanks for a dance across the ocean. My ocean of despair. You held me as I danced atop the ocean that I'm used to drowning in. Thank you for helping me stay afloat. If only for a moment."

Instead, I blurt out, "I'm sorry," and run into the fitting room I finally spot to my left.

As I change quickly, looking into the mirror, the scars on my arms turn into ghastly tattoos with mouths and eyes and arms—tattoos that perform a dance of victory in my blurring vision. I pull my green long sleeve back over my arms, wanting

151

to hide the faces and muffle the taunts. Forgetting about the burns, I yank the sleeves down, and like power returning after a blackout, the pain of my recently scorched skin returns instantly and intensely. My knees buckle under the surge, but gauze and ice are out of reach in this tiny space I'm locked behind.

Knowing I cannot stay here all night, I gather myself off the floor, gritting my teeth as I hug my arm to myself, friction heightening each sensation. My hands shake as I fumble to replace each dress correctly on its hanger.

I can't help but blurt out my anger in a train of questions: "Why? Why did you take away my pain? Only for a little while? I'm hurting. It hurts. Will this pain ever go away?"

An answer comes. But not the one I expected. The pain was paused for a moment. *To give you time to feel other things.*

"But I thought when the pain disappeared... Actually, I don't know what to think anymore." I tell the truth.

I am shaking my head no. I want more. I don't know if I have a right to ask. And I'm not sure how much longer I can wait.

I open the door to return the dresses and sweater to the nearest sales clerk, asking her to discard the tights. I spot Lagan by the store's exit. I'm ready to leave, too. School lunches will be served in less than ten minutes.

Lagan looks outside, one hand on the door, the other fiddling with his car keys. Disappointment tastes less bitter when you dine alone. I wince in pain when a shopper bumps my arm in passing. Feeling vulnerable inside and out, I wish I could walk back to school on my own, but time robs me of even this tiny mercy.

"We should hurry back." I break the silence as we walk across the parking lots to find the Civic.

We've been circling around the mall outdoors, Lagan walking slightly ahead of me, silently. Once again, I'm rich with doubt and affliction. Poor in hope and time. Story of my life.

"I'll never forget today..." Lagan finally speaks as he opens my car door and closes it when my feet firmly set themselves on the mat. "For the rest of my life." Lagan takes the driver's seat. "Talia?"

"Yes." I stare at my lap.

"You're precious." Lagan touches my arm.

"Ouch!" I let my pain slip out.

"What's wrong?"

"Nothing."

"I hurt you. Your arm hurts. What happened?"

"Finish what you were gonna say." I beg him with my eyes. "Don't worry about my arm. I'll be fine..."

Lagan tries to roll back my sleeve, but I pull my arm to me quickly and slide the cloth over my arm and hand. I can't be exposed. I'd have no out.

"What I was gonna say..." Lagan begins again awkwardly, then pauses. We are talking about things that we can talk about, because my reaction bolts the door he cannot walk through, yet. And maybe ever.

"What I was gonna say was that you don't need a crown to prove anything. You're precious to me."

The car ignition starts and we're back at school in less than five minutes. We pull into the driveway, and Lagan lets me walk back inside alone. He'll see me tomorrow. I'll finish the day out. Alone.

I sit in the cafeteria and push my food around the plate with my plastic fork. I hunger and thirst for things not on the menu today. Or ever, for that matter. To voice my desires always seems so futile. My arm throbs, daring me to ask. The tattoos taunt louder. I swallow, pick up my imaginary boxing gloves and hear my heart take three swings: "I. Do. Dare."

The cursing images mute with shock. I've never talked back before.

I begin inside my head with my eyes lowered to my lap. I need Lagan. I know Lagan will come if I invite him. I feel like a little girl about to cross her first busy intersection. I need a hand to hold. I guess that's what I'm really asking: *Can I hold his hand? So I don't have to cross alone?*

I don't hear an answer, but I'm glad I asked. And I'm not scared to ask. For once in my life, I'm not scared. I own this moment. And no one—not even Dad–can take this away from me.

I reach down into my bag to grab a Sticky notepad and pen. I begin writing out a quick question to Lagan before I chicken out. I'm so absorbed in how to word it that I don't notice Lagan approaching my table.

Until he speaks, startling me. "Is that for me, by any chance?"

The e in the word *please* ends off the paper when my pen slips. Good enough. I peel the note off and smooth the note down in front of him before I walk out of the cafeteria. I'm probably the only person in Phys Ed, so I don't bother swinging by my locker to retrieve my uniform.

Before I ascend the stairs leading to the gymnasium, Lagan's voice echoes from behind, calling my name. I turn around to face him.

"Yes. On one condition." He shakes his head, dimple in full effect. "And you thought you were the only one with conditions."

I laugh. My mind fast-forwards to May 17. In the garden. I hope it doesn't rain.

"Aren't you gonna ask what that condition is?" Lagan prompts me.

"Okay." I say my line on cue. "On what condition?"

"No more secrets."

I look down. I know he's talking about my arm.

His voice softens to a husky whisper. "Unless you tell me what's going on with you, I can't really know you. And I want to know you. I don't expect you to tell me everything all at once. But will you tell me the truth, little by little?"

I swallow and look away. Then take a deep breath, look down at Lagan, and nod. I know it's the only way. I turn and walk up the rest of the stairs. Panting as I reach the top, I accept that the actual journey I agreed to travel with Lagan makes this climb look like an anthill in comparison.

I turn to look back, and Lagan still stands at the bottom of the steps. He holds up one finger and then seven using both hands, as a smile releases that heart-stopping dimple. Yup. May 17, 7:00 p.m. About one hour before sunset. Two weeks away. I hope my arm and lips are fully healed by then.

I plan to get all my work done in order to enjoy the last hour before the garden closes with Lagan—under our waterfall willow. Funny how numbers have never been significant to me, like how some folks have a lucky number, but I'm tickled at the fact that we are both seventeen years old right now. If I choose a favorite number today, right now, that number is one-seven. Seventeen.

~TWENTY-TWO~

May 17 on the calendar takes up so much space inside my head that I actually forget about the letter I stumbled upon on Dad's desk until I pass his den on my way to Jesse's room after school. Tempted to see the envelope to make sure I hadn't dreamt the whole scenario, I turn the knob to find it locked. The glass windows reveal Dad's desk is clear, bar a few stationary items. The pile of letters no longer covers the corner. Dad came home once already today. Maybe twice.

"Jess?" I call his name, worried Dad might have seen him somewhere besides his bed.

I find Jesse in his bed, lifting his body up and lowering it, his face muscles tense when his elbows lock. He lowers himself and turns to face me, sweat beading off his forehead. "Talia." He says my name perfectly for the first time since the accident.

"Did Dad see you?" Small talk can wait. "Did he see you? Stronger? Trying to walk?"

"No." Jess shakes his head at the same time. "But I almost...got...busted."

My anxiety level drops and surges like a car's revving engine. "What do you mean by almost?" I need the whole story—quickly.

"I inched...to the kitch-en," Jess says slowly but clearly. "Fal-ling. Pull-ing back up. Hold-ing walls, furn-i-ture. Push-ing my legs. I fell a lot. I wasn't giv-ing up. I kept going. Know-ing I'd have to crawl back. Well..."

"Can you fast forward to when Dad shows up?" My enemy—the clock—fiddles with its trigger finger, and my arm cannot handle another bullet so soon.

Jesse shakes his head at my impatience. Then he speaks. Broken phrases, but I understand. "I heard Dad. Unlocking the door. On my way back. My legs felt like jelly, but Dad was home. So I lifted back to my feet. Lunged toward my room. Landed on the floor. Face down, near my bed. Dad saw me and assumed I had fallen. He put me back in bed. Cursing how lucky I was that he stopped by. Then he left again. That's all."

"Wow." Sigh. "That was a close call."

"Yeah." Jess agrees with a wide grin. *Is he proud of his adventure?*

"He locked his office," I say.

"What'd ya expect? After catch-ing you in there yes-ter-day."

"That's true."

I don't have time to tell Jess about the letter. Or my arm. Or my slow dance with danger. Soon, maybe at night after Dad goes to sleep, I'll sneak to his room and tell him everything. Or even better, when summer vacation starts while Lagan leaves for his internship and Dad works late.

***

The future reels toward me like an animated movie. Days turn to weeks. May. Then June. Lagan and I secretly meet under our waterfall willow twice, but each occasion leaves me wanting. On June 23, graduation arrives and leaves like a ghost. I barely notice, because my family doesn't attend. Dad had a very important meeting with a client from New York. So important, you couldn't reschedule for your daughter's graduation. No surprise there. The school mails me my diploma. I'm official.

Lagan's graduation party is on June 30, not on the seventeenth. If I find some way to visit, I risk unraveling future opportunities with him, but he reminds me every day up to the last day of school. "It would mean a lot. Just stop by for a quick minute."

On June 30, I dismiss any chance of leaving the house when Dad arrives home on that Friday like clockwork, at 4:45 p.m. By seven o'clock, dinner is done, the dish rack sits empty, and the floors sparkle. Dad reaches in the fridge for milk to add to his nightly cup of chai right before the startling bellow of my name leaves his lips. "Talia?"

I jump, thinking maybe cleaning out the fridge was on the list and I forgot to throw out old leftovers. "Where's the milk? I just bought a jug two days ago."

I shrug, but Jesse points to the kitchen sink while Dad's head remains buried in the fridge.

"Oh yeah." I steady my voice. "Jess accidentally knocked the jug over this morning from the counter after I poured some into his cereal. Don't worry. I get paid this week. You can take the money out of my salary to cover the loss. I'm sorry, Dad. I should have paid attention to Jess's clumsiness."

My brother and I exchange a stolen glance. Dad slams the fridge door shut.

"I am tired." Dad bores holes into me with his eyes. "Not in the mood to run out to the store just to buy milk." Then he glares at Jesse and says, "So the one time you decide to move, you waste my money? What a waste you are."

Dad, just because he can't walk and talk, doesn't mean he can't hear you. I swallow my words and wait for the fire in Dad's eyes to simmer down, just a tad, before suggesting something I've never offered before.

"Dad." I choose my words carefully. "Do you want me to run over to the nearest deli, across from the high school, and pick up some milk? It takes about twenty minutes to walk there, and it doesn't get dark until close to nine these days. I'll bring back the receipt and exact change, and I can make you a fresh cup of tea when I return. If that helps?"

"Okay." Dad blurts out as he marches past us to his office. "I'll be busy at my desk. Just leave the change on the counter and put the kettle to boil when you get back. And, Talia?"

"Yes, Dad?" I speak to his back.

He turns to look at me from down the hallway, holding a ten-dollar bill out, and warns, "Don't talk to anyone. Get the milk and come straight home."

I approach him, palm open to receive the money. Dad drops it a few centimeters in front of me. The bill sails to the floor, and Dad turns to enter his bat cave. Except he's the evil Joker, and Batman awaits at his graduation party, a few blocks from the high school. My mind swirls as I pick up the cash and stare at my dingy jeans and stained green sweatshirt.

I run upstairs and change my clothes to my nicest jeans and a clean white, button-down, long-sleeve shirt. Wearing a dress, the one black dress I own from Mom's funeral, would draw too much attention. This will have to do. I brush my hair and slip on my black flats, anxious and terrified to see Lagan in a social setting.

Think Cinderella. Get in. Say hello. Get back. And don't forget to buy the milk. I decide to buy the milk first, afraid that after seeing Lagan, my mind will malfunction, and I'll run home empty-handed. The carriage turning back into a pumpkin does not compare to the consequences of a botched up return.

Self-talk accompanies my entire jog to the store, taking all the shortcuts I've learned and arriving in under six minutes. Only one person stands in line at the cash register. I check the expiration date on the milk and pay, holding my tongue from making small talk. Thanking the owner, my stride slows with the jug at my hip as I race toward the south street neighborhood behind the high school. Thinking back, I'm relieved that Lagan made me memorize his address when I told him I'd try to attend his party. If my mind remembers correctly, his house is only two blocks from the playground where he pushed me on the swings. I cross the yard, aware of the changing sky and ticking clock.

I can do this. *Slip in. Smile. Slip out.*

A few houses down the street, I hear music pumping, and I slow my pace as I approach a sea of twinkling lights, forming a canopy across the backyard of the house. I'm here. Lagan told me his cousin Rani planned to create a Milky Way experience for him and his friends. *Impressive.* The sights and sounds of how I always imagined a party envelope me. And the music, streaming from large speakers in different corners of the yard, moves me like I've arrived on the moon.

The words to a song I have never heard before play. But for some reason, I recognize the lyrics. Of course. Lagan's voice playing through the sound system confirms my suspicions. He left his notebook in class once, and I didn't know it was his song-writing composition book until I skimmed through a few pages before slamming the book shut. I felt guilty that I never asked his permission. Wow! His voice sounds like a cross between Jason Mraz and Swedish House Mafia. Plan to suggest he learn to carry a guitar on the back of his bike so I can hear him sing more often. As I enter the gate, I stash the milk jug by the side fence, and scan the crowd. Everyone in the whole school must be here.

As I stroll toward a speaker, the music pulls me in like horizontal gravity. Lagan's voice streams across my ears as if he were singing to me. The words return and I sing along, softly, not wanting to draw attention to myself. I close my eyes for a moment, disappearing in between the strum of guitar chords around me and the starry lights above.

When I open my eyes, Lagan stands in front of me and time stops. I am still mouthing the words, wanting him to know I love his song. The poetry of his heart. His voice. He shakes his head in disbelief, perhaps that I showed up. Or that I knew the lines to his song. I don't know what overcomes me, but I want to remember this moment. Every detail. The sights. The sounds. The scents. So I lean forward, my cheek grazing his jawline, close my eyes, and inhale. Deeply. Until I can inhale no more. I allow the aroma of a peppermint-sprinkled summer night to wash over all my senses. Satisfied by the nibble from this surprise sample of a life I thought I'd never live, I turn to leave.

"Wait," Lagan begs. We both know I can't.

Someone, maybe Lagan's mom, pulls him away with the words, "Time to cut your cake!" and we lock eyes for a moment before a crowd follows the man of the hour to the cake table.

I continue out of the gate, scooping up the milk on my way out. Glancing at my watch, I have about ten minutes to enter the front door void of suspicion. I hold the jug close to me and run the whole way home, squealing every few blocks, replaying Jesse's gift to me. Lagan's gift to me. I feel rich tonight.

I wipe the sweat off my forehead with my sleeve as I unlock the front door. One minute early. And as I enter the kitchen to place the change in the correct location, Jesse sits in his chair, exactly where I left him. Smiling. He knows. I put the kettle to boil after placing the milk on the counter. Jesse holds up the age-old sign for okay with his thumb and first finger kissing. I look down the hall toward Dad's office. Nothing. He's absorbed in his work.

I turn back toward Jesse and mouth two words I have not said enough to my little brother. Thank you. I lean over him and hug my baby brother, and his arms squeeze back. Watching the clock continue to tick, I realize that my heart rate takes longer to return to normal than the entire length of the brief clandestine encounter. My heart pounds even as I lay down to sleep that night. Escaping Dad's radar whets my appetite. For the sparkle of stars. The scent of peppermint.

And the melody of Lagan's voice, a lullaby that ushers me into my dreams.

~TWENTY-THREE~

The routines of my life post-graduation are driven by one day alone. The seventeenth of each month. Consistently, Dad works late into the evening, sometimes returning past midnight. And Lagan and I meet one last time before he leaves for overseas. At the garden, we share stories of growing-up years, most of my stories about my fondest memories of Mom. We share sunsets, each time a completely new display of colors washes across the same canvas.

And on that last day, Lagan sings in my ear as he attempts to teach me two steps, and we waltz under our waterfall willow, the shadow of entwined arms our only audience. I muddy his shoes with my fumbling, but he continues to sing. Tuning out the world. Tuning me into his thoughts. Writing songs on the Post-it notes of my heart. Lyrics I memorize and replay when I need a gita for my lost Gita. *Mommy, how I need you more than ever.* I don't know the way to move from girl to woman, and yet I'm here. At the crossroads without a map.

Soon college will begin and schedules will change again. My hours will cut back, but perhaps I can request to work on the seventeenth of the month, even if it falls on a weekend. I need something to look forward to. One thing.

A week into August, Lagan gone and a note from Dad alerting us that he won't be home for hours, I decide a better time might not come. So I tell Jesse everything. About meetings with Lagan at the garden and our brief encounter at his party. About the gardener. And about the pain in my arm mysteriously disappearing for a short while. He doesn't say anything at first. I can't tell if he's processing, or if I've upset him.

I also outline what I remember of Amit Shah's letter—the information I long ago dismissed as depressing and useless. Our grandparents' apparent search for us surges unusual energy in Jesse's eyes, but I remain skeptical. A home where we're wanted but we'll probably never know creates one more taunting key beyond prison bars, just out of reach.

"Were there any letters from Benton Harbor?" Jesse's question confuses me.

"As in, our old neighborhood? School? Not that I recall. Why?" Is Jesse keeping in touch with someone? Expecting someone to find us? Him?

"It's nothing. Forget I asked." Jesse shuts the door before I can open it.

But I'm not that easily swayed. "Who would write you from back there? Come on Jess, you know your secret's safe with me."

"What's the point? She's gone. And she never tried to find me." My brother's confession opens a window to his heart. Broken by a girl I never knew. "It's my fault anyway, so just drop it. Don't wanna talk about it anymore."

"Just tell me her name. Maybe I knew her from school." I just want a name. A name makes her more real. I want my brother's chance at love to be real. Even if the chance is long gone.

His silence answers for him. And I'm sorry I pushed so hard. Some stories are too painful to share. Because sharing means remembering. And remembering slows down the journey to forgotten. Something tells me this girl is someone Jesse will never forget.

He doesn't say much to me for many days following. I allow the silence. The very mention of the gardener makes his eyebrows wrinkle. Like he's stuck behind a wall of anger so high he can't see over it. Nor think of a way to climb over it.

The tragedy of Mom's separation still fails to explain why Dad turned out the way he did, although my grandparents' poverty might have spurred their decision to let Mom travel overseas alone. The age-old myth that America is the land of promise. But still. What promise did you make them, Dad? I could draw up a long list of the ones you've broken.

One night, when Dad strolls in nearer to the 1:00 a.m. clang of the grandfather clock, I'm wide-awake with thoughts of Lagan. He's been gone for three weeks, and my aching for him paces like a marathon runner through my mind.

I decide to rise and empty my bladder, but when I exit my room, I hear voices. Dad's not alone, and the voice sounds awfully familiar. Jed! That sounds just like the cowboy who said those crass things some time ago. And he speaks with the projection worthy of a Broadway show. I decide to leave the bathroom door slightly ajar so I can listen in.

"Geri, she's older than most of the girls, but she's beautiful and ready, if I do say so myself."

"Shut up!" Dad sounds furious. *Beware the kitchen, Jed. Wouldn't put it past Dad to turn the kettle on you.* Literally. "I already told the boss that she's damaged. Just like Gita was. So she will never be an option. Am I understood?"

"Boss always picks the cream of the crop when it comes to lawyers. Bet he didn't bank on one brilliant enough to write his own contract. Doggone it." Jed sounds annoyed and a muffled thud suggests someone banged the countertop. "You and the pilot make a secret pact? Cuz his girl, now there's a blond beauty I wouldn't mind for myself."

"You disgust me," Dad retorts. *So why bring scum like Jed into your castle, Dad?*

"I think it's a little strange that all the women in this house have been crossed off. Just sayin, my friend."

What kind of friend makes creepy propositions like that?

"Discussion over. And don't call me 'friend.' My family is off limits. Good night." Dad's voice speaks with finality.

"What about the plans? The new hotel? There are plenty of girls—er—cases, we have to discuss. I'm flying back tomorrow, Ger—"

"I said good night. E-mail me." A slam of the front door puts a period on the sentence. More like an exclamation point.

What was that about? I close the lid gently and leave the toilet unflushed before tiptoeing back to my room. As I pull the covers over my head, I wonder what kind of debt Dad, the financial-genius himself, could possibly get himself into. Who owes whom? And what the heck were they talking about when Jed said I'm ready. *Ready for what?*

~TWENTY-FOUR~

The first day of college arrives, and I'm a nervous wreck. Here I go again, having to weave my way through new crowds, inquisitive professors, and nosy college girls. Ironically, no one really bothers me. Some students race from class to class while others stroll at a snail's pace, the absence of late slips offering a new type of freedom, I suppose. And everyone is in his or her own world, including the teachers. Students like me frantically copy every detail from droning lectures, and others just lean back their heads and catch up on missed sleep. I might not sleep well, but I can't risk getting poor grades and Dad taking this away from me.

My favorite class is Intro to Shakespeare, because the playwright didn't shy away from tragedy—the one thing I can relate to. I find myself daydreaming about Lagan any time I read about a hero, and then suddenly start wondering if my modern day prince has a flaw. Even a tiny one?

Autumn willow dates bring early sunsets and chilly nights. Frost canopies Chicago, and by October 17, the garden stands void of flowers but not of color. Reds, yellows, oranges, and browns paint every tree, and our waterfall willow glitters a perfect blend of Crayola's mango tango and laser lemon. After raking the fallen leaves into a cushiony pile, Lagan and I sit side by side to watch the sun dip behind the horizon.

When the ground grows frigid, we move to the bike rack after brushing the leaves off our clothes. I miss one.

Lagan reaches over and slips a tiny leaf out from under my sleeve. "Saving this one as a memento?" he asks, holding the thin, yellow leaf up in the air.

"If you only knew what else is up my sleeve." I lob back, eyebrows raised.

"Are you offering a peek?"

Hold up. How did we get here? Instinctively, I pull my sleeves down, and refrain from responding. I'm tempted to hide behind the pink and purple clouds overhead, the sunset inviting me away from Lagan and his question.

But my promise dictates my response. No more secrets. With the absence of fresh wounds, I slowly pull up my sleeve, just an inch or two, and reveal scars that I'd never shown anyone. I watch his eyes move up and down my wrist. He instinctively reaches in my direction, but I pull back. I don't want him to touch my splotchy, rough skin.

His hand retracts, and Lagan's eyes moisten as he exhales one word: "Why?"

I guess by now he's figured out the who in this irrational equation. "Remember the lists I mentioned to you once?" I preface my explanation.

He nods, still unable to take his eyes off my arm.

"Dad." I wince at the sound of his name. "My dad doesn't like it when the lists don't get done. On time."

Lagan's concern turns to anger in the pitch of his voice. "So why haven't you left? Called the cops? Run away? Why do you stay?"

I hear his pleas, but asking implies that answers exist.

"I can't leave Jesse. Plus, when I, we, do leave, I want it to be for good. Forever. No looking back and no way that Dad can ever find us. Disappear. But..."

"If you're thinking of me," Lagan answers, "don't."

It's not his fault I choose to stay. I just haven't figured out all the side effects. The one side effect, really. The one I can't accept. Losing him. I want both. And I don't want to settle.

Hope keeps me thinking someday an escape offering both will materialize, and a burn here and there is worth the price of waiting, if waiting means both. Jesse and Lagan. I want to keep both. I plan to keep both.

"Forget it. I'll be fine. Let's talk about something else." I'm ready to think about anything else.

"Talia, I'm not looking away. I did that once. I can't. I won't make that mistake again. I'm calling the cops." Lagan pushes his resolve on me, but I'm not ready. *Don't you see?* A tiny corner of a picture fails to reveal the entire story.

Pushing myself off the bike rack, anger heats my ears. "You can't." I burst his bubble. "I never asked you to fix my life. Or me."

"So you want to tell me *if* and *how* and *when* I can help? Did it ever occur to you that you're not that different from him?" Lagan's questions don't just sting. I feel ripped in half.

"I'm sorry," Lagan says when I don't respond. "That was uncool. Stupid. Uncalled for."

He reaches for my hand, but my clenched fist refuses to open as I turn from him and face the willow, my mirror.

How dare you? Cuss words torpedo to the tip of my tongue, bracing for takeoff like divers unable to control their fall. Instinct wins when my teeth bite down on my lower lip. Minutes pass in silence, my emotions duking it out inside me. Lagan's response pierces me where I didn't know I could hurt. In the space between us. Spreading like the darkness of the night. Each time I think I'm ready...

"Right now," I say, my voice barely audible. "I need a friend. Not a hero." That's the best I can do. He has no choice to put his sword away, because this is my fight.

That's all I share, and Lagan goes quiet when I step on the brakes. Sitting side by side on the cool, metal bar, again—we watch the sky change shades and the faint twinkle of emerging stars brighten. Staring at the painted clouds as they roll by, the faint honk from passing geese reminds me that winter fast approaches. Silently we leave the garden that evening, hand in hand, together and alone.

Lagan drives me a few blocks from my house when he stops the car to let me out. But not before he reaches over, tenderly circling my wrist with his hand. This time I let his fingertips trail down the length of my covered arm. Leaning across the gearshift, his lips place quiet kisses over the back of my hand—the shoreline to my ocean of scars.

Then he wipes his face on my sleeve. I hadn't noticed his tears in the dark. Our combined sadness weighs down my already heavy heart, so I briskly exit his car and jog home, my scars throbbing with the rain. My rainy world.

Like a branch plunged into deep waters, Lagan means to rescue me.

He does, even if he doesn't see it. Each moment with Lagan is a moment I don't drown in my pain.

And he kissed me. Imperfect me.

If he meant to kiss it better, he did. He does. More than he knows.

~TWENTY-FIVE~

Winter term of my freshman year of college whirls in, and I witness Jesse birthing unfamiliar courage as he accesses our neighbor's unsecured wireless Internet and renews his relationship with the outside world via the Web. He spends hours upon hours reading and researching, steering clear of any traceable social networks. If he isn't reading, he's working out, strengthening and relearning, stretching and lifting, building and rebuilding. The wonder of escaping Dad's preying claws eludes both of us. In fact, each narrow victory, whether by hours or seconds, fuels us to do the forbidden: *live*.

Jesse helps me with his list more and more these days as his mobility increases and he can hold himself up longer, even helping with dishes without his legs giving way. His new abilities give us both more time. Jess uses the time to learn. He starts by reading through all my high school notes and workbooks from senior year. I help him when he gets stuck with a math equation or a physics formula. We work at the dining room table. Jess sits in his wheelchair, always prepared for Dad's surprise arrivals.

My brother's perseverance births miraculous results. The doctors predicted Jess's complex hip fracture and head trauma would cause immobility and speech delay, possibly for a lifetime. Jesse's will begs to differ. His self-rehab results in slow but definite ambulatory progress, his academic skills sharpen, and he develops a ravenous hunger for knowledge.

But Jesse's definitive goals elude me. We both crave freedom. That's a given. But another hunger burns inside the intensity I find in his stare. Afraid to ask, the busyness of my new schedule pushes worry to the sidelines as I justify that Jess is no longer a boy. I keep meaning to ask Lagan to speak with him. Do the big brother thing or something like that. If he's up to it, of course. And Jesse would have to agree to it, too.

With my job hours at the garden and my professors who add extra assignments when least expected, every second seems accounted for. During most winter workdays, I desk job it alongside Jason in the office as we prepare for spring planting plans. More pressing than gardening, Jason and I spend many hours shoveling walkways for winter visitors. Dad receives my paychecks and funnels them straight toward my tuition—the portion the scholarship does not cover. Once in a while, when Jess or I bring up the notion of running away, the combination of finances and the fear of being caught and returning to our very own Alcatraz roadblocks each conceivable plan.

One particular Friday morning in February, Loyola campus' switchboard rings our house early enough that Dad hasn't left for work yet. Dad knocks on my door, mumbles that my school cancelled classes due to an incoming snowstorm, and to make sure I finish weekend chores today instead. I nod my robotic sign of obedience and resist falling back asleep to begin the long list ahead of me. I'm thankful that as soon as Dad's car leaves the driveway, Jess can and will help me tackle the house.

Dad's practice never closes due to inclement weather. When he has a meeting downtown, he usually parks and takes the Metra into the city. Financial gain seems to dictate his drive. I can honestly only remember one canceled trial in all these years, the day of Mom's funeral. Apart from that I can't recall a sick day, a vacation day, or even a personal day taken by Dad. Even if he was under the weather, he preferred to be in his office. Dad makes the average workaholic look like a sluggard.

Dad wasn't always a lawyer. I only know this because my fifth grade teacher called to ask if Dad wanted to speak at the school Career Day. Mom answered the phone. She made a lot of excuses for Dad, and then gave Mrs. Knox her two-minute rundown of Dad's rise to fame as one of the top immigration lawyers in the country.

According to the little I overheard Mom say, he started out as a volunteer in the Federal Visa department located at the Detroit-Windsor border while in undergrad at U of M. Mom and Dad got married when he was just a paralegal who pretty much wrote the documents the lawyers were too busy or too lazy to write. As higher ups recognized his talent and relentless spirit, they promoted him to manager, and then paid for his law school on the condition he returned to work for them. Somewhere along the line, Jesse and I were born, and with the growing expenses, Dad opened up his own firm in Benton Harbor.

Before we knew it, the Law Office of Gerard Vanderbilt quickly attracted high profile clients that poured in like a fresh pot of coffee. When Dad called to tell us about an impending visitor, he'd instruct us to stay in our rooms. Dad clearly had no intention of showing off his kids to his colleagues. More like blowing off. If only those fellows sporting three-piece suits knew what kind of man he really is. I wonder how many would consider stripping Dad of his power and putting him on trial. A girl can dream.

Shortly before Mom died, Dad's clients flew in from all over, willing to come to him, making the decision to move to Chicago all the easier, with access to O'Hare and Midway saving time and money for everyone. When a windy city nor'easter blew in, it didn't make a difference how close we were to any airport. O'Hare and Midway would both shut down today if the predicted snow actually showed up.

This particular snow day seems a hoax at six in the morning. A few flakes swirl here and there. By nine in the morning, the air is empty and still. I rethink my decision to call Jason to change shifts, because I can't foresee not making it home. Not if the weather stays this calm. I postpone my final decision until I cross off the final item on the list, and I proof, print, and pack away my English essays.

By noon, Jesse and I complete double-checking every inch of every room. The house looks impeccable. Time to play. I open the front door first, and the sky resembles a herd of polar bears charging with their eyes closed. The sea of white blanks out everything more than five feet away, and the lawn is covered by at least three inches already. The weatherman's Doppler radar functioned correctly after all, and I close the door to prevent more snow from blowing indoors.

Jess stands behind me, and we shake our heads at each other. The speedy accumulation demands shoveling. Without a snow blower, we both know the futility of a manual attempt. Layers will reappear on our heels. And if the threat of frostbite doesn't deter us, the gift of stolen time does.

"Or not." Jess stares at the sea of white outside the kitchen window defiantly, reading my mind. "I mean...it wasn't on the list. Right?"

"Good point." Possibility boomerangs between our nods. "What do you want to do then?"

"Break into Dad's office." No hesitation in Jess's words. He's thought about this for some time.

"Not funny. What do you want to do that won't get us in trouble?"

He repeats the response, his face set in grim lines. "Break into Dad's office. You can go off and meet lover boy Lagan if you like. I'll make sure I put the door back on before Dad gets home."

"You're serious?" A chill of fear coats my arms with goose bumps. "What's the point anyway? What do you want with Dad's office?"

"More clues about our MIA grandparents, why Mom came to America, how Dad tricked her. If there's any way to contact Mom's parents? If we run away to India, I doubt Dad would come look for us. It could be our ticket out. It's worth a shot."

Jess's mind unravels a foolproof plan of escape that he's determined to carry out. "With or without you."

I can't let him risk this alone. We're a team. "With me, of course. I'll get the toolbox from the garage."

"I've been reading up on breaking computer codes in order to hack Dad's e-mail. I'll bet Dad's business files hold clues. Just remind me to erase our activity history. He notices every little change. Are you sure you want to do this with me? If I get caught, I have nothing to lose. If you get caught...you know what I'm saying. You have to think about..."

"Lagan." I fill in the blank. "We stick together. So if you found an escape route, we work for it together. And we escape together. Maybe...maybe Lagan can help us."

"No," Jess says without blinking. "We can't risk that."

"I just mean, if the door is heavy or you think you need a tool that we don't have, I know Lagan will do whatever he can to help us. He wants to help. He understands."

Jess stops in his tracks. "What do you mean by 'he understands'? Did you tell him about Dad? Are you nuts? How much did you tell him?"

I look down. Lagan's arrival into my life broke more than one unspoken pact. Other than that one peek at a tiny section of my arm, when it was more healed than burnt, Lagan knows nothing, really.

I return from a short detour down that October evening under the willow back to today. "He doesn't know much. Just that life isn't perfect. Only perfectly hard. For me. For us."

"And he still wants to be friends?" Jesse's voice softens and his stare is wanting.

"I know, right? He's not like the rest. Lagan doesn't see it like I thought he would." I had dismissed the conversation, filing it away like I did everything else. "He doesn't see me like...I see myself."

Jess hmm's my conclusions and turns away, like he's looking into the future. Or maybe it's the past. Was there someone who saw him like Lagan sees me?

"Know what I'm talking about?" I fish. Baiting my little brother with the option to open up about the mystery girl from Benton Harbor. Knowing he probably won't.

"Sure." He shrugs his shoulder matter-of-factly. "Did I forget to mention how the ladies lined up outside the door when I made cover of *Hot Teen Male Gimp of the Year*?"

"All it takes is one." I throw my line out one last time. Time might never be on my side again.

"Enough chit-chat. We have a crime to commit. Let's roll."

Jess shifts gears and wheels toward the garage, his legs tired from cleaning. I follow, wondering if Jesse will ever tell me her name. The girl who chased his heart. A friend he once ran to. If we run away tonight, we both know that Dad will hunt until he finds us. And then, the words or else would result in unthinkable consequences.

How would a life in India alter the future? In my mind, the story always ends with both Jess and me ensnared in Dad's poisonous web. Maybe Jess hopes to build a spaceship and shuttle us to the moon with affordable materials found overseas. Doubt muddies my hope. I shake my head. Focus on Jesse's mission to open the office door. First things first.

After finding straight and Phillips screwdrivers, along with a hammer and wrenches of various sizes, we return to the den. The view out the kitchen window reveals about a foot of snow accumulation. Whoa! The wind is whipping, and a growing snow mountain leans against our front door. Jess dials Dad's cell and hands me the phone.

Dad's voice is immediately demanding. "Talia, make it quick. I have a meeting in five minutes, and I just made it downtown with the cab driver cursing me out for asking him to do his job."

"Dad." I steady my voice. "The snow is really bad. Are you sure you shouldn't just postpone work and drive home before the storm gets worse?"

"Is that it?" He sounds annoyed. "I'll worry about myself. Just finish your chores and stay indoors. I'll taxi it home if the trains stop running. Okay? By the way, my five o'clock was moved back due the client's flight delay, so you and Jess have dinner without me. And don't wait up."

"Okay, Dad." I try to sound disappointed while fireworks launch inside me. "Will do."

"Yes!" Jess says, pulling himself up and steadying his weight on his right leg.

His right arm also seems stronger than his left. I work on Jess's left side, so he can use my shoulder for balance. Since he demonstrates knowledge if not experience, I make like an OR nurse, handing Jesse tools while he operates on the doorknob, then the door hinges. After popping out pins, the door begins to fall toward us, but we push together and ease it toward the wall on our side.

We have a short window in which to explore, invade, reassemble, and clean up. With the plan of attack in conjunction with our decoy assignments, each task depends on the prior one's success. We decide on a five-minute turnover when we hit a roadblock. And we expect to hit roadblocks. After five minutes of trying to maneuver around or through any setback, we have to move forward to the next task. The entire process should take no longer than an hour, and if we do this right, everything will be back in its place long before Dad's return.

Jess pulls out latex gloves for both of us as if we're members of *Ocean's Eleven* minus nine. "Not a trace, all right? Not even a fingerprint can prove we were here."

"And I'll keep my clumsy factor in check today." I swat away images of swirling files in the air with my imaginary bat. I can handle this.

Door removed, I follow Jesse into Dad's lair. The desk proves void of further clues regarding our mom or grandparents. When I pull the bottom right handle toward me, the sight of Dad's gun startles me. It's still here. Flashbacks of that afternoon finding Jess in here floods my thoughts, and I sense the urgency of our mission. I slam the drawer shut and move toward the file cabinet. Seated in Dad's chair now, Jess looks over from the monitor. He knows what I saw in the drawer. Silently, he returns to tapping on the keyboard, scrolling through screens, and searching Dad's saved files and documents for clues. Any clue.

I move to the drawers of Dad's file cabinet against the furthest wall to find letters in the middle drawer. Memorizing their position in the drawer, as well as the top address, I pick each envelope up and begin to meticulously sort through them, looking for any overseas stamps or labels, especially those from India. Sheesh. There are so many from India. I return them and move to the next drawer. Same thing. File upon file with female names that read "Joyti, Kavitha, Sagel, Manisha, Mali," and on and on. *Does Dad only deal with female clients?*

Pulling open the last section, my fingers almost flick past a file that sends a shiver down my spine. I back up the manila folder to read the name under my breath. "Gita Shah." That's Mom's name.

"Jesse?" I'm afraid to remove it as if lifting it could detonate a bomb.

"Find something?"

"Mom's name." I turn to see him moving toward me. "There's a file with Mom's name on it."

Jesse could care less about bombs exploding. He yanks the file out without giving me a chance to memorize which name it belonged after. Thankfully a small space remains between the names Farah and Henna. I'm still thinking about how Dad filed alphabetically when Jess let's out an emphatic string of cuss words.

"Jesse?" Cursing could only mean one thing.

"It's useless. The file has one sheet of paper with a bunch of law jargon all over it." I'm looking at the paper too now. There's that word Mom told me was misspelled on the magazine, saying the word was skirt. "Escort." Mom lied to me.

Trying to decipher the legal jargon, it seems like an official document giving Mom permission to work for a one-year period in the States. *Did Dad hire Mom to escort him to places?* That might explain how she ended up with him. I mean, you couldn't pay me enough to stay with the man if I had a choice. Dad's handwriting runs atop the line marked for the representing attorney, although it's another lawyer's name— Michael Meyers, Esq. I'd recognize his handwriting anywhere. I shake my head in disbelief.

Mom never worked a day in her life as far as I could remember. My mind scripts a hundred more questions of what I've always assumed to be true. I begin to wonder whether my parents even wanted children. Maybe I was an accident. And Dad's treatment, or should I say mistreatment of me, is his punishment for me showing up. Like it's all my fault.

I'm lost in thought over this deeper level of rejection that I contrive with the slightest suggestion of Mom's mistake— Mom's foolish choice to pick Dad as her lover. *Now look at me.* I'm as bad as my father, blaming Mom for everything. Maybe Lagan was right. Repulsed by the comparison, my foot kicks the drawer shut. The loud ting of metal hitting metal punctuates our attempt. It's over.

Just like that. No further clue regarding our grandparents or Mom's history or our heritage exists in Dad's office. Perhaps he just hadn't had a chance to toss the most recent letter that I stumbled upon. Wish I had taken the time to memorize the return address. Add that to my long list of coulda, shoulda, woulda's.

Another plan dissipates into oblivion, and it's time to reassemble and clean up. Jesse's eyes express loss beyond words. Without seeing the original letter, it feels like a hoax to both of us. We go back to being alone—together—unwanted and alone. Neither of us speaks as we return every item perfectly and finish by reinstalling the door and its lock. The door seems heavier as we align the angles in order to replace the hinges. Why did we have to remove the hinges if we removed the doorknob? Does it matter now?

"I'll put the tools back if you want to rest a bit." I feel terrible. "Your legs must be exhausted."

Jess complies by wheeling to the stairwell, dragging himself up to his room and pulling the covers over his head. He's more disappointed than me. I return the tools, shut the garage door, and decide to start dinner. My stomach's growling reminds me that we skipped lunch. When I see the snow whisked up to the kitchen window, I'm shocked at the volume. And it's still coming down. I don't see any snow plows. They're probably busy trying to keep the highways clear. There has to be over a foot of snow out there. I turn on the radio on the counter to listen for the latest weather update.

"Jess!" I run to tell him the news. "Jesse! The weatherman says that sixteen inches of snow have fallen, and they're expecting three or four more before midnight when it will finally slow down!"

"So?" Jess responds from under the covers.

"That means, I hope, that Dad cannot get home! There's no way! Not even cabs can drive in this insane weather. The radio guy advised everyone to stay indoors. Even a lot of the train lines stopped running due to ice on the tracks. This is insane! Insanely awesome!"

"What are you so excited about?" Jess sits up in bed and looks at me curiously. "One day of freedom doesn't cut it for me. I want out. I want to get out of this hell for good. Are you so clueless that you missed the bit about no info? No grandparents' address? No way to get to the two people who might exist that actually want us? I'm going back to sleep. Wake me up if you get some real good news. Like the police find Dad in the storm. Frozen to death. Until then, leave me alone, okay?"

I swallow. *Okay.* I return to boiling water to make rice. Salty rice soup appeals to me on cold wintry days. Any soup really. I fish through the fridge for what else I can throw into the soup and find green onions, leftover chicken, spinach, and fresh basil. I chop each item up, toss in some paprika, salt, and black pepper, and hope the warm aromas of basil and spice might lure Jess out of bed to eat with me.

Dad calls while I slurp my soup, trying not to burn my tongue. "I'm stuck at work." I bite my tongue to keep from squealing aloud. "The cab companies aren't driving to the suburbs until the snowplows make their rounds, and they might not get to it till the morning. I'll crash on my couch here in my downtown office for the night if I can't make it home. You two behave, and I'll see you tomorrow evening after work. Even if I manage to fetch a cab in the morning, I'll waste time commuting right back through the mess. If anything changes, I'll call."

Will this qualify as good news to Jess? I don't care. I run back to Jesse's room and announce Dad's message. "Maybe it's just one day, but let's make the best of it! Let's go and play in the snow! Let's build a snowman! Let's goof off! Come on already!"

I pester Jesse until he finally rolls out of bed and gets up. "Fine, but if my legs collapse in the snow, you're responsible for carrying me inside. Deal?"

"Dealio! Can I get help?" I press my hands together. "Can I ask Lagan to come over?"

Jess points out the obvious. "How do you plan to call him without getting the call traced or tracked by Dad? And second of all, how do you think Lagan would manage to get here through the snow when Dad can't get home?"

"Hmm." He makes two very good points. "For the first question, I'll tell Dad that I needed homework help. He won't see the number again. He'll forget about it. For the second problem, maybe he owns a snowmobile? He only lives a few blocks away. It's worth a shot!"

"You're gonna do what you wanna do." Jesse shakes his head as he plops down into the wheelchair. "Do whacha gotta do."

I follow my brother as he shuttles down the steps on the conveyer he rarely uses these days and then rolls into the kitchen where I ladle a bowl of soup for him. Staring at the phone, I realize that I don't know Lagan's number. Another grand idea swirls down the drain.

Dishing up another helping of steamy soup, I join Jesse to wash down another serving of warm goodness. Next, I dig out winter wear and snow boots for my brother and myself, reminding him to layer up before we go out. We exit our house from the back door resembling Eskimos, every inch besides our eyes covered. At first Jesse lightly steps atop the close to two feet of snow, but too quickly. His feet sink deep into the snow. I have no choice but to follow, and I'm out of breath just trekking to the front of the house.

No one is out, except for a few kids on their sleds racing down the empty street, no traffic to worry about. I look back to see Jesse picking up his legs one at time to work his way toward me. His eyelashes are covered with dainty snowflakes.

Neither of us has ever made a snowman. How hard can it be? I fall back onto an untouched area in the yard, and sway my arms and legs, then stumble forward as I rise to look back. My first snow angel. I blink away flakes on my eyelashes that get immediately replaced with fresh ones.

As I circle the scene, my eyes can barely take in the beauty. The whole earth, every branch, every inch of earth, is perfectly white. Perfectly clean. Perfectly lovely.

I close my eyes, pull my scarf down, and stick out my tongue. I'm in my own world when...ouch! A snowball hits my back. Jess declares war from a bank he's hiding behind near the front hedges. *Forget the snowman.* Revenge calls my name. I hop from spot to spot and head for the biggest tree in our yard. Jesse nails me two more times before I dive for cover. I eat a little more than a few flakes in my ridiculous Mission Impossible reenactment. I form several snowballs before I turn to fire them toward my enemy. Jesse catches them like baseballs and shoots them right back at me. *Not fair!*

We're so consumed by our war, neither of us stops to greet the abominable snowman making his way up the driveway. The mailman? Except that he has no mail.

When he turns, and I recognize his eyes, I point at Jesse and scream for help. "Lagan! Get him!" I need help. I have yet to hit Jesse once! Lagan drops down and produces power-packed ammunition within seconds. *Finally!* A little testosterone to show Jesse he can't push me around!

"Ouch!" A snowball nails me in the arm, and I realize that I gloated too soon. "Lagan! You're supposed to be on my side!"

"My bad." He laughs out frosty steam puffs. "I thought you said boys against girls!"

Next thing I know, Lagan and Jesse fire away while edging up on me, and I barely rise to my feet to run away when I'm tackled face first into the snow by the boys' team. My second snow meal today. Yum! Cold! Glad it's not yellow.

"No fair!" I spit snow out of my mouth and try to wiggle out from under the weight of two sets of bulging teen biceps. "Time out!"

"We'll let you out if you…" Lagan shifts slightly toward Jesse, holding out an open hand while keeping the other tightly wrapped around my knees.

"If you agree to make us hot chocolate and homemade cookies when we go inside." Jess fills in the blank.

"Not a chance!" I retort. "I am not rewarding this unjust behavior!"

"Okay then…bacon. I'll let you go for a few strips of perfectly crisped bacon." Lagan throws a gleeful grin my way and burrows his head into my back like it's a pillow. "Or we'll just lay here till you can't feel your toes!"

Jess chimes in. "No can do on the bacon, but I know we have the stuff for cookies." Then he turns to me. "Last I heard, it's pretty hard to bake with frostbitten fingers."

I weigh my options, as if I have many, and cave in. "Okay! Just let me go already!"

We play in the snow for a while longer, until Jess feels his legs giving out, and then we make our way to the back door. Shaking off the snow before entering, Jess keels over when the back door opens. I remove my snow gear quickly and race to retrieve the wheelchair, dry clothes, and a blanket. Jess is so tired that he lets Lagan help him peel back his shoes. A sweater and slippers with a blanket over his lap do the job. He starts to thaw, and I leave in order to get myself into dry clothes. Lagan hasn't removed his layers besides his gloves and hat when I return downstairs.

"Should I stay?" Lagan needs permission.

"Of course!"

I fill him in on the details of Dad's delay. How I wanted to call him. How he came. "By the way, how did you know my dad wouldn't be home?"

Lagan looks pleased with himself. "Well, I hoped he'd be at work. But if he wasn't, I planned to offer to shovel your driveway. Teenagers always try to make a quick buck on snow days."

"Hmm." I nod, impressed with the simplicity of his idea. "If Dad does somehow show up, we'll have to explain why we're feeding this teenager before he shoveled the driveway!"

"That's easy. Teens always work harder after eating." Lagan raises his eyebrows playfully. "I'll happily shovel for a cup of hot cocoa and a couple of warm, out-of-the-oven goodies."

Jesse jumps in to agree. "Of course. Dad will buy that explanation hands down. So we—I mean you—best get to baking."

"I'll help." Lagan hangs up his snow gear on the back door hook. "But I have to warn you, I need a lot of guidance in the kitchen. The only reason the last brownies I baked turned out was because my cousin is a pro when it comes to baked goods. Rani says you never stick to the time on a recipe. A few minutes beforehand work better since things keep cooking on hot trays even after you pull them out. But I'm a by-the-book type of guy. Anyway, where do you keep your flour? And measuring cups?"

Lagan opens cabinets while Jess and I just watch silently for a moment. Jess's eyes say what I'm thinking. This feels right. Company. A friend. Baking together. A day of freedom tastes even sweeter than either of us expected. Never thought it would occur inside the beehive. When the king's away, the peasants will play. Something like that.

That evening, we feast on oatmeal raisin cookies and frothy hot chocolate. Everyone takes seconds, and then we finish off the soup I made earlier. When Lagan checks his watch, he jumps up to start clearing dishes.

"You don't have to..."

"Yes, I do. It's the least I can do after such a scrumptious dinner. But I should get going before my parents start looking for my name listed under the newspaper's list of SCD—Snowplow Collateral Damage. Those guys drive half-asleep when they've been up all night salting the roads."

Jesse chuckles and rolls himself into the living room to watch TV. We've never had so much free time on our hands. Maybe we'll stay up all night too.

The clock reads 8:00 p.m., and it's dark outside. As if reading my thoughts, Lagan nudges my shoulder at the kitchen sink. "Don't worry. I'm a big boy. I'll call you when I get home to let you know I'm safe after dialing star sixty-seven. That way my number stays blocked from the caller ID. Okay?"

"Okay."

Our hands collide in a soap-filled sink, and I couldn't have asked for a happier day. Especially since Jesse genuinely allowed Lagan to be a part of our lives today. Lagan shakes hands with Jess, telling him how proud he is of his progress. "You got a killer throw, dude. You should think about baseball. In the spring, of course, after all the snow melts."

"Of course." Jess smiles big, then wheels himself back to the living room on cue to allow Lagan to say goodbye to me.

"Thanks, umm, for coming by." I fumble for words, suddenly aware it's just the two of us.

"Hey." Lagan raises my chin with his hand. "I did have a reason for coming over."

"All right." I shrug my shoulders. "Are you gonna tell me, or do I have to guess?"

"Well..." Lagan looks away for a moment. "You see, I wanted to ask you something. And I had to do it in person. I want to know if you'll let me W4U?"

"W4U?" I chuckle at his newest acronym. "I'm guessing it's pretty serious for you to chance turning into Frosty just to ask in person."

"You could say that." Lagan tips his head, like he's searching my eyes for permission to continue. "It stands for Wait For You. Because I will. Wait. For as long as it takes."

"W4U, huh?" I'm trying to make light of the weighty words that linger between us. The questions I can't answer. A timeline I can't predict. "It might take a long time. A really long time." I'm so close to saying it, and then he does.

With his hands turned up and animated, he turns on a thick, Italian accent and says, "For what? For you? Forevah!"

I can't help but giggle at his antics, and then Lagan steps closer. Gently kisses two fingers and then places his fingers on my lips and rests them there. My broken lips. With his pulsing, unscathed fingers, he kisses me. And I cannot breathe.

"And for the record, forever isn't too long." Lagan's fingers playfully swirl off my lips and down my chin, and then he turns to open the back door. "I'll see you soon. The seventeenth, if not sooner."

The door closes and I stand there, my trembling hand resting over my mouth.

Nothing like a snow day to make my first snow angel.

To taste a kiss on my lips.

To flirt with forever.

Nothing like a snow day.

~TWENTY-SIX~

The last time this much snow surrounded us was the winter before Mom died. The fall preceding that bitter Benton Harbor December marked the last season Mom had hair and the last time Dad yelled at her. Jesse and I were thirteen and fourteen years old, respectively. The neighbors across the street had moved out a month before, and a Penske truck pulled up one October day unannounced. We watched the moving guys take trips back and forth between the truck and the house from our kitchen window. Dad wasn't back from work, so all three of us finished our chores and enjoyed a few moments of peace while the driveway lay empty.

I saw the way Mom's eyes shifted from our driveway to the mom across the street. She wanted to meet her. She needed an excuse. She looked at the clock, wondering if she should gamble. I'd seen this look in her eyes before. She had an idea.

Mom opened up the cupboards, pulled out a platter and asked Jesse and I to quickly grab one of each type of fruit from the produce basket in the fridge. Jesse washed the fruit while I found the extra cutting boards stored under the kitchen sink. With all three of us chopping away, we had a colorful ensemble ready in no time. Mom fiddled with the Glad wrap while Jesse and I washed the dishes, threw out peels, and wiped down the counter—experts at getting rid of evidence. Stealing glances between the clock and the movers, I knew that Mom only had fifteen minutes to play with if Dad returned at his usual time of 4:45 p.m. The clock on the microwave flipped to 4:31.

"You two run along to your rooms and do your extra reading," Mom said. "I'll be right back."

Jesse and I exchanged glances, and then looked at Mom, wishing her luck with our eyes, and scurried on up to our bedrooms. As soon as we heard the front door shut, we raced back down to watch Mom meet the family through the kitchen window. Seeing Mom make a friend was better than watching TV. Jesse put his arm around my shoulder, and for a brief moment we tasted the crumbs of possibility.

Instinctively, my eyes shifted among three spots: from Mom, to the clock, and to the driveway. "Hurry," I whispered, as we watched Mom smiling and our new neighbor giving her a side hug.

Dad's black Acura pulled up into the driveway. Early. The clock read 4:40. And just like that, the sun turned black and the crumbs turned poisonous. Death came a-knocking, and Jesse and I flew like our tails were on fire up to our rooms. We knew better than to be in each other's room, but I so wished for Jesse's hand to squeeze. My nails dug into the pages of John Green's *Paper Towns* when I heard the front door slam shut. *Dad.* Seconds later, the door opened and shut again. *Mom.* The air smelled noxious with uncertainty. Only thing I was certain of: it was gonna be bad.

A little over two years after the closet incident and Mom's crazed recovery, when the new neighbors moved in across the street, the wind changed direction again—this time into a twister that none of us would ever recover from. I heard Dad's footsteps making his rounds to his office, then to each room, checking and double-checking our workmanship. When he made his way back to the kitchen, I snuck down to the first floor to peek in, staying hidden by crouching in the stairwell. I could see Mom standing with her hands gripped on the sides of the kitchen sink. The water was running, and someone had pulled the curtains shut.

Dad was at the other end of the kitchen, and I watched his back as he opened the cabinet to remove a stack of Corning Ware plates. He held a single dish up in the air, smashed it against the granite top, and then—to my horror—he turned and threw the jagged, broken plate like a dart at Mom's back. The dish made a dull sound against Mom's shirt before it shattered to pieces as it hit the tile floor. She buckled over the sink, and then pulled herself back to a stand like a wounded soldier trying to save her dignity. Then a second. My eyes blurred instantly and I couldn't watch any longer. I bit my lip to keep from screaming and ran back up to my room and waited for the sound of the last breaking dish. They just kept coming. And with each sound wave of broken glass, I punched the carpet floor by my bedroom door, wishing for the impossible. That Dad's sadistic appetite could be quenched sooner rather than later. For Dad to cut himself on a broken dish and bleed to death. For time to rewind.

Minutes seemed like hours, until the piercing clamor came to a sudden halt. I held my breath until I saw Mom's head emerge from the stairwell. She crawled up the steps, dragged herself past my room on her hands and knees, and continued toward the hallway bathroom. Blood seeped through the back of her white floral-printed blouse. The flowers were bleeding. And so was my heart.

I needed to get permission from Dad to help her, and I knew it wouldn't be easy to ask. I just wanted to "clean up the mess," I'd say, hoping his OCD nature would grant me this one small liberty. I'd pick up the broken dishes first, and then I'd attend to Mom, using the minimum amount of Neosporin, simply to prevent blood from getting on the carpet or bedroom sheets. I had this whole conversation in my head, planning a strategic backdoor rescue, naively thinking I could outwit the tsar.

Little did I know that Dad had his own plan to throw Mom down a well where no rope could reach. He walked past my room, carrying a small, black, leather bag. Dad entered the bathroom and locked the door behind him. I swallowed another ocean of tears as I ran over to Jess's room. "Let's clean the kitchen."

"That's true." Jess's voice was hoarse and his eyes red. "It'll be on our lists anyway." Jess headed for the vacuum in the hall closet while I raced down the stairs for the broom.

When I reached the opening to the kitchen, my mouth fell open. Not even an inch of the kitchen tile was visible. Broken glass lay everywhere, and I knew we'd be eating off paper plates until we all saved enough imaginary allowance from our chores to buy new dishes. Nothing happened in the house without Dad's approval, especially purchases of any kind. He did all the shopping, and new dishes would be added to the wish list in Mom's head.

We—Jess, Mom, and I—all had our invisible wish lists that we only voiced when Dad was absent. Mine included trendy clothes in place of the thrift shop wardrobe I owned. Jess's wish list had video games he had only heard the kids at school rave about—the Xbox or Wii. Anything would do. Mom simply dreamt of hair accessories. She longed for rhinestone slides, colorful hair bands, and silky ribbons for her hair, but Dad never encouraged the expression of either her femininity or her beauty. So I often closed my eyes and imagined rainbows and glitter, silk and stones, when I looked at Mom's flowing hair.

Thinking of ways to reach Mom and attend to her wounds, I worked with Jess to diligently restore the kitchen. With the noise of the vacuum whirring loudly, neither of us heard the sounds coming from the upstairs bathroom. When we finished throwing out the last double-bagged load of broken Corning Ware, mopped the kitchen floor, and wiped down the countertops of all the shards, I cautiously climbed the stairs and sat at the top while Jess left to return the vacuum to the garage. Dad passed by me on his way down to his den, a look of satisfaction plastered across his face. Not sure where Mom was, I checked the bedroom first. Then I noticed the light in the bathroom where she originally entered. The door remained partially closed, and as I approached, I heard muffled whimpers.

"Mom?" I asked while knocking softly. "Is it okay to come in?"

Silence. More soft moaning.

"Mom?" This time I pushed the door open to see her for myself. To my horror, a trail of long black hair lead up to my mother sitting on the toilet lid. Mom's long black hair. All. Gone.

"Mom!" I cried as I ran up to her. "Your hair? He didn't? How could he? Why?" I bent down and hugged her knees. Her mouth had duct tape over it, and her wrists were bound with a single layer of tape, too. The clippers were lying on the edge of the sink, and Mom's glory surrounded her like fallen petals. She looked naked. Awful. Ugly. She was bald.

I wanted to pull the duct tape off, but I knew waiting for Dad's approval would minimize further damage. How much *more* could he hurt her? Or me? If I swallowed a river of tears earlier, I looked at my Mom's bare scalp and pushed through the ocean of my sadness to reach her. I couldn't get stuck in my shock. There was no time for that. I only had seconds to help her, if Dad gave me even that.

I quickly took the tweezers out of the medicine cabinet and went to work, picking out glass pieces from her cut-up back, finding it impossible not to keep glancing at Mom's head. Her hair all over the floor. And, all the while, I prayed for a miracle. I prayed for lightning to strike my father dead, instantly. I prayed for revenge. I prayed for awful things. Unspeakable things. I hoped and prayed for all sorts of horrific, drawn-out acts of retribution to fall upon Dad. Dad would have a heart attack if he read my mind. That would work for me just as well.

I redirected my energy to cleaning up Mom's back, but the immense task before me could not be tackled in the few minutes before Dad returned and punished me for helping her. I thought of how I would transition to picking up her hair when I heard footsteps, and even as I thought it, someone approached quickly. I covered the First Aid kit with a washcloth and moved to a crouched position and began gathering Mom's long black strands into piles.

Jess came up from behind, and I nearly jumped out of my skin, thinking it was Dad. Confused at the scene, the hair, Mom's back, the duct tape, Jess went into a rage.

"I'm gonna kill him." He spoke to no one in particular. "I'm gonna kill him in his sleep. Tonight. I'm gonna find the sharpest knife in the kitchen drawer and slit his—"

"Throat." Dad finished the sentence as he pushed open the door and sauntered into the bathroom.

I thought Dad threatened Mom's life that evening. At that moment, I knew Dad planned to destroy Jesse as well. Dad would punish him for breathing words of treason. But Dad controlled us with his unpredictability. He simply snapped his crocodile teeth shut when we least expected it.

The air was thick with murderous intentions, and I wished for the courage to call for help. To call the police. An ambulance. Child Services. Anyone. There had to be laws that Dad had broken, and the law was supposed to protect us. In the real world, fathers protected their offspring. Instead, ours seemed to revel in every chance he had to cut us. Sure, I heard the kids at school complain about their chores. But no one ever mentioned consequences other than being grounded or losing electronics or TV time.

Worse still, Dad convinced us that no one would ever believe any accusations of abuse. He strategically chose weapons that could just as easily be connected with accidents:

boiling water, a hot iron, broken glass. Plus he had friends in every profession: cops, judges, and politicians. He was the go-to lawyer guy of so many men in authority, the one time we tried to run away, the man in uniform who promised to help us, helped us right back into the arms of the one who hurt us—Dad. So we found ourselves imprisoned, and none of us knew how to escape without abandoning the other, a covenant we would not break. Until that night.

That night Mom left us. Verbally, at first. She never spoke after that night. No more gitas left our bald Gita's lips after that day. Not even a sad song. She also ceased to look me in the eyes. She walked around the house like a mobile stone statue, despair permanently chiseled into her form, even her shadow. Her list became shorter and shorter, and mine grew longer and longer.

Not even a week had passed and it became apparent that Mom had mentally deserted us as well. She retreated to her bed for larger portions of each passing day, and one morning, she simply did not get up. Mom lay there, sleeping with her eyes open, not shifting sides. She stopped eating, but I never told Dad. She'd drink from a straw when I forced her to, but only the bare minimum. That's when my list included Mom's name on several lines. Wake Mom up. Feed Mom. Give Mom a sponge bath. Clean Mom's bedpan. The rest were the usual household chores. It was hard back then, but I realize now that I miss back then. I miss Mom terribly.

Mom never recovered from her second nervous breakdown. On the night before New Year's, I went into Mom's room to do the usual nighttime routine of brushing her teeth, massaging her head and legs, wiping her down with a washcloth, and kissing her goodnight. Her forehead was cold. Her eyes were closed. The fluttering had stopped. I felt her wrist and knew she was free.

Mom died in her sleep, and we buried her on New Year's Day morning. I made a haphazard wig with her hair save one strand and Scotch-taped it around her face in a futile attempt to cover her shame. I even applied pink lipstick to the thin broken line where her smile once laid. And I dressed her in blue. It wasn't the sparkly blue sari in her picture she once allowed me to steal a glance of, but it was blue. And wearing blue was how I wanted to remember her. When the mortician told me time was up, I kissed her cold cheeks, the top of her eyelids, and the palms of her hands. Tears rolled down my cheeks onto her open lines of life. I closed her fingers around my final gift to her before I tucked her hands back by her side. If only she could bury my sadness with her.

Jesse and Dad carried the casket with the help of the funeral personnel. Dad picked a cemetery two blocks from our house, like he planned to keep an eye on mom, even in her grave. Under a heavy winter coat, I wore a black dress Dad allowed me to buy from the clearance rack. Piles of mud-mixed snow lay all around. The air temperature was so frigid that it hurt to breathe. My tears froze before slipping off my cheeks, as if to engrave the sadness there forever. No one came to her funeral. As far as I knew, no one was invited. When the casket lowered into the frozen earth, I pictured myself jumping in to join her. One glance at Jesse and my feet took two steps back. When the dirt-snow mixture hit the top of the casket, Mom's words to me when I was seven returned, as if she were right there speaking to me: "No matter what happens, promise me that you'll take care of your little brother."

Yes, Mom. I promise. *Happy New Year, Mom. And sweet dreams.*

~TWENTY-SEVEN~

My waterfall willow changes colors right before my eyes. From her naked branches of winter to the pale yellow blossoms of spring, her paint seeps from within her and reminds me of the hourglass. Time stops for no one.

On March 17, a couple months after our snow play day, Lagan and I meet at our designated time, and after a simple dinner of cream of potato soup and turkey and avocado sandwiches, Lagan catches me off guard with a question. Or actually a request. "I need to talk to you about Rani."

My shoulders tense with the sound of another girl's name.

"Remember Rani? My cousin?" I bust out laughing at the word cousin.

Of course. Lagan mentioned her time and time again, but I haven't met her yet. I stop rustling with the Ziploc bags and empty paper containers to turn and give him my full attention. He isn't laughing.

"Sorry for laughing." I feel stupid. Something terrible might be wrong with Rani, and I'm getting unstuck from the quicksand of jealousy. Sheesh. You'd think knowing Lagan's W4U quest would be enough to keep me afloat. Insecurity just feels familiar to me, like the scents of cleaning products.

Lagan shakes his head. He's at a loss for words for once. So I wait.

I take a seat on our branch bench under the willow, something Lagan and I assembled together with a few saved limbs that Jason allowed, and quickly glance down at my watch. I have about fifteen minutes left to my break. Plenty of time.

Lagan clears his throat and begins to share a story about the girl he calls his best friend. "Since we're cousins, we grew up together, seeing each other at least once a week when our parents decided to settle in the Chicago area in the same neighborhood. Prima, my baby sis, is closer to Rani's age, but she's your typical hair, nails, heels, girly girl, so although I know they totally care about each other, Rani never really connected with her. Or any of the other female cousins. But we clicked. Right from the start." Lagan stops and squints his eyes as he looks up at me, as if to gauge whether I understood thus far. "You know how it is? I mean, do you? Know how it is?"

Glad he doesn't assume, I press my lips together and shake my head no. I have no idea. "The only family I know is Jesse. Maybe I have cousins out there, but I've never met them. My mom's parents are out there somewhere, on some remote farm in India. Doubt I'll be visiting them anytime soon."

Lagan sighs. The look on his face makes me think he's not sure if I'll get it. His story. His relationship with Rani. Or whatever he needs to tell me about her.

"Yeah." Lagan smiles a small but definite smile. "But you're a girl. So you should be able to relate, I think. Actually..." Another hesitation as he picks up a branch off the ground and moves closer to where I'm sitting. Lagan leans against the Willow's trunk, breaking off little bits of the branch and tossing them into an imaginary hoop. Always practicing his shot. Can't seem to help himself. Like this little physical act is helping him to formulate his thoughts.

Near the end of his story, tears glisten in his eyes. He's never told anyone before. About seeing things he shouldn't have. Staying silent when he should have spoken up. Failing to defend Rani when she didn't even know she was being hurt.

"Rani was seven. Only seven." Lagan punches the bark. Then puts his hand flat on the willow's trunk, as if to apologize. "What kind of guy does that to a little girl?"

His voice trails off. He doesn't want to talk about it anymore. It's a debt he can never pay back. His averted gaze tell me he's not sure he should have told me. Or maybe his silence says, "Now your turn."

Not yet. I'm not ready to undress. My heart still has a few layers to get through before we talk about Dad and all the skid marks. The kind that even the strongest of street cleaners can't get out.

"Anything else?" I ask, keeping the focus on Rani. On Lagan. On anyone but me.

"Yes." Lagan looks up into my eyes for the first time this afternoon and says two words: "I'm sorry."

"Me too." I sigh. Nothing like a good ol' confession to derail the steadiest of trains. Lagan, the locomotive that lost his lungs. For a guy who rarely lacked words, when his sleazy uncle slipped his hands between Rani's little girl legs, Lagan hid in her closet, staring silently. They were in the middle of a game of hide and seek. Lagan hid in shame when his cousin stopped seeking. He only came out when the room was empty. The game was over. Reminds me that we all fall down. Some more often than others. But in the end, we all fall sometimes.

"Rani doesn't know. I haven't told her. It happened when we were kids. It's been so long. I don't know that I have to tell her."

I put my hand on his arm. "She knows you're there for her. That you care. That's all that matters."

And that's what I seem to know as true these days. Nothing gets our attention like the curveballs of life. I've been hit so many times, a soft lob is what throws me for a loop. But it's weird how when others get a surprise pitch, I ache inside as if the wind struck me out too.

"You're right." Lagan speaks with a dose of renewed confidence.

"And you know what else?" I'm just chock-full of good ideas today. Talk about a switcheroo of roles. "You can tell her. Someday. You have to tell her. Someday."

Lagan lets out another huge sigh and sits down next to me. "You're right. I know you're right. Someday."

We don't talk much after that. I don't know where Lagan's mind drifts off to when he lays his head on my lap. I run my fingers through his hair and think of Rani, a girl he loves that I have never met. A girl who was touched where you're not supposed to know touch so soon. By a man who isn't supposed to touch you like that. A girl whose heartaches bring pain to this boy I love. Maybe someday our paths will cross.

A squirrel scurries into our willow cave, and another follows right on the tail of the first. Daydream over, the chase is on. I watch for a moment and even Lagan looks over, and we both laugh at the simplicity of life. Of how simple life can be.

"If all I had to do was chase you up a tree and nuzzle into the back of your neck to tell you how crazy I am about you..." His voice trails off. I wonder if he feels guilty about changing the topic.

I glance at my watch. "OMG!" I stand up in a frenzy. Lagan rolls off my lap to the ground to his hands and knees. "Oops. Sorry." I have got to remember to turn down that panic button when Lagan's around. "I need to work on that." I offer Lagan my hand, and he takes it and then pulls me to the ground.

"We can't be having you looking all spiffy and clean. You need to look like you've been doing some work around here." And with that, he smears some dirt on my cheeks and nose as I try to loosen his grip and break free. He has my good arm by the wrist, and I scoot back on my bottom to try to broaden the space between us.

"Truce! Mercy! Time-out!" Whatever it takes to say I don't want to play. "I'm gonna get fired! My break was over five minutes ago!"

"You should have thought of that before you dropped me like a hot potato." Lagan lets go, giving me a chance to get to my feet, but the chase is on. Those darn squirrels. Talk about bad timing for inspiration!

"I can't climb trees!" I yell ahead of me, although this lanky-legged athlete is on my heels like there's no tomorrow. I squeeze through a break in the wispy branches, but I feel Lagan's arms around my waist just as I exit out onto the green landscape outside the willow. "Okay! You got me! You win! Game over! Let me get back to work now."

"Not until I get my prize."

"What is it with guys and their trophies?"

"A small prize will do." Lagan's locked fingers cement themselves against my back, and I have no choice but to comply.

I bend down and quickly grasp an acorn, and then I turn toward my man as his strong arms embrace me. Face-to-face with no space between us, I see myself in his eyes.

"Close your eyes and I'll give it to you." His eyebrows raise, his dimple dances playfully on his cheek, and the twinkle of anticipation lights up his eyes.

"All right. Closing." Lagan has his eyes shut, and I wiggle one arm from out of his grip, stand up on my tippy toes, and move my face close enough to breathe in the scent of that sweet peppermint gum he carries almost as reliably as those Post-its.

I inhale deeply and then exhale slowly as I run the tip of my nose across his cheek, back toward his left ear. Down to his jawline. His lips spread into an unmistakable smile, and he licks his bottom lip. Perfect. I shove the acorn into his slightly parted lips, break loose, and run for my life!

"So wrong!" I hear behind me. And he strolls toward me, laughing and shaking his head. The game is over. For now.

"You said, 'small.'" I remind him as I pick up my gardening gloves. "I'll see you next month! I'll W4U, okay. Gotsta get back to work."

"I'm keeping it, you know." I look up after I retrieve a rake that fell to the ground during our antics, and Lagan holds up the acorn between two fingers. "It was a gift after all. And a hint." Lagan tucks the acorn into his inside jacket pocket.

"Whatever," I say. Hint or no hint, I will see you later. Before I get fired and there is no later to look forward to.

"Mine." Lagan says, patting his chest where a bump outlines the acorn in his pocket before bending down to pick up his bike.

And so am I.

Lagan mounts his bike and rides off, leaving me under the willow, heart racing, mind swirling, lips longing. Can't wait till next month.

~TWENTY-EIGHT~

In early April, Lagan transfers from DePaul to Northwestern's downtown campus to keep pursuing his pre-law degree. He also picks up a job as a paid intern at his uncle's law office in the heart of the city. The funds help pay tuition, but leave little time to do much more than work or study.

We share our dreams under our springtime willow in the garden while new blossoms sail through the air to create a pink and yellow sprinkled blanket around us. He dreams about creating positive change in society through the government—if the people vote him in someday. I dream a writer's dream. God knows I have enough material for a trilogy on pain. But I'd rather write make-believe tales, the kind with happy endings.

The scents of budding flowers and the earth after a rainfall remind me of second chances. Jesse needs a second chance more than anyone I know. Lagan and I brainstorm how to help Jesse move his mountains, both seen and unseen. I can't lie. When I think for Jesse, I see a mountain fearfully higher than his secret mobility. His anger drives his every action.

"I'll happily do the forgiveness thing—once I get my justice. Have to live up to my name after all." Jess tells me this time and time again.

Jesse can practically run now. He doesn't use his wheelchair at all, except when Dad's around. Hiding his healed

SWIMMING THROUGH CLOUDS

body from Dad frustrates Jess more than ever. But we both know his secret better creates the possibility of a stealth escape. Luckily, Dad works more hours than ever, giving us siblings plenty of time to breathe. Jesse even finds a free online site that helps him prepare for his GED. He'll get a high school diploma and then think about the next step: how to escape Dad or how to convince Dad to let him attend college. After telling Dad he's been miraculously healed. *Yeah.* The details remain hazy at best.

Sitting under the willow on April 17, I tell Lagan my latest and greatest. "Jesse will be eighteen in a month. We'll both legally be adults, and regardless of our financial stability, we could run away and start over. Just not sure how far we have to run in order to find safety beyond my dad's claws. Across the ocean makes sense to me. Perhaps India in order to trace our roots and hopefully find our grandparents. Learn about what it was like for Mom to grow up in Kolkata. We can both work to that end, making due with our earnings, keeping life simple. Simply perfect describes any life absent of my dad."

Lagan listens silently each time I mention leaving. Disappearing from his family, Rani, and life in Chicago is not a realistic option for him. I would never ask him to leave. How can I have both? I ask myself each time we meet. When Lagan tells me that his new college roommate is a medical student named Reggie, I come up with a perfect solution. Perfect if life were as black and white as a Shakespearian play.

"Maybe your roomie can drug us both, Romeo and Juliet-style, and we can wake up in a cemetery. Jesse could dig us up and then we could all run off to India together. Sound appealing?" *Except the part about waking up in a coffin, I'm guessing.*

"What makes you think just cuz he's in med school he has access to illegal drugs? Or any drugs for that matter? You've been watching too many episodes of ER, haven't you?"

203

"Haha. Very funny." The last time Jess and I spent any significant time staring at the tube was the infamous snow day when he asked if he could wait for me. W4U.

Besides, Shakespeare wrote the classic catch-22. He never came up with any workable solution. Sigh. How could I think to take Lagan away from his loved ones? He actually has people other than me who love him. The price is too high. I cannot ask. I will not ask.

May 17 is three weeks away, and when it comes, I'll leave campus, take the 'L,' and then transfer to the bus that takes me a few blocks from the garden. Midterms are underway, and I cannot focus. I am so anxious to see Lagan. This past month proved the longest time period without Dad's wrath, and my lips look almost normal. Almost pretty.

Jesse asks me when I return from class on April 24 when my next workday is.

I tell him tomorrow night. "Why?"

"I just want to know when you won't be around. I need some space."

"I won't bug you about your anger anymore." I feel a need to apologize. "I told you I dropped it."

"That's not the problem," Jesse reassures me with a smile. "I just need a few uninterrupted hours." The fire in his eyes seems ignited with a new idea.

"Dad's not working late tomorrow night." I point to the calendar to remind him.

"I know."

Wait. "Jess? Are you gonna tell him that you're walking? Talking?"

"If you must know..." Jess pauses for a split second. "Yes. I plan to tell him. And I don't want you around to feel his back hand when it starts flying."

"Jesse." My lips are quivering. "What if? What if he doesn't know how to handle the news? What if he hurts you? Badly? I'm scared, Jesse. Just wait a few weeks. You'll be eighteen. We'll run away as legal adults. Dad won't have any rights on us then."

I beg Jesse to reconsider, but he's made his mind up. He wants to take his chances. Just not with me around. If I couldn't study before, now my mind spins a whirlwind of horrific outcomes all leading to Jesse being hurt by Dad so badly that his progress returns to square one. Learning to walk again. And talk again. Dad could do that.

I'm trembling inside my sheets at night. Maybe I should call in sick. Stay close by when Jesse tells Dad. I toss and turn late into the night, aware of the hurt and pain that wall us in and threaten to lock Jesse in for years to come. I have no plan to stop him.

I talk to the gardener, hoping sleep will eventually find me. I talk to the gardener without words. Like truckloads of coal, I carry my load back and forth, a miner familiar with the darkest of caves, and lay them at his feet. First, doubt. Then fear. Then anxiety. Then repeat. I'm searching for that place of still. Where my heart no longer threatens to leap off a cliff. So here I am. Again and again.

I awake, shirt damp, feeling exhausted. When did sleep find me, I wonder? I dodged the demons of possibility all night. Jesse's demons. They taunted me with images of his falling from the roof. Broken fingers clutching to the list that pushed him over. Bloody knees from crawling across the floor. I take my shower before the sunrise, my pounding heart still fighting to find still.

Jesse lies in bed when I begin my morning chores, Dad already off to work for the day. My little brother with the big plans is not in the mood to help me today. Perhaps he hasn't slept well either. I hug him tightly, his head turned from my face. Just as I reach his bedroom doorway, I hear Jesse's first words since last night: "You're right."

"What?" My hand catches the doorframe as I catch a curse before it leaves my lips. "What did you just say?"

"I said, 'You're right.' In fact, you've been right all along." Jesse swings his legs off the side of the bed and sits up, then stares at his hands, cracking his knuckles like a boxer about to enter the ring.

Dropping my bag to the floor, I return to Jess's bedside, giving him the green light to say more. I'm still not sure what we're talking about, but I know my brother well enough to wait it out.

"Fire." Jess says a word—the one word that has penetrated our lives above the rest.

"I'm gonna set the house on fire." Jess lays out his plan like he's reading the directions on the back of a Betty Crocker cake mix. "I'm gonna burn Dad's perfect world to the ground for all the times he burned you. And Mom. And me."

"Jess." I actually don't know what to say. I close my eyes and envision the bed sheets below me engulfed in embers. Orange dances in my eyes. And maybe I imagine it, but a sensation of heat rises over my ears. Wallpaper peels, spreads out, and patterns erase like a fading dream. Teakettles blacken, melt, and vanish. And just before Jesse and I flee the house of fire, I rip up the list. Then every list ever written. Into hundreds of pieces and throw the shreds up into the air. Lashing flames lick them up before one scrap hits the ground. Then we run. And run and run. Never looking back.

"It's the perfect plan, really." Jesse's words tell me this daydream is about to become reality. "You leave the house. Don't show up to work. Take nothing with you. Not even the shoes you usually wear every day. You can't let anyone see you either."

"When?" I know now where he's going with this. "Because..." And I know he's right. The only way we can truly escape Dad is death. Or rather, the appearance of. But I can't leave without saying goodbye. And Jesse knows this.

"I was gonna say now. I'm ready. I was ready yesterday. Heck, the day Mom died. Why didn't I think of this sooner?"

Jesse shakes his head and punches his hand. Time is something we can never take back. But we have tomorrow, if—and that's a huge if—we can pull this off.

"Give me one day. Let me have one last day at the garden. And say my goodbyes." Really one goodbye. "And then. Then we can..." And my voice fails to say the word go. Because I've seen these crossroads a million times. In and out of my dreams. Lagan and I never had a fighting chance at happily ever after. The fight has always been between Dad and me. Jess and Dad. And even when we win, we lose. I lose.

"One day." Jess's words linger in the air as I head out the front door. I have one last day to live. To love. Then to let go.

~TWENTY-NINE~

During the commute to campus, I change my mind and stay on the train as it heads downtown. I don't know Northwestern's campus at all, but I know Lagan is there, somewhere. I can't waste my last night alive staring at a whiteboard of quotes by Thoreau and Emerson. Our own Walden Pond awaits out there, wherever Jesse and I decide to run away to.

Why would anyone attach the word *good* to *bye* puzzles me. Angers me. And then saddens me. Because, ultimately, this sucks. But maybe it's better this way. Jesse decided the *when* so I wouldn't have to.

As soon as I exit the Metra, I walk several blocks, following signs pointing to NU's downtown campus. Finding a courtesy phone inside the Northwestern Medical School Library, I stand nearby to wait my turn. A short blond woman has the receiver to her ear. I can't hear her conversation, but anyone a mile away can see her chomping on bubble gum like it's going out of style.

I dial Lagan's number from memory in my head. Over and over again, so I won't forget it. After that winter snow day, when the boys snow-piled on top of me, and we feasted on cookies and cocoa, I learned all of Lagan's numbers—home, dorm, and cell by heart—for such a time as this.

As I wait in line for the blond who leans against the wall like she's settling into a nice long chat with an old friend, I force myself to stay calm by thinking about the snowball fight, the ridiculous tackle, hands colliding in warm dishwater, and my first fingertip-delivered, peppermint kiss. Jesse's words, "Don't take anything with you," bring on new meaning when I think about the kiss I will never know, because my lips never healed in time. Running the back of my index finger along the scabs of my bottom lip, I clear my throat loudly, hoping bubble-popping Blondie takes a hint.

She turns her back to me and continues to jabber. I have no choice but to keep waiting. I rewind to the winter scene in my mind, Jesse and I dressed from head to toe in snow gear, Jess's legs strong and ready to live again. Silently planning who would make the first brave move to the front of the house, we stood motionless, dazed and confused by deep slopes of snow mounded up against the siding.

"Step on top. Think light!" Jesse muffled the words from under his scarf-covered mouth. "Try to step over it." But the moment he took his third step, he sank. Knee deep.

I wanted to laugh. But I knew I was next. And there was no way around it. If I wanted to play, I had to go through it.

"Through," I said as Jess plowed onward. "That's the only way to get there." And even as Blondie hangs up and saunters off, I stare at the phone for a second before picking it up. Because I know it like my frostbitten fingers on that winter snow day. There's no way around this. Jess's plan is foolproof and the best shot at freedom from Dad's iron clutches. *Through*. I have to go through with it.

"Hello?" Lagan's voice works like a tranquilizer, sending a wave of peace straight into my pounding heart.

Followed by a second set of waves, and in flood the hows: How much do I tell him? How much is safe for him to know? *How will I help you to let me go?*

"Hi. I'm sort of in the neighborhood. Can I stop by for a minute?"

"Talia? Are you okay? Sure. Of course. I'm at work. Where are you?"

"Just tell me the cross streets where you're at. I figured if you weren't in class, you might be at your uncle's office today. Do you get a lunch break or something like that?" I recall how Lagan asked me the same question the first time he snuck up on me at the garden.

"Are you asking me out on a date? To what special occasion do I owe this surprise visit? Did Christmas come early this year? Hold on a sec. I have another call coming in on the office line..."

As I think about how to answer Lagan's questions, I realize that another student has lined up behind me, waiting for the use of the phone. I motion to her with one finger and hope that Lagan will keep me waiting less than a minute.

"So, as you were saying..." Lagan's voice comes back on the line.

"You were about to tell me the cross streets. I'll meet you at your uncle's office, and we can talk when I get there. There's someone waiting to use this phone."

"The office is at the corner of S. Wabash Ave. and East Harrison Street. Sure you don't want me to meet you where you're at? I can clock out early today."

"Don't worry 'bout it. I'll be there soon." I'm moving the phone away from my ear.

"K, I'll see..."

Click.

Finding the cross streets on a wall map near the library exit, I gauge the distance to decide if walking makes sense. It does. I find the law office just as Lagan described, next to an Asian restaurant with red paper lanterns hanging in the window. Standing outside, I'm not sure if I should knock or just walk in.

The doormat displays golden balance scales. The two trays are labeled *Justice* and *Mercy*, and they seem almost perfectly balanced. Mercy tips the scale to the right. Too bad there isn't a third choice. The choice of impossible.

The door sounds a stilted chime of dysfunctional bells when I turn the knob and push. An attractive Indian woman wearing a purple, silk, button-down blouse with a black, pleated skirt rises from behind her desk to greet me.

"Welcome to the law offices of Justice and Mercy. How can I help you?" she says properly with a tone suggesting memorized words that she greets every visitor with. She can't be much older than me. "Do you have an appointment today, Miss?"

"I'm sorry." I stare at her perfectly manicured lilac nails. "I'm looking for someone. Does Lagan—"

"Lagan does indeed work here." I see Lagan's face pop up from behind a nearby cubicle. "I thought I recognized that voice. Come into my office. Rani, she's cool. She's with me."

"With you?" Rani glances at me suspiciously. "Is there something you forgot to tell me, Cuz?"

Lagan looks at me, waiting for me to say my name, maybe. But I can't. "I'm just getting some homework help. I can come back..."

"No, no, it's cool. You'll have to excuse my cousin. She's just..." Lagan waves me over.

"Getting back to studying for midterms. Nice to meet you." Rani walks around her desk and stretches a hand forward to shake mine. "Any friend of Lagan's is a friend of mine."

I don't know what comes over me, but instead of taking her hand, I move forward and give Rani a quick hug. "Really nice to meet you too."

Lagan stands speechless for a second. "I'll take my lunch break now and wrap up my correspondence on this case afterward. If that's okay?"

Rani smiles warmly to me before folding her arms across her waist and shaking her head toward Lagan like she's heard that one before. Wonder how different things might have been if I weren't leaving? *Is she the one who will comfort you when I'm gone?*

"Sure." She shrugs her shoulders and clickity-clicks back to her seat. "Dad calls the shots around here, so if you miss a deadline, Cuz, the cost will be off your brown-skinned back."

When Rani's resumes reading her textbook, I ask, "Hey, can we take a short walk?"

"Of course." He stops typing and glances in the direction where his cousin sits. "Can I tell Rani that we're…together? She's cool. You could hang with her while I finish up."

"Today's not good." I say honestly. Or any other day, ever.

"Is everything okay?" Lagan stops typing to search my face for answers. "I'll tell her another day. No worries. Only when you're ready. Give me two minutes. Let me finish this e-mail to a client, and I'll take an early break. Hang tight. I'll make this quick."

"Should I wait outside?"

"Nope. Take a seat. I'm just proofing the message to make sure I catch any typos. Be with you in five, four, three…"

"You don't have to count." I sit down. "I can wait two minutes."

Two minutes stretch to five. Not until my eyes begin to scan my surroundings do I realize the gift before me: a first and final peek into Lagan's world. I spend the long seconds memorizing every detail of Lagan's cubicle. There are funny little doodles of stick figures on Post-its everywhere, pinned to his corkboard. One Sticky has two figures drawn sitting side by side next to a willow tree, watching a sunrise. Or is that a sunset? Hmm. Another has two stick figures dancing under an umbrella. A third sketch confirms my suspicions: two stick figures swimming through clouds, hand-in-hand, the sky a mix of rain and sunshine. In addition, photographs of dewdrops on the tip of autumn leaves fill in spaces. National *Geographic* cutouts perhaps. The only other significant details to his cubicle are the quotes everywhere. Some printed out on postcards. Others handwritten on three-by-five card stock. Still others on, of course, Post-it notes.

I can't read the fine print, except for the one taped across the top of his computer monitor, typed in larger font than the others: "<u>The Beautiful Fight</u>: Life is a battle you don't fight alone."

I recognize the title and reread the words over and over again, until the letters blur. I don't know if the tears evidence that I believe the words, or if they foreshadow the battles ahead. Maybe both. I peel off a blank Post-it from Lagan's desk, scribble two short words and slip it into my back pocket while Lagan continues to tap away on the keyboard.

The word battle reminds me of a dream I had last night. Jess walked the tightrope above Dad's jailhouse courtyard, and when Dad recognized his son's legs and arms balancing perfectly above the prison walls, angry snakes spewed from Dad's mouth, wrapping around and amputating Jess's arms and legs—irreparable, bloody limbs spread around like uprooted trees after a hurricane. The images disturb more than my vision. I don't hear Lagan's voice until he puts his hand under my chin, lifts my head, and wipes his fingertips across my cheeks.

"Talia? Where are you? Did you even hear...? Forget it. Let's get outta here."

"I'm sorry." I'm back. "Done?"

"Yes." Lagan places some Kleenex in my hands.

I fish my shades from my purse to cover up. Her eyes glued to a book, Rani doesn't budge from her seat when Lagan says, "Hey, I wrapped up my case and am calling it a day."

"Manana, Cuz," Rani says.

"Laters." And with that, Lagan pushes the bell-sounding door open and waits for me to pass through first.

The afternoon sun greets me like a flashlight looking for a dropped diamond. Time to pull back the shades.

213

Hiding your heart, Talia. Part the curtains and let Lagan see you. It's time to tell him the truth. The whole truth. The gardener speaks clearly through the sun, and I know that it's now or never. Never was an option yesterday.

The seals on my leaky eyes keep lifting. Lagan leads me a few blocks down to the lake, toward Buckingham Fountain, and it's crying upside down. A visual of my life, only the opposite direction. An upside down well, once deep and dark, I have no choice but to leave my hiding place. The impending farewell stunts my speech, and I can't help but turn and bury my face in Lagan's shoulder. So much lies behind. And so much ahead. Only a day away.

When my breathing steadies, I start with one word: "Jesse." His name sputters from my croaking throat.

"Yes?" Lagan squeezes my hand gently.

"I'm scared."

As Lagan wraps his arm around me and leads me, my fingers follow behind him along his belt line and my thumb slips through a loop. Oh, to hold on just a little longer.

Linked at the hips, we move clumsily over to a bench opposite the fountain where Lake Michigan lies to our right. Traffic blurs by on Lakeshore Drive, the world going nowhere fast.

Lagan listens intently as I relay conversations with Jesse, my fears, and my nightmares. Sometimes he looks off to the lake, shakes his head, and turns back to hear more. Other times, he rubs my cupped hands, failing to arrest the shaking. The tremble spills from my insides out, as I outline details of Dad's violent past and the memories that frame my life of terror. That Jess, Mom, and I have faced our entire lives. I say too much.

I know this when Lagan lets go of my hands. He begins to punch his left hand with his right, attempting to injure an enemy just out of his grasp. I recognize the frustration in his repetitive pounding. Jess and I have spent our entire lives swinging at invisible adversaries in our dreams. Neither of us has ever dared to fight the real evil while awake. Until now. Until today.

I'm awake now. And I have no choice but to fight for our flight.

"And that's why we have to leave. Dad has to believe that we're—" And I can't say the word. Because I know the word implies death to a lot more than just me. It's my time to give Lagan a little, square yellow paper. The words *The End* stare up at me from the Post-it note I pull out from my back pocket. I hand it over, because I have no choice. "I always knew it couldn't last." I knew this from the beginning, but never wanted to face it.

"I always knew it would be hard..." Lagan's words trail off as the note sits on his palm like a weight that cannot be lifted. "I just never knew it would end like this."

I rise and walk over to the edge of the fountain. The spray mixes with my tears, and I know nothing will ever wash the brief time I had with Lagan from my memory. Like days with Mom, I will file away the pictures and pull them out when I want to remember. I'm forcing myself to move to the other side of *later* when Lagan's arms wrap around my waist from behind to bring me back to *now*.

"Have you thought about calling the police?" Lagan asks the question Jesse and I answered years ago.

The police are not on our side. Dad has too many cop friends. My silence answers for me. So Lagan reels off a few more impossibles, because that's all we have left. The impossible. He just hasn't accepted it yet.

"There has to be a reason why he never just got rid of you and Jesse." Lagan throws in another line. "Why would any father who hates parenting that much hold on to his kids? Some things just don't add up."

"He's mentioned the word debt, but I never got the whole story. Not like I could outright ask him. Whatever it is or whomever he owes, it has to be bad enough that he threw a guy out of our house once over it. I don't know, Lagan..." Because I don't. "I just know I can't, we can't, live like this anymore. You don't understand." I hate to say the words. Because more than anything I need Lagan to just understand. There is no other way.

"Sure. I don't get everything, but I can't just sit back and watch you disappear. Not like this."

"LIG." It's my turn to give Lagan an acronym to face life with.

"LIG?" Lagan turns my shoulders to face him, and I can feel his hands move to my back and link.

"Let it go." I look into those dark brown eyes, and I'm swimming. He in my pools. Me in his. "Or LMG—Let me go."

Like a lifeguard who thinks he can rescue the Titanic, Lagan shakes his head no. "No. Not this time. Not when we've come so far. Not when I know what I know. Not now, when I know how much I love you."

"And that's why you have to let me go." I stand my ground, even as the words I've never heard from a boy stream into my heart into my vault for safekeeping. I'll take them and keep them forever. He loves me. He loves me.

Lagan shakes his head more and lets go of me this time. "It won't work. Jesse'll get caught. You can't just set a house on fire and get away with it. Police investigate that kind of stuff. They'll find out it was arson. And when they don't find any bodies in the house, your dad will know you're both alive. You won't have enough time to run to the next state, let alone another country. And then Jesse will be in jail. How does that make any sense?"

"You have a point." Several, in fact, that I had never thought about.

"What about India? You and Jess could leave on a flight tonight. I'll borrow money from my parents. And you can search for your grandparents."

"Any plan where Dad can find us was crossed out already." I guess I have to spell it out.

"There are things for that." His math brain refuses to accept that this is not a simple equation. Nothing adds up and no solution exists.

"Like what? And don't say magic shows where the girl in the box is first sawed in half and then she disappears." I'm through with bleeding. Fire woos me like a friend who promises freedom from Alcatraz, and I'm following—whether Lagan approves or not.

"Changing identities. Witness protection programs. Home for abused..." Suddenly feeling ashamed at hearing the word spoken out loud about me for the first time, I turn away, but Lagan pulls me close. He's grasping at me like one trying to save water in his hands, aware that even as he holds me tightly, I'm slipping away.

"How would I find this sort of place, if it existed? How would they keep Dad from finding me and taking me back? And would Jesse be able to stay with me? That's the only condition I would even consider." That's the most I've ever thought out loud. I just want to be far away from Dad. That's the bottom line.

"You have to tell the truth. That he hurts you. They'll let you in then. They can't refuse you." Lagan is not giving up. "It would just be for a little while, until they can help you find a safe way to come back..."

To you. That's what you want, isn't it? Of course, that's what I want too, but I accept that no matter what happens tomorrow, I'm leaving and probably never coming back. Maybe Lagan doesn't have to know that. Maybe it's easier this way.

"Okay." Who said that?

"Really?" Lagan exhales a nervous chuckle. "You're considering it? You're willing to find another way?"

"It's worth a shot, right?" I hope. "Let's find a place. A homeless shelter or something like that where they take cases like me. And Jesse. And if they have some way of hiding us. Then, maybe, someday..."

"For now, I'll know you're safe. And that's what I want most of all." Lagan pulls out his iPhone and begins to Google options.

I find my way back to the park bench as my mind goes back and forth. Where would Jesse and I run to, anyway? Taking nothing with us means I can't touch the account my checks get deposited in either. How far will we get without money or IDs? How long before someone reports us as runaways and tries to reunite us with Dad? Maybe Lagan is onto something—a way for us to leave without Dad being able to trace us. We could try it out. Use fake names. Test out a shelter. Let some time pass. Any night of sleep under a roof where Dad does not sleep sounds heavenly, really.

"I think I found one. Or two. Actually, there is a bunch. But this one sounds promising. The thing is, Talia, and I know you do not want to hear this, but if, for just a little while, you went to a women's shelter and let Jesse go to a men's shelter, you'd throw off your dad. He's expecting to find you together. What if you separated, just for a little while? I think it only makes sense."

"Jess will never go for it." And neither will I, for that matter.

"But if it means you're really free of your Dad for sure, wouldn't that make a difference? Actually, from what I can tell so far, you might not have a choice."

I know he's right. "I just don't know how I'll convince Jesse."

"Let me do it." Lagan wants to play knight all day long. "I'll talk to him. And if you're already safe at a women's shelter, he won't have a choice, and he'll agree to camp out until it's safe—safer. You know what I mean."

"Do you think they'll let me keep in touch with Jess? Call him? Check on him? See him once in a while?"

"I'm sure they decide things like that on case-by-case basis. There are probably different rules at different places, too. But I don't see why not," Lagan says.

After making some calls, finding some shelters with no empty beds and others requiring police reports, Lagan finds one that allows anonymous entry upon completion of an interview process. Seems like they have a different approach.

"Yes, I think I understand." Lagan is verifying what he read online. "So you're saying that as long as the shelter personnel can determine that she's not trying to contact her abuser, they don't see a problem with her calling her brother. Great. Nope. That answers my question. See you...maybe...today? Okay. I'll tell her to stop by today before eight."

"Today?" Everything's happening so fast.

Lagan plops down on the bench next to me and puts his arm around my shoulder. "She said if you want to come by and talk informally to see if you feel comfortable, you could even show up at the head office today, tell the registry that you're living in an abusive situation, and they'll begin the interview process. The main condition they require is all new residents must sign a contract to protect you and the other women, in which you agree never to disclose the location of the actual shelter."

Listening to Lagan explain how it works breathes life into the idea. This is quickly becoming much more than just an idea. Am I really doing this? Rising to my feet, I ask, "Are we doing this?"

"Do you have any reason not to? And, Talia..." Lagan stands and cups my face in his hands. "Whatever Jesse says, whether he agrees or not, promise me you won't go back.

Ever. You have to promise me that you will never go back to your dad or that house."

I gulp. Because I have never so happily agreed to something my whole life. "I promise." A tear slips down my cheek into his palm. "Jesse, too. Make Jesse promise."

"I'll try. And I'll show him the site on my phone where you'll be. It's gonna work out. I really believe it's all gonna work out." With a lifting scoop, Lagan picks me off the cement, and I squeal with hope I've never tasted before.

"Wait! Wait! Put me down!"

"Never." Lagan's dimple returns, and I feel like I'm falling. All over again.

"Come on. I just have to do one thing." I wiggle enough that Lagan lets me slide down to where my toes touch the pavement.

"I'll LYG on one condition." And the tables are turned on me! How does he do that?

"Yes." I'll agree to anything at this point.

"You'll find me when the time is right. And not before. You'll put your safety above my need for you. Because, Talia, I need you like I need...peppermint-flavored Trident. More. Much more. Promise me that. And I'll let you go."

"That's technically two promises." For the record. "But, yes, I get the sense that they won't exactly let me just leave whenever I feel like I want some fresh air. That's the point of a shelter, after all. I promise to stay put until the time is right. Now LMG!"

As my feet find firm footing on the ground, Lagan still holds me close to him. So close. Too close. "The Post-it." I fill the space between our lips with a request. "I need it back."

"Oh, that ol' thang. I threw it away."

"I was gonna rewrite it." SUS for See You Soon. Because any possibility of a possibility counts as soon in my books.

"We will. You and I." Lagan leans in and our noses touch. "The future awaits. Bit by bit. We'll write it together. Apart and then together again. Okay?" As he nods, searching for my approval, his lips draw dangerously close to mine.

"Now?" Lagan asks.

"It's not that I don't want to. I just..." And I'm embarrassed to admit it. Deep breath. "I just always hoped my lips would be perfectly healed before my first kiss."

"You are. Perfect for me." Lagan's hands brush my hair back, his fingertips swirling a trail to the back of my neck. I'm shaking my head no when he stills me, closes the gap, and rests his lips on mine. "Now?" he mumbles, exhaling the wish into me.

A giggle, a tiny nod, and we're swimming through clouds to our first kiss. So sweet, so sweet, I can hardly breathe—my heart wide open, because I don't want to miss a thing. The prickle of his goatee on my skin, the scent of peppermint on his breath, the softness of his lips pressing on mine.

The cool breeze of Jesse's words, "Take nothing with you," nudges me to slow down and step back. Lagan steps back too, his hands finding mine.

Grinning, he asks, "Well?"

"Pretty perfect. Yeah." We both chuckle, and I would love to stay in this place.

"Alrighty, then. I guess we don't have to practice." Lagan's eyes dance with mischief. "Unless...well. There'll be plenty of time to practice."

I'm still out of breath from the kiss. My first kiss. Wow.

"I'm gonna stop by the garden to say my goodbyes." Time to shift focus. Away from gush and mush to cards and ducks. Have no choice but to get everything in order. "Then take the subway to the shelter office. By then, you and Jess will have had enough time to talk, I'm hoping. And Lagan...thanks. For everything."

Nodding, his dimple-lit smile says of course while his worry-flooded eyes remind me we haven't crossed the finish line.

"Oh, take my key." I give him the front door key before I change my mind. "You don't have to break any doors down. If Jess doesn't agree... What if?" And I can't breathe the words of failure. How will I live if the two men I love fail to return to me?

"No what if's. I'm just gonna pick up your brother and roll outta there MJ-style."

"I'm..."

"Scared?" Lagan says. "I'm scared, too."

"You should be." Shivers return. "Dad's a freakin' lunatic. What if he's home already? I don't know how I feel about him knowing your face and meeting you for the first time. It'll be the guillotine first, questions later."

"Later is not our problem. Look at me." Lagan waits for my eyes to meet his, urgency coating his every word. "No more clouds. I can't have it. I won't have it." Lagan shakes his head and looks at the sidewalk.

"What are you saying?"

"I can't explain it clearly, but something in my gut tells me you need to get far away from your house. Somewhere your dad can't find you. He's hurt you enough. For once, let me fight for you."

Time is ticking. I've never had someone fight for me. "How will I know you're okay?"

"Let's just face this, one battle at a time. We agree that the number one priority is to get both you and Jesse away from your dad." Lagan releases a big sigh and takes my hands again. "You have no idea how glad I am that you finally told me everything. You did, right? Tell me everything?"

Lagan squeezes my hands, and when I don't answer, he says, "Look, if your Dad tries to hurt—"

"Not try." I correct him. "He will."

"Fine. If your dad happens to be there or he tries to hurt Jesse or me, how do you know his rage won't spill over to you for keeping Jess's legs a secret? No matter what happens, I want you nowhere near the house."

"I don't know anything for sure. I just know that somehow we always got through it." There it is again. That word. Through.

I wonder if Lagan is thinking what I'm thinking? What if this storm turns into a hurricane that leaves no survivors? Lagan knows enough now to suspect correctly. If Dad could find a way to kill Mom without a gun...

"Well, then it's settled." Lagan breaks my train of thought. "If anything goes down, I'll have a text message reporting gunshots and violence already set to send to 911 with one press of a button." Lagan punches in the drafted text with his head down for a moment.

"Speaking of gunshots," I swallow a picture of the shiny weapon in Dad's drawer. "Lagan, my dad owns a gun."

Defeat seems inevitable if Jesse doesn't get out before Dad comes home. We hurry to the subway station and step over the gap into the Metra car just as the conductor closes the doors. Fairly empty save a few passengers with their heads buried behind newspapers, the afternoon rush hour won't happen for several hours. Sitting on the bench nearest an exit, I silently read the Zipcar ads that stretch across the top border, my right leg bouncing involuntarily. One arm around my shoulders, Lagan's free hand tops my kneecap, stilling my leg. My heart races on.

Can't believe I've waited this long to try again. When Dad foiled our escape with Mom, for years, Jesse and I were too young and scared to try again. Lagan's right. Why go home to misery for one more night? Why not run away now? While we all still have our legs.

Lagan tries calling the house from his cell again to let Jesse know he's on the way. But he still doesn't pick up. Why isn't Jesse answering the phone?

"Should I call my parents?" Lagan asks after the train picks up speed. "Ask them if I can borrow the car."

I lower my voice even if no one sits near enough to us to hear. "If some neighbor sees your car in the driveway, the plates will make Dad think you helped us get away. And that could help him trace our whereabouts." Plus how will Lagan quickly explain all this to his parents? "Just talk to Jesse. I'm pretty sure he'll listen to you."

Lagan's hand feels like a wet ice cube in mine. I stare at our hands when Lagan pulls me to my feet. The stop closest to the house remains two away. I'll stay on the train and backtrack to the city, transfer trains, and head out to the garden.

Lagan takes a step toward the doors, moving me with him. Perhaps edging toward the exit helps him to assume the battle position. I imagine his armor full of bullet holes. Strange how I've never felt more safe than in this place. His arms wrapped around me.

"Go to the shelter, okay? The office. You know what I mean. Wait for me," he says.

It's my turn to W4U. I see that now.

"For us." Lagan corrects himself. "I'll get Jesse. And we'll get through this. I love you, okay? Don't forget that." Lagan's lips rest on my forehead till the train comes to a jarring halt. A tight squeeze. A slip of a Post-it note into my palm with a whispered, "Read it later." A peppermint-filled kiss, and it's my turn. To let him go.

I stuff the Sticky Note into my jeans pocket and watch the train doors open. Then start to close. As the love of my life moves forward and walks through, I rush to the window, wanting to hold on to the sight of Lagan as long as I can. He turns and looks for me. Finding my gaze, he raises his hand. I think he's waving, at first. As the train rolls forward, he lifts four fingers. And then points to me. I nod as my palm kisses the window. With four fingers up, my thumb curled under.

For what? For you...? Forever.

~THIRTY~

As the afternoon hustle and bustle of commuters bumps me to and fro in the Metra train car headed uptown, the crowd cushions my resurging breakdowns. I've second-guessed my decision to let Lagan get Jesse a million times before I exit at my stop in Glencoe. Walking the last mile to the garden entrance always clears my head, but today I jog the entire route like a fugitive escaping the police.

Shivers race down my sweaty neck as the image of the silver gun in Dad's desk drawer returns to the forefront of my thoughts. *Oh, how I hope Dad moved it!* Really praying Jesse doesn't try and take it with him when he shuts the prison doors behind him, once and for all.

I haven't even begun to think about what it will take to remove Dad's invisible handcuffs. As I rub my wrists instinctively, I imagine the cuffs transforming into a charm bracelet with miniature clocks, teakettles, and hair clippers on it. The bracelet melts into my skin, burning a tattoo around my flesh. Because the truth is, visible or not, I will never forget.

I wonder if I'll ever know what true freedom feels like. I do know that I'm not done wanting. And I will wait for the hands that held mine only hours ago to hold me once more. I need to empty my locker, say my goodbyes and head to the shelter office. Start up the interview process before I chicken out. And wait it out.

The garden office is empty. Everyone must be on break or on the grounds right now. Perfect. As I turn the dial on the combination lock, I think about those first days when I first met Lagan, and how he used to leave me Sticky Notes on my school locker. Seems like forever ago. I never saved them for fear of Dad using them as ammunition. Additional ammo, that is.

When Jason first showed me my locker, I never put anything in it. For months I took everything with me and kept it under the willow where I spent most of my time. Then one day it rained while I was on the job. Everything got muddy.

"You do have a locker," Jason reminded me that evening when I walked past him wearing my mud-splattered coat and backpack.

That was the first time I realized Jason was in cahoots with Lagan. Because I would often open up my locker and find something fun on workdays that didn't fall on the seventeenth. Usually something to eat. Something untraceable. Lemon-flavored cough drops. An apple. A Ziploc with cucumber slices. Once I found an empty water bottle with a Post-it that read, "Fill it up with your dreams today." I tossed the note and refilled it at the water fountain before I started digging that day.

The locker should be empty, save one book and my most prized possession—Mom's strand of hair. I left Lagan's book in here weeks ago when winter slowed down the workday. I retrieve *The Beautiful Fight* from the top shelf and slip it into my backpack.

I'm also here to leave a small note. A small Post-it note telling Jason goodbye. Thanks, really. I write only one word on it: Thanks. Because I'm afraid if I say it to his face, I might start crying.

He's been the big brother I never had, giving me my space but showing me the ropes and giving me the freedom I needed by the willow to find my way. I'm sure he knew I was lost. But he also seemed to know there were some answers I had to find on my own. Lessons learned from a waterfall willow, once weeping. Thoughts of my own personal tree of life remind me that I have one last goodbye to say before I leave.

Jason catches me racing past the garden office, headed straight for the willow. "Hey! Wait up!"

"Jason! Sorry. I didn't see you. I can't stay today."

"No worries. Just wanted to make sure everything's okay with you. Everything's okay with you, right?"

"Everything is…fine." *That sounded convincing.*

Jason looks me over. "Are you sure you're all right? You look a little...distracted. Or something?"

The thought that has burned in my mind since I left Lagan slips off the tip of my tongue, one word at a time. "I'll be...back."

"Excuse me?" Jason's eyes narrow. "Going on a trip or something? You said that like you're not even sure. You okay?"

My silence speaks for itself. I can't speak if I want to. I'm not okay. And I'm not okay talking about it.

"Whatever it is, I'm here to help if I can." Jason shuffles his feet and makes his way back toward the office, talking to me over his shoulder. "Didn't mean to pry. Back to work I go."

And just like that, my window of opportunity to say more dissipates like a popped soap bubble.

I lift my feet and move slowly to my waterfall cave, accepting more and more that the only safe place until I see Lagan and Jesse is a secret shelter.

Before I move under my willow, my silent friend speaks inexplicable peace as the wind dances among her branches. I run my fingers along the outside of her flowing arms, little pink and yellow blossoms sailing to the floor with my touch. I only wish her arms were human and could wrap around me with the strength of Lagan's arms—an embrace I wish I were more familiar with now.

The gardener is here. I know. But I can't lie. I need arms I can feel right now. I need heat, and pulse, and unmistakable squeeze. I'm alone. Waiting and wanting.

I keel over to my knees, now under the willow. My fists hit the dirt floor, and I beg the invisible voice once more for arms that will hold me again. And Jess's legs to run, and run free. And for the first time, I think about Dad. And it's not for his death, for once. Just tears. I weep with my willow for the man in my life who has probably never shed a single tear for me.

My promise to Lagan to never go back to the man or my house rings like an alarm to remind me I can't stay here. Reluctantly, I shake my shoulders and rise to my feet. It's time to move on.

The train ride back to the city is packed. Everyone's getting off of work and heading home. Home. There's a word that's about to undergo an address change. I look down at my watch, then out the window as the sun begins to set behind the bustling train. The sun falls below the horizon, leaving dark red streaks across the darkening sky. Even the sky bleeds tonight.

As the train draws me closer and closer to my destination, I rehearse my story. Lagan is the first person I ever told. The only person.

"Who will believe me?" I wanted a way out.

"I believe you." He never failed to remind me.

And that's why I'll wait for you.

And SUS. Soon, come already.

The address appears just as the Google map I memorized earlier had it laid out. Caddy corner to the Starbucks, next to the Rite Aid on Wacker Drive. The front door appears as any other office suite, with numbers and names on a chart behind a glass-encased frame. I double check the suite number and begin my trek up the stairs. The elevator will take me to the sixth floor too quickly. Still not sure I know what to say.

Opening the stairwell door, I'm greeted with the name, *Hope Now*, painted in simple, solid blue letters across the door. I push, but the door doesn't budge. An intercom system buzzes, and a female voice sounds from the small speaker built into the wall to the right of the entrance. "Hope Now. This is Diana speaking. How may I help you?"

Deep breath. "My name is Talia. I'm hurt. My dad hurts me. I need help. I, uh, I was wondering—"

A click sounds the release of the locked door. I turn the handle as the voice on the intercom welcomes me. "We're so glad you came, hon. Come on through."

EPILOGUE

My mind refuses to stay anchored, always wandering, like a hot air balloon cut from its tether. The invisible winds of *what if* lift me from *what is* now. I frequently float away to cloud ten— cloud nine is for traditionalists—and find myself looking past his eyes while nodding my head. He thought I heard him. In the beginning, I did. Just not totally. Not selectively either, because that would imply choice. And I'm more convinced than ever that if I had a choice, I would never have chosen this divided existence. It is simply exhausting.

Jesse walks. Jesse runs. And Jesse flies in my dreams, a fire blazing behind him. Back to me, swoops me up, and we sail away together. Through the clouds of yesterday. Today. And tomorrow. I count the clouds as they roll by the shelter windows, wondering when I will see my little brother's face again. Clear blue skies make waiting especially hard.

I hear the voices of the other women around me fade as I walk through the motions on this first night at the shelter. When the last light dims, I lay down to sleep, and my mind takes flight to visit Lagan, returning to that time that happened and didn't happen. All that was and could have been and might never be. Somewhere between my memories and my dreams.

I close my eyes as my mouth spills out details in an attempt to tie up another story. He gently slows my words with two fingertips running down my forehead, over the bridge of my nose, down to my soft, perfectly curled, lower lip. There he rests them. Until my lips come together. I like his fingers on my lips. He leans forward till our foreheads kiss and whispers, "To be continued," and we part ways.

I open my eyes. *Now* offers me three door prizes for showing up. One I can't let go of and the other two I keep tucked under my pillow: cold wrists, peppermint-flavored Trident, and Lagan's last yellow Post-it note:

me + you = us three

He always did love math.

I once asked him, "Why Sticky Notes?"

"Because they're compact, square, and...sticky."

I think he hoped his words would stick with me. They do. I have a slideshow of every last one in my head, reminding me of those first days. When words were few, opportunity scarce, and we lived out our fairy tale under a waterfall willow.

RAJDEEP PAULUS

ACKNOWLEDGEMENTS

Excuse me while I pull out my speech.

First of all, I'd like to thank God. Without God, I would have no dreams. And without those dreams, there'd be no stories.

To my parents, thank you Mom for teaching me that it is sweeter to give than to receive. I love you for laughing at my stories and generously supporting my dreams to be a writer. You're my Super-Mom, and I'm so blessed to be your first princess.

And Dad, you're my inspiration. You taught me the very art of story telling with all your anecdotes you told me as I was growing up. Thank you for reading my stories and challenging me to never stop learning. Daddy's girl, yes, I am.

To Amma, my second Mom and story-telling friend. I love that we became friends when I fell in love with your son. Thank you for your daily help and your love for reading and writing. You inspire me! And to Appa, my second dad, I know you always dreamed of writing a book. Your stories will always stay with me.

To my baby sis and best friend, Sandi, my sounding board on so many days—thank you for laughing with me and crying with me. I cannot imagine going through this life without you. Love you so much and thank God for every day of good health he continues to give you. Like my morning cup of coffee, yes, you are!

To my princesses—Hannah, Nitha, Lydia and Sarah—thank you for letting Mommy write, giving me so much material, and cheering me on. Mommy knows no other place I'd rather be than with you four in my arms. You're my jewels, my treasures, my most precious gifts from God. Don't ever forget: You is smart. You is kind. You is important.

To Roopa, my BFE and first official reader. Where do I begin? Even if you didn't like chocolate or laugh loud or love to read, I'd still love you. Because you tell me the truth. And you love me. And I don't know that many people discover this kind of friendship in their lifetime. Just so thankful I found you. And we got through the awkward, high school, she's so different from me, roadblock. You are the green in my life! :)

To my Literary Agent, Chip MacGregor: Chip, thanks for that first email, when I freaked out after sending you a message with a typo, and your response was, "Reelly? I didn't notic. :o)" Seriously, thanks for taking a chance on me. For looking past that fumbling introduction and believing in my writing. For reminding me to be patient and making time to answer my one hundred and one questions about all things writing.

To the late Miss Trosko, my high school English teacher, for giving me an F in English but telling me I had potential. And for giving me the courage to pursue my passion.

To my late grandmother. For making me laugh and telling others, "Kamali kuri nae kamali kiana lickna." Translated, "Of course a crazy girl like you would write crazy stories!" Biji, I miss you so much.

To Stancy, Roy, and Anna—for the countless hours of babysitting. Thank you for loving the girls and freeing up time for me to pump out the pages. You all are family. Love you so much!

To my family, Uncles, Aunts, Siblings, Cousins, Nieces and Nephews—all of you contribute to some of the best chapters of my life.

To Pat Matuzek, my first editor. For all the work you put into making this story cleaner and stronger. And Kyle Waalan, my second editor, for the finishing touches before I sent my first baby out into the world.

To my crit group, Renee, Liz, Emily, Selene and Lisa. You ladies Rock! You've helped me to develop thicker skin and made me a better writer. Thank you for challenging me to answer the hard questions and inspiring me with your stories too.

And to the Playlist Fiction crew: Jennifer Murgia, Laura Anderson Kurk, Laura Smith, Stephanie Morrill, Amanda Luedeke and Sandra Bishop. You took a chance on this newbie writer, and I am so grateful. And the Playlist Fiction Street Team! Thanks for investing in our team and enthusiastically introducing us to the world! Bonus for me—I discovered some pretty cool authors and made some new, fun reader friends.

Finally, to Peter and Liz at the GLY cafe. Thank you for taking care of me while I camp out and type away for hours. I'll never forget the day I had my Goldilocks moment, finding the perfect table and chair to write at in your coffee house. And the quinoa brownies...yum to the yum!

This Thank You Note is also to You. Really, It is!

You know that moment when they call your name at the Oscars, and all you can think is, I hope I don't trip on the red carpet as I strut up in my floor length evening gown. And I really hope I don't forget to mention my mom. Because then she might move and leave no forwarding address. And that would be bad. Really bad.

Yeah, me neither. (Love you, Mom!)

Truth be told, I've been dreaming about this "thank you" list for years. Decades, really. I think I rewrote the list several hundred times before I wrote my first book. Because I am huge on saying, "Thank You!" Simply, because you don't journey the madness of this life alone. You weren't made to. We were meant to walk—together.

So, at the risk of sounding cheesy and We Are the World-ish, I sincerely want to thank anyone and everyone who made my little dream a big reality. If you're holding this book because you heard from a friend of friend that its a must-read, or you just clicked the download button by accident, and it was too late to hit cancel, this book is dedicated to you too. Because, I'm not all about karma, but I do believe that things happen for a reason. And you're here now, and I'm so glad you came.

So dive in. Hang out. Linger when a line makes you think. Find me on social media and ask a question. And share if you feel compelled. Even a two sentence review helps shape my writing and helps others to discover a new book!

Happy swimming, all. Because as surely as the sun rises each and every day, we all have our clouds. But we can swim through them. Together.

Sincerely aware that great stories change lives,

Rajdeep

ABOUT THE AUTHOR

Rajdeep decided to be a writer during her junior year in high school after her English teacher gave her an "F" but told her she had potential. She studied English Literature at Northwestern University, and she writes masala-marinated, Young Adult Fiction. For more, meet her on Social Media @rajdeeppaulus and rajdeeppaulus.com.

When Paulus is not tapping on her Mac, you can find her dancing with her four princesses, kayaking with her hubs, coaching basketball, or eating dark chocolate while sipping a frothy, sugar-free latte.

Made in the USA
Middletown, DE
09 August 2017